MY BEST MISTAKE

by Sylvie Grayson

GREAT WESTERN PUBLISHING c/o
sylviegraysonauthor@gmail.com

Copyright © 2016 by Sylvie Grayson

All rights reserved.

For information contact

sylviegraysonauthor@gmail.com

www.sylviegrayson.com

ISBN: 978-0-9947345-3-2

Great Western Publishing is a registered trademark of Sylvie Grayson.

Cover art by Steven Novak   novakillustration@gmail.com

Other books by Sylvie Grayson

contemporary romantic suspense

Suspended Animation

The Lies He Told Me

Legal Obstruction

sci-fi/fantasy

Khandarken Rising,
The Last War: Book One

Son of the Emperor,
The Last War: Book Two

Truth and Treachery,
The Last War: Book Three

Praise for Sylvie Grayson's books

I've been reading Sylvie Grayson - can't seem to put them down. How do you come up with these exciting mysteries? Very fun reading!!

Suspended Animation

Wow! This book is amazing, its very well written and the characters are very well developed. This is my first book by Sylvie Grayson and it won't be my last. I was hooked from the first page and this book was very hard to put down.

Interesting characters, family conflicts and divided loyalties make this a book that kept me up half the night

Legal Obstruction

I loved this book! I've found my new favorite author. Emily is a fiercely professional woman who is on her own and determined to protect her little family. Joe is a solitary guy who often doesn't deal with problems until they are front and center. But boy does Emily wake him up and does he take notice. Add in a wildcard assistant and a few unsavory characters and I was up all night finishing the book to find out what happens.

The Lies He Told Me

If you are a fan of the heartwarming craftiness and domesticity of a Debbie McComber romance, and the intense intrigues of Danielle Steele, you'll enjoy the writing style of Sylvie Grayson; where the bad guys are not heartless, and the good guys are virtually flawless.

Just a quick note to let you know how much I enjoyed your book. You drew on your vast experience as a result of being a female, a wife, lover, mother, business woman, lawyer, friend, gardener, homeowner, compassionate and caring individual. It was an intriguing read which kept me guessing and very interested. Well done, Sylvie.

The Last War: Book One, Khandarken Rising

The General of Khandarken sends his son, Dante, to investigate the situation. When Dante meets the lovely Beth she eyes him with suspicion. But he won't stop until he solves the tangle of motives, fueled by greed, which threaten Beth and her family. I enjoyed this book very much. The well-developed characters and sensuous love scenes make this a page turner. I look forward to reading Book Two and Book Three

... this story is one of a kind in its own and couldn't be truly compared to anything but itself. It has so many unique characteristics to it. The personal relationships are intriguing and different from many other fictional relationships. The names are cool, the plot gets thicker with each page, and I loved the author's style. It became evident that I was addicted to reading the book once I was sad to be finished. I'm going to give this a strong recommendation. It's my kind of book.

The Last War: Book Two, Son of the Emperor

I am a big fan of The Last War series. I loved Book One, the story of Major Dante Regiment and Beth Farmer. The dystopian world Grayson has created, where women are scarce and Clones are used to replace them, where the Emperor has finally been defeated but his son takes up the fight, just gets better in this second book. ...Thrills abound on the race to freedom and home. I really enjoyed this book and can't wait for Book Three. Grayson has great imagination, the fantasy series is awesome.

DEDICATION

I am blessed with wonderful support that has enabled me to write. To my husband, who is always ready to listen, read and lend a hand with difficult passages. To my children who had faith in me and helped with their interest, support and practical suggestions.

To my critique group who supported me to polish the words for publication, my many thanks.

Any errors or omissions are mine alone.

Sylvie Grayson
www.sylviegrayson.com

MY BEST MISTAKE

CHAPTER ONE

Jenny rolled onto her back and blew out a long sigh, then wriggled to find a more comfortable spot on the tattered grass mat. The gentle warmth of the sun touched her cheeks, and the smell of the damp earth rose around her. Slowly she opened her eyes. So still and peaceful, so private.

This was absolutely the perfect spot to start a tan. She didn't want to get burnt to a crisp when she finally arrived in Greece on this up-coming trip that Izzy had talked her into. When had she last really relaxed? She took another deep breath, closed her eyes and revelled in the sun's unseasonable warmth, if not heat, in the Pacific northwest this time of year.

Lying naked in the sheltered spot felt just a touch vulnerable. That niggling feeling was back. Her eyelids flashed open as she craned her neck. No, no one could see her here. Although some pervert could have snuck up from the beach and be peering at her from the bank. Her gaze darted in that direction and encountered nothing but blue sky and dead grass on the edge of the low cliff.

Be rational. The house protects you on one side. She relaxed slightly. *Then, there's the huge rhododendron behind.* She screwed

1

her face up to peer back at a bush that would take a lumberjack to hack through. And there was a solid hedge of cedars, aromatic and heavy, down the other side.

At her feet all she could see was sky. If she raised her head she would look out over the low overhang to the ocean glittering below in one of its rare moods of tame ripples and lapping waves. What a beautiful day, so unexpected for late-winter in Victoria.

She sank back on the mat to the sound of the water seething below, sucking at the sand through the tangled kelp. But that feeling was back. When her eyes flew open, she spotted a flash of movement in the cedar hedge.

"Jordie! Jordie Cochrane!" she shrieked. Vibrating with indignation, she leaped to her feet. "Come out this instant!" She hopped about on the grass mat in a rage until she remembered her naked state. Snatching the bath towel, she wrapped it around herself in swift jerky motions.

"Jordie! I *knew* it! I'm so mad…"

"You could scream?" Jordie's low voice came from right behind her. Jenny whipped about, wild brown hair flying, to confront the amused gaze of her cousin. "You *are* screaming, Jenny."

Jordie's red hair curled thickly on his head, his heavy dark-red beard covering the lower part of his jaw. Startling blue eyes were keen in his face. He hadn't changed a bit, even when they were kids he'd teased her unmercifully. Except for the beard, he hadn't had that then. But she didn't allow the thought to slow her down. Rage returned in full force.

"I don't have to put up with this!" She pointed an indignant finger at his chest and the towel slipped dangerously.

Jordie just stood there and grinned.

2

She lowered her brows at him. "What were you doing, sitting in the hedge like a peeping Tom?" she hissed, face hot. "Do you have to spy on me?" She was alarmingly close to crying.

"Ah, Jenny." Jordie reached out his hand in a futile gesture in the face of her ire. "I wasn't peeping at you. I was working in the yard and heard a rustle in the hedge. When I went to investigate, I spotted you lying naked as a jay bird, soaking up the sun."

She clutched the towel tightly to her chest in the face of his searing gaze. "You have no right, Jordie." Jenny curved her shoulder away and bent to pick up her mat, struggling to hold back the tears. She could have sworn she felt his hand on her back.

When she turned, his head swung back to her. "I need to talk to you about something." His mouth firmed determinedly.

She huffed and sniffed but couldn't quite decipher his expression through the heavy beard and half-closed eyelids. "Talk to me? About what?"

He shifted his stance defensively. "It's about Maggie."

"Maggie?" she shrieked in alarm. "What's wrong? Is she hurt?"

Jordie shook his head. "No. Calm down, Jenny. Your daughter is fine."

She frowned. "Then why do you have to talk to me about her? Maggie can speak for herself."

"Your mom called me. Maggie's been talking to her grandma."

Jenny's heart beat hard in her chest. This didn't sound good, and probably wasn't. Maggie didn't return most of her phone calls these days. "So," she waved her hand as if it didn't matter. "Tell me."

"This is difficult." He pressed his lips together and seemed to gauge her with his gaze. "It's just that... Maggie told your mom that you're angry all the time. And she can't talk to you, because everything turns into an argument." He must have seen the hurt in her face, because he stepped forward and tried to take her hand, but she shook him off.

"Jenny, she misses you. She needs her mother."

She turned abruptly and stalked down the yard to the back deck. "Don't be at me, Jordie. Just because you're my cousin doesn't give you the right to harass me."

"I'm not really your cousin, Jenny." His gravelly voice followed her retreat.

Jenny glared at him over her shoulder. "Well, you aren't, but you are." And with that oblique response, she marched into the house and slid the glass door closed with a thud.

~*~*~*~

Jordie watched Jenny disappear through the door. How had he put himself in this situation? She was so beautiful, the quick glimpse of a naked woman had just confirmed that, although it wasn't news to him. His temperature had gone up about ten degrees in the time it took her to grab the towel and cover up. But she was impossible to deal with.

He rubbed his wrist across his eyes and pushed back through the hedge to where he'd been pruning the fruit trees in his yard. Her daughter Maggie was a delicate little thing, pretty and a bit timid. It was no wonder she was cowed by her mother. Jenny was a roaring inferno these days. Since she'd moved next door, he couldn't figure out where the old

Jenny had disappeared to. She used to be fun, friendly, a little shy and willing to try just about anything. And very lovely.

She was still lovely. But a lot of the other qualities seemed to be eaten up by a rage that never quit. It was that bastard, Bobby, of course. She'd married Bobby right out of high school and things had not gone well. Up until he left her and the kids, when it went further downhill from there.

Jordie hadn't been looking forward to passing on that tough message from Maggie. He'd seen the hurt on Jenny's face, even as she tried to hide it by lashing out at him. If only she would take it to heart. She loved her kids, she just needed to rein in the emotion.

And the last thing he needed was to fall in love with her again.

He glanced at his kitchen window and picked up the pruning shears. Linda wasn't home, and he had no idea where she'd disappeared to today, which was no different from any other day. Why did she stay? He slashed viciously at a stray branch. She'd moved into the spare bedroom years ago, but didn't want a divorce. *It would be embarrassing,* she claimed. *It would be demeaning. How would she support herself?*

The same way she did now. He broke another branch off and threw it onto the pile. *He would support her.* Meanwhile, he was in limbo. With Jenny living right beside him.

CHAPTER TWO

A t Sentinel Security's offices in downtown Victoria, Jenny swung her chair around to face the window. She stared down at the street two floors below and watched the rain bounce on the sidewalk. If it weren't for Isabelle, she never would have agreed to go on a trip. Good old Izzy. And it was hardly spur of the moment. One of the few high school friends who would still put up with her, Isabelle had harassed her for months to go away, and when Jenny finally explained that the timing was bad, Isabelle promptly changed the travel dates. That had effectively backed her into a corner. With her son Rob travelling somewhere in Europe, and her baby girl Maggie off at university, she'd run out of excuses.

She smiled as she remembered the sly look on her friend's face when she arrived at Jenny's house with the new flight schedule. "Do you suppose you can arrange the time off? Your boss, Frank, doesn't seem to think it's a problem, I ran into him last night in the grocery store, by the way. He was shopping with Ms. Icicle, his tender and compassionate wife."

Jenny snickered at the jibe. However, once she was committed to the trip, the decision immediately sent her into a tailspin. Her life always seemed hung together in a precarious balance at the best of times, and vacations had never been part of the plan.

She rose and knocked on Frank's door.

"Come in," his gruff voice responded.

Frank, her boss and major shareholder, was sitting in his creaky old chair, a file open on the scarred desk before him. He didn't bother to lift his head.

Jenny dove in. "Have you been conspiring with Isabelle on this travel plan she has going? She said she talked to you about it."

"Conspiring?" Frank's head popped up, and he flipped the file closed with his beefy fingers. "Conspiring! I didn't tell Isabelle you'd go. But have you been on a vacation since you and Bobby divorced?"

Jenny scowled, noticing that Frank never alluded to the fact that Bobby left her, ran off, slunk away. He always insisted that they had 'separated' and 'divorced', determinedly neutral words. "If you mean, have I traveled since Bozo dumped me, the answer is no. I've been too busy, and you know it." Her voice turned sharp, her expression purposely cynical.

"Well, everyone needs a break now and then." He shoved his head forward aggressively as his eyes questioned hers. "Come on, take a chance! Wouldn't it be great to take off for a few weeks with nothing to do but lay around in the sun and wander at the local market? We'll be okay without you. It'll be a struggle, but we'll manage." His smile teased. "I know it'll come as a surprise, but we managed before you started work here."

Jenny stared at him accusingly for a moment longer, then gave a little laugh and threw up her hands. "Okay, I give up. And no, the trip probably won't do me any actual, physical *harm*." She sighed and sagged back against the sofa, looking at him with a wry expression.

Frank gave his deep laugh and walked around the desk to plunk his square solid body down beside hers on the cushions. He grabbed her hands in his gnarled fingers. The grooves deepened in his face as he smiled. "Jenny, you're like my own daughter. We work well together, you and I. You've changed this business beyond my wildest imaginings. I'm fond of you and you know it."

He drew a deep breath, and let it out with a sigh as he gazed past her toward the window, staring sightlessly at the brick wall across the alley that blocked any possible view from his office. "You and I have a special relationship, more than just business partners."

She squeezed his tough old fingers. "Now, don't go all maudlin on me, Frank. I'm just taking a two-week vacation, not selling out on you or dumping this shabby company for something bigger and better."

He returned his attention to her face. "I know. I don't know what's gotten into me. But I worry about you. You don't look after yourself, never have any fun. I know there's another side to you. Why don't you buy some new clothes, get your hair done, have an affair? You can afford it. Don't forget, I happen to know how much money you take out of this company."

"And not a cent more than I'm worth, either," she muttered. "Have an affair, indeed!" She punched him half-heartedly in the chest as thoughts of Jordie crept involuntarily into her brain and she tried to shove them away.

Frank laughed and freed one hand to swing a burly arm around her shoulders in a hug.

The office door opened behind them at the same time as the phone on his desk buzzed. Frank turned his head and Jenny felt him tense before he released her and rose, smiling and holding out his hand.

"Good afternoon, my dear. How nice to see you here. You seldom come down to the office. Are you out shopping?"

Jenny craned her neck to see Alita, Frank's wife, standing in the open doorway.

~*~*~*~

Alita was flawlessly groomed, her tailored suit the perfect blue to match the striking colour of her eyes. Her pale hair was wound in a chignon low on the back of her head, every strand in place. Her black clutch purse and espadrilles were of matching eel skin. She stared at them coldly.

Jenny drew a breath and forced a greeting. "Hi, Alita. You can be among the first to hear the news. Frank is booting me out." Alita's face warmed with interest, then cooled quickly as Jenny continued, "I'm taking a trip, two weeks in Greece. First vacation in years."

Jenny smiled wryly into Alita's unresponsive expression, then turned her attention back to Frank who'd dropped his hand. Jenny thought he suddenly looked older than his seventy-three years. His curly, slightly grizzled white hair still rose in a high crest off his forehead, his bushy brows shadowing his intense brown eyes. But his face looked tired.

"Well, I can't stay here lollygagging around, like some I could name." Jenny headed for the door. "There're things to do if I'm ever going to be able to get away. No one else seems to work around here." With that parting shot at Frank in the hopes of nudging him back to his good humour, Jenny walked toward the doorway.

Alita was not about to give an inch. There had never been any love lost between them, and Jenny felt belligerent enough to bowl her right over. "Nice to see you. Sorry I can't stay."

The woman stared straight into her eyes, hatred making them glitter coldly. "What a shame, Jenny. And I see you've just had your hair done."

Jenny's hand rose involuntarily to her heavy lopsided bun, but she smirked and nodded. "Same hairdresser you use, I guess. Excuse me."

Frank's wife flushed and took a small step to the side to allow Jenny room to pass. As she closed the door, she heard the low hiss of her voice. "What were you and that woman doing there on the couch?"

Jenny shook her head and felt her bun slip even lower to the left. She automatically felt around for a wayward pin to re-anchor the mass. As she passed Queenie's desk, the secretary looked up. "I tried to buzz him, but she got in there before I could warn you." She noted the high colour in Jenny's cheeks and raised her carefully penciled brows.

"Never mind, Queenie, I gave as good as I got. Call him on the intercom in about two minutes and tell him he has a long distance call. Otherwise, he'll come out covered in blood and claw marks." Queenie nodded and Jenny swept past into her own office, slamming the door.

CHAPTER THREE

Jenny threw herself into her chair, leaning her head against the high padded leather back and twirling in an angry circle with one toe. *Bitch!* She fumed and rocked.

Even when she'd been promoted to Frank's assistant, she'd been invisible to Alita. Then as Jenny helped expand the business, eventually buying an interest, Alita had become openly antagonistic. Today had just been unlucky timing. Frank's wife had happened on a scene that could easily be misconstrued. But the die was cast. Jenny was not about to toady to that witch.

Let her think what she wants. Frank's too good for her. He treats her like royalty. And she's as mean as... Jenny couldn't think of anything mean enough to liken her to.

She stopped the chair with her toe and stifled a laugh. She was acting like a child. As if jabbed by an electric prod, she leaped up and stormed over to the mirror hanging on the back of her office door, gazing with sudden interest at her reflection.

What she saw made her pause. A woman no longer in the first blush of youth, no makeup, clear skin and a decent

11

face. Dark marks under wide hazel eyes. Reddish-brown hair pulled straight back and wound in an indifferent knot that leaned hazardously to the left. Plain white blouse, navy blue polyester jacket. Frank had always said she looked like a prison matron in the outfit and she'd taken his comments as a joke. Now she hesitated as she looked closer.

Maybe he was right. Even Alita, devil that she was, might have had cause to give her a dig about her hair. She grimaced. Her gaze swung to her navy purse sitting on the corner of her desk, plain, serviceable, many compartments. She bragged that she didn't need a briefcase. Made of sturdy vinyl. Matched her flat plain loafers, same navy, same vinyl.

Late thirties and looking sixty. It's a wonder Izzy even wanted to go on a trip with her. She hadn't always been this dowdy. She could remember men watching her as she walked by, skirt swinging, legs flashing. Why, when she and Bobby...

Jenny stopped those traitorous thoughts with a furious burst of energy. Grabbing that sensible plastic purse, she hooked some keys from her desk drawer and marched into the hall. "Queenie, I'm out. Don't know if I'll be back today. Take messages."

As she flashed past toward the entry, she heard Queenie's husky voice behind her, "But, just a minute. Jenny?"

She didn't stop. The elevator doors were closing and she dashed through the opening with seconds to spare, waving to one of their security guards who was checking in. She grinned impudently at the self-important looking three-piece suit that occupied centre stage in the elevator, and he moved over immediately to make room for her. When the elevator pulled to a stop on the ground floor she darted out, down the steps of the old office building and onto the sidewalk amidst the mid-afternoon pedestrian traffic. *Where was the nearest hairdresser?*

~*~*~*~

Jenny staggered into the hallway, dumped her bags on the floor and kicked her door shut. She flicked on some lights and walked through to the kitchen to check her answering machine. Two messages. The first was from Frank, hoping she wasn't upset about what had happened at the office, Alita sent her apologies. At that comment, Jenny snorted aloud in patent disbelief.

The second was from Isabelle, did she want to meet for dinner, seven o'clock, the Emporium. She'd try her cell phone. Jenny glanced at her watch and shrugged, knowing her phone had been turned off. *Nine-thirty. Too late, sorry Izzy.*

Dragging her shopping bags into the living room, she piled everything on the sofa. A new purse, leather, sleek and stylish. Still navy, but it was a start. A pair of shoes to match, wonderful soft leather, medium narrow heel, pretty racy compared to her usual choice. A beautiful lightweight wool suit in royal blue. It looked fabulous. And a soft pink silk blouse to wear with it that the salesgirl had talked her into buying. Silk wasn't as expensive as she'd thought. Not that she would know.

Well, that was going to change. Frank had jolted her out of a rut today. He might live to regret it. She'd be looking for more dividends from the company to pay for her new lifestyle! She giggled.

Shaking her head, she admired the new swing of her hair. She wasn't used to it yet but the hairdresser had done a fabulous job, cutting it to just above the shoulder in staggered layers. She'd spent as much time in the shop dressing rooms looking at her hair as she did at the clothes she was trying on.

The phone rang and Jenny grabbed it. It was Margaret calling from Vancouver on her Sunday duty call. Jenny barely gave her a chance to say hello before she launched into a tirade about how rude Alita had been.

Maggie eventually fell silent, finally reduced to answering questions in monosyllables, and then rang off, saying she could hear a friend calling. Jenny hung up the phone, frustrated anew. This was her fault... Jordie had warned her.

She shrugged in irritation and hurt. As she allowed the thoughts to come, the familiar wash of panic welled up and she struggled to beat it back.

When things fell apart between Bobby and her, Rob had been eleven and Maggie a very young nine. They were hurt when their father moved out, and Jenny was angry. Looking back, she'd probably done as much harm with her anger as Bobby had done by his actions. Her reaction to that was more anger. It was a familiar energy surge that kept her from sinking into remorse or sorrow, or a hundred other emotions that waited with open jaws to snatch her with their jagged teeth and drag her down.

Leaving her new purchases on the sofa, she yanked on a pair of jogging pants and grabbed her running shoes. A good walk should drive away this heavy feeling. Walking got her out and this was a perfect place to do it. The ocean in its many unpredictable moods was a constant draw and the streets and paths were picturesque. It was a physical outlet for all the emotional turmoil in her mind.

Spotting Jordie on his deck next door, she turned her head away, in no mood to be sociable. Maggie with her short perfunctory phone calls hurt her heart, and her son Rob making contact only once in the three months he'd been off in Europe only added to the misery. Was he unable to afford postage for a postcard?

She *needed* a run.

CHAPTER FOUR

Jenny's new look met with such wild success at work that she panicked and locked herself in her office for most of Monday, coming out when the reception area was clear of everyone but Queenie. The secretary nailed her with a look. "You can't sulk in there all day. You look great, it's just going to take people a while to get used to it."

Jenny laughed and grabbed the long-nailed, scarlet-polished finger Queenie shook under her nose. "Okay, Ms. Know It All, I'll come out of hiding and I'll even be gracious. *Thank you, Frank, that's very sweet. Thank you, Mr. Knowles, most kind of you.*" She minced around the room and executed a curtsy toward the desk, just as Frank's office door opened and Mr. Knowles emerged.

Jenny jerked erect and gave some files on Queenie's desk a close perusal as the client looked quizzically around. "Oh, Jenny, there you are. We've finalized the security coverage for the store for the next couple of months. Frank has the details. I especially liked that young man you sent over last time. He's very productive, seemed to catch at least one shoplifter every time. Oh, and I like your hair, is it different? Looks wonderful."

Jenny turned and smiled, ignoring Queenie's snicker as she held out her hand. "Thank you, Mr. Knowles. I'll try to make sure the same security person is available for at least part of the contract."

That night Izzy arrived to see her new purchases. "Can't stop now, Jenny," she said. "Your hair looks great, some women would sell their kids for a cut like that. But you need travel clothes."

Jenny eyed Izzy fondly. Isabelle Riley had hardly changed in the years since they'd been friends in junior high. Her long black hair hung down her back in a flat sheath of dense colour, high cheek bones inherited from her Spanish mother. Isabelle was a dancer and went off at sixteen to study at the Royal Winnipeg School of Ballet. Now she taught at a studio in town.

"So, let's have a look," her friend continued. "You simply can't wear that beautiful royal blue suit one day, and the polyester navy thing the next."

"But it has pants as well as a skirt," Jenny mourned. "I can't throw it out, now can I?"

"I certainly don't see why not." Isabelle scowled at the three-piece polyester outfit laying offendingly across Jenny's bed. "You can't give it away, because no one will take it. How long have you had it?"

"It was my first purchase as an employed woman in Victoria."

"And the last, too, I'll bet. Well, it doesn't owe you a thing. I swear you've worn it every day. It has to go." Isabelle swept it off the bed and into a bag. Then she turned purposefully toward the closet. "What else have we got here?"

Jenny dashed across the room and threw herself spread-eagled in front of the closet doors. "No, Izzy! Back off, or I'll have to get violent. I'll clear it out, but in my own time. I can't totally change overnight."

"Okay, as long as you promise to get ruthless," said Isabelle. "We have to go shopping. You need more work clothes that don't look like prison uniforms."

Jenny slunk down the hall to get her purse. "Have you been talking to Frank, by any chance?" she asked.

~*~*~*~

Standing in the back warehouse of his store, Jordie pulled the cell phone from his pocket and punched the button.

"Uncle Jordie?" The voice was hesitant.

"Hi, Maggie. Good to hear from you." He grinned at the short pause. This was a very careful young lady.

"Well, Grandma told me she'd talked to you."

"Oh, okay. That's great." Was this good news or bad? Had Jenny gone off the rails again with her daughter? "I talked to your mum a few days ago. How is it going?"

There was a little laugh. "It's better. She's not as pushy on the phone. I just wanted to thank you for saying something to her. I was kind of afraid to."

"Hey, Maggie. You're more than welcome." Jordie felt a flutter of protectiveness in his chest. She needed his backing, just like Jenny did. He wouldn't let them down. "Your mother loves you, you know that, right?"

"Yeah." She sounded breathy on the phone. "I know. I've missed her too."

Jordie nodded and walked into the lumberyard at the back of his store. "She's missed you as well. Don't be a stranger, okay? Make sure you talk to her before she leaves for Greece. It might be hard to be in contact while she's away."

"I know." There was a pause. "But isn't this exciting? Mum never takes a trip. Anyway, thanks Uncle Jordie."

"You're welcome. How are your studies coming?"

"Oh, you know. They're coming."

He laughed. "Okay, talk to you soon. Call me if you need anything, okay? Or just to talk. I can do that too."

She laughed and hung up.

As he pressed the *off* button and shoved the gadget into his pocket, he sidestepped a customer heading out the overhang door at the back of his store. He wasn't thrilled about this trip Jenny was taking. What if she didn't come back? What if she met someone over there? His chest felt tight. He needed to sort out his own life, because he wasn't going to live in limbo forever, and when Jenny came back from Greece, he was going for her with everything he had.

He glanced across the yard at the forklift driver who was trying to load two lifts at once, stupid young buck. "Hey," he shouted. "Not that way. Hold it," and he trotted across the blacktop.

CHAPTER FIVE

J enny pushed back her office chair and shoved her bangs
off her forehead with an impatient hand. Her fuchsia silk
skirt was wrinkled and the multi-coloured mohair sweater
was too hot for the office. The sun was beating in her
window in an unusual appearance for mid-winter. She shoved
up her sleeves, then rose to open the window. She still
couldn't believe her new clothes. She'd catch a glimpse of her
reflection and it never failed to catch her by surprise.

She even felt different. The staff seemed to respond to
her in a changed way. Before she was just a manager,
responsible, capable, organized, an office fixture.

But her new image had altered that. Queenie always
had a big smile when she arrived at work, and Frank's eyes
gleamed when he caught sight of her. Esley Moro had been
the funniest though. Esley was head of property security and
had been with Frank for years. A retired armed forces man,
he ran his department with military precision, much to the
amusement of some of his guards. He'd always dealt with
Jenny in a straight-from-the-shoulder style, his full droopy
mustache bristling impressively as he delivered his reports.

When he met with Jenny for the weekly update this time, he was actually rendered speechless. He stared at her hair, then her face and his mouth remained open. Jenny stifled her snicker and began the meeting without his participation. After everyone left he congratulated her gruffly on her new hairstyle and backed stiffly from the room.

Now she waved her arms to cool off and sat back at her desk to focus on the pages in front of her. The accounts didn't make sense, but she was no accountant. She'd ask Queenie in the morning. There were more funds in the bank than there should have been. Maybe Queenie had posted several months at once. Or Frank had some new accounts he hadn't told her about. He had fingers in so many pies, she had trouble keeping up. It was the kind of problem most companies would be glad to have. Jenny grimaced. Still…

She sighed and glanced at her watch. If she was going to meet Isabelle for dinner, she'd better get a move on. Izzy hated it when she was late. Flicking off her reading lamp, she shuffled the pages over to the side of her desk. As she reached for her jacket, she heard the outer office door open.

"Hello," a low masculine voice called. "Anyone home?"

She walked out of her office, purse under her arm. "We're closed, but maybe I can help you. Are you lost?"

"Not lost, not hardly." Norman Suffron looked down into Jenny's startled face.

"Norman!" she stammered, glancing at her watch. "What are you doing here at this time of night?" She backed up a step. "Can I do something for you?"

Norman Suffron was Alita's only son by her first husband. When she and Frank married, Norman was already grown and living away from home, so the connection was not close. But Jenny had met him several times at office functions held at Frank's house.

He was striking looking, with his mother's fair colouring paired with unusually dark eyes. According to Frank, the father was Mexican.

In spite of his attractive looks, Jenny always felt a coldness about him that made her distinctly uncomfortable. She tended to act on instinct when judging character, and she always noticed a distinct lack of it in Norman.

Moving behind Queenie's desk, she rested her hand on the telephone. "I was just locking up and calling in my report to Frank."

"A report to Frank?" His eyes widened with interest. Moving forward casually with manicured hand on hip, he leaned his thighs against the desk on the other side. His subtly textured jacket hung perfectly from his shoulders, accentuating his athletic build and lean waist. "I was just in the neighbourhood and noticed the lights on. Thought I'd stop by on the off chance that Frank was around, check in with the step-pater. Keep on his good side."

He looked at her quizzically. "How did you ever convince him to change the name of the company, by the way? I know Acme Security was as plain as peanut butter, but he seemed wedded to it. Sentinel Security Group has a certain distinctive flair that is quite unlike Frank."

She glanced down. "It just seemed appropriate to change the name while we were changing the image. It was a business decision."

"Hmmm," he mused. "Frank really listens to you, doesn't he? Mother should watch out if she knows what's good for her." He gave her an insolent grin.

Jenny ignored that. "Frank's gone for the day but I'm just about to call him. If you'd like to talk with him be my guest." She made a show of picking up the receiver but Norman waved a hand in dismissal.

"No, it's not that important. I'll try to catch him later. By the way, have you done something with your hair?" His forehead wrinkled attractively. "You look fantastic!" He smiled down at her.

Jenny moved back jerkily. She hated this kind of come-on, and Norman tried it every time she met him. "Thank you," she murmured, beginning to punch numbers into the phone. "And now I really must finish up. You can see yourself out, Norman."

His brows rose, but he finally took the hint. As the office door swung shut on his well-groomed back, Jenny let out her breath in relief and placed the receiver back in the cradle, moving quickly around the desk to lock the front door. She'd never been caught alone in the office before. Maybe she'd better take steps to make sure she wasn't caught again.

~*~*~*~

The view through the glass doors off Jenny's back deck was peaceful. The ocean glinted and flashed in constant movement under the glorious winter sun where hordes of seagulls soared and dove into the water. A blue heron perched in disgusted solitude on a low rock that was barely visible at high tide. Jenny always thought of them as cranky old men. They paced back and forth, stately yet awkward on their long stick-like legs in the shallow water, searching and striking, then took off in a flurry of wings and water, croaking hoarsely.

She caught sight of Jordie. He was standing in her yard on a ladder with pruning shears and saw hanging from his belt, working on the old apple tree. It had been that way ever since she moved in after his father had left her the house in his will. Jordie mowed her lawn and clipped the hedge, cleaned the moss from the roof. It was like having her own personal handyman and tears came to her eyes at the way he took care of them.

Sliding the door open, she leaned out. "Would you like a coffee when you're done?"

Jordie turned on the top step of the ladder and grinned at her. "That would be great. Thanks."

Presently he clumped onto the deck, prying off his boots and carrying them inside to warm on the mat near the door. He padded into the living room and stood looking out the windows at the islands near the horizon.

"Still gorgeous, even in winter, isn't it?" Jenny had come up beside him with two cups of coffee.

"Yes, it is," he said, his head swinging slowly to take her in, his eyes steady on her face. He took the coffee over to the sofa. "Maggie phone you this week?" he asked as he carefully plopped down on the cushions, mug in hand.

"Yes, we had a nice conversation last night. It's the second time she's called since Sunday." Jenny gave him a guarded look, then glanced uncomfortably away. "Thank you for talking to me. I guess I've been a bit defensive and it couldn't have been easy for her to deal with."

"Come here," he said, and put an arm around her shoulders as she settled beside him. "Not easy for either of you, right? It's okay, Jenny."

A sob leaked out and she leaned against his familiar chest, clinging to his thick sweater. "How could she think that I was angry with *her*? I was angry with Bobby, and all the hurt and humiliation..." She ran out of breath and Jordie pulled her tightly against him, his big hand caressing her hair.

"Do you know," she gasped, "one of his affairs was with the mother of Maggie's best friend in elementary school in Nelson? If Maggie had found out, she would have been devastated. Nelson is a small town. I was terrified someone would tell her." The tears finally slowed.

Jordie held her, rubbing her back. He pressed her hand against his chest in comfort. "Jenny, it's okay. Bobby can't hurt you now, he's not in your life anymore."

"But he is," she blubbered. "The kids are still hurt when he doesn't call, or remember their birthdays. When he doesn't see them at Christmas, he still hurts them." She became aware of the comfort of his arms, his familiar beard brushing her temple, the kisses he pressed to her hair. She heaved a watery sigh and lifted her head. "I'm sorry Jordie, what a mess." Pushing off the cushions, she went to the bathroom to blow her nose.

When she returned, he was finishing his coffee. "Don't go away, now, Jenny. Come back and sit down. Let's talk this out."

Jenny gave a quavering laugh. "You sound just like Uncle Neal. Your dad always used to pat his knee and say, 'sit down here, Jenny, and let's talk this out.' I was usually crying because you'd been teasing me."

Jordie actually flushed under his beard. "I know I teased you a lot. Did I make your life miserable?"

She plopped down beside him on the sofa. "Not miserable, just normal I guess." She took his hand. "You're a kind man, Jordie. You've taken good care of me since I moved here. And I know I haven't made things easy for you. I'm prickly and stubborn."

"No, not easy, but very worthwhile. Now, don't go off on tangents. Let's talk about Maggie. She needs her mum and she's hurting, Jenny. What gives?"

She watched his big fingers as she played with them. "I guess I'm always so angry about everything, that's all she sees. The last few times she called, I didn't give her a chance to talk before I jumped in with a tirade about something. Last time it was about you peeking through the hedge while I was sunbathing."

His fingers tightened momentarily in her grasp and Jenny peered impishly at him. "So by the time I asked her how she was, she'd stopped talking. I guess it was me who shut her up, wasn't it?"

Jordie nodded. "Maybe. I know you're hard to talk to sometimes when you've already decided it will hurt you. Right?"

Jenny nodded, her eyes downcast but her fingers still in his grasp.

"So think how hard it's been for Maggie," he said as she looked up at him questioningly. "She loves you, and she's young. Maybe she felt you didn't really hear what she had to say."

Her head lowered again and nodded.

"Jenny." He lifted her chin with his other hand to look at her and his mouth turned down at her sad expression. "This isn't about you being a bad mother."

She reached over to get a tissue. "I know my anger has been getting in the way. It must be time to let it go, huh?"

She studied his face for a minute. "I'll bet you weren't too thrilled when Mum phoned. I'd already chewed your head off half a dozen times." She stroked his beard until he grabbed her hand and abruptly pulled it away.

His smile seemed strained as he gripped her fingers, then released them and stood. "Time to go. Got my own trees to do."

Jenny nodded silently and watched him walk over to his boots by the door. He walked like an old man sometimes, like a man who had nothing to look forward to.

Then she bounced off the sofa at the shrill sound of the doorbell. "Oh, no, that's Izzy! She's here to take me shopping, and I'm not near ready!"

He laughed as she flew in a panic down the hall.

CHAPTER SIX

Jordie stepped out onto the sundeck and sat down in one of Jenny's damp deck chairs to pull on his muddy boots. He paused to gaze out at the ocean. His fishing boat was anchored in the next bay, tucked inside the shelter of the cove and he often escaped to head out onto the water. Not just to fish, but to relax and get away from Linda.

He sighed and leaned down to finish lacing his boots. Marrying Linda had been a mistake, maybe the biggest mistake of his life. She'd never been happy. Sometimes he wondered why she said that *yes* to his hasty proposal.

She didn't like intimacy, at least not with him. He'd long ago given up trying to entice or persuade her into his bed.

Jordie had been concerned and then dismayed early in their marriage when she didn't become pregnant. It had been a blow to his self-esteem but he went for tests, only to discover that the problem wasn't his. He'd assured her they could adopt.

He remembered the fury that engulfed him the day he discovered that from the beginning of their marriage his wife had been on the pill. Linda was calm when he confronted her. She liked her life platonic and peaceful. He'd winced involuntarily, but agreed behind his determinedly impassive expression that she knew exactly what she was talking about. Their relationship was platonic.

With despair he thought of his mother and step-father. It had been obvious to everyone that they loved each other. Jordie had realized that his own life was to be different, that kind of relationship wasn't for him. When his wife moved into the spare room, he'd buried himself in work.

But Jenny's return, living right next door, had aroused all those old feelings. It was difficult having her so near, yet still out of reach. He was a man torn by his conflicting emotions. And yet he couldn't stay away from her. She drew him like a magnet to her door.

~*~*~*~

Jenny ran her hands through her hair as she leaned out the door of her office. "Brad," she bellowed, "have you got that list yet?"

Queenie glared at her as she tried to talk on the telephone through the noise.

Jenny mouthed *sorry* and stalked down the hall. The back office was larger than the front rooms and housed the old office furniture Jenny had replaced a while ago. It had taken a bit of work to pry Frank free from his beat-up desk, but he was very pleased with the antique oak one that she found, huge, slightly battle-scarred, with locking file drawers. The top was polished to a beautiful sheen. She'd bought a great old brown leather chair to go with it. Queenie reported that several times she'd found him smoothing his hands down the soft padded arms.

She'd taken away the uncomfortable wooden chairs with the thin spindle backs that she remembered perching on for her job interview with Frank and replaced them with a comfortable couch and two upholstered armchairs. Frank complained that it was just like home. Every time he came to work his office had been re-arranged. She ignored his comments.

For the secretary she got a government- issue desk with computer wing, adding shelves and new filing cabinets to her space. Queenie was in heaven. A long sofa for one wall, several upholstered chairs, a low coffee table, all made for a comfortable but businesslike setting in the entrance.

Then she'd found some good prints for the walls, and turned her attention to her own office. Her walls now glowed with warm peach-toned paint, there was a pine table and chairs in the corner, and a low bench below the window loaded with plants from home.

The big back office was still a barren wasteland. Brad, Jenny's assistant, and Esley both had desks here, as did Pat Rooke, the supervisor of the 'theft experts'.

Jenny rushed through the door and Brad looked up from his papers. At twenty-two, Brad Foster was the type of guy who seemed to blend into the woodwork. He was average height, mousy brown hair cut short and parted on the side in a manner reminiscent of old FBI movies. His clothes were like Jenny's before her makeover. White polyester shirt, thin tie, brown polyester pants, brown shoes and socks. At least his shoes were leather.

He'd come on board just when Jenny was getting into full swing. He only worked as a theft expert for four months. He wasn't any good at it, and although he blended nicely into the crowd at any retail store, he got bored and lost interest in watching the customers.

But he was a wizard at organization. When she started a new project, Brad would take a lot of the load, leaving her free to do the management that Frank hated so much. Now there were three department heads, Pat Rooke with about forty people working as part-time theft experts, Esley Moro who managed twenty-eight security guards, and a new man, Dave Powers, that Jenny had just hired.

Dave was ex-police, about fifty and in good physical shape. He was possessed of a keen inquisitive mind. He'd made detective and taken early retirement. Jenny was positive she had the perfect job for him in her new baby, the private investigations department.

Brad handed her a piece of paper listing the names and qualifications of all the applicants they'd received for their new branch. Jenny glanced quickly down the list. It was long.

"Yes, but which ones do you recommend?" she asked impatiently.

He handed her a second list without looking up, and she smiled in spite of herself. She hardly ever caught him off guard, although sometimes, like now, she actively tried. This second list was much shorter, three names.

"Ah," she said, "that's more like it. Powers is coming in this afternoon and we can go over it with him. We need to find him a place to work as well. I've got my feelers out for another desk." She looked around the room critically. "Can we really fit another one in here?"

Brad nodded. "If we move Esley over, there's room near the window. Esley and Pat don't spend much time here so it shouldn't be too crowded." He consulted his notebook. "I've also been thinking that it would be better if we left this room for the department managers. We could wall off part of the reception area, then I'd be within reach of your office. We could build a filing room behind," he continued. "Queenie would have better security and the files shouldn't be out in the open anyway."

Jenny narrowed her eyes. "Have you talked to Queenie about this?"

Brad nodded again. "She suggested it. It'll be more important than ever with Mr. Powers here." He looked more serious, if that were possible. "Queenie thought her files have been disturbed lately, they were out of sequence when she came in. I thought you might have been going through them." His look was questioning, small creases showing in his young forehead

Jenny shook her head. "I don't touch her files. She hands me what I need before I have a chance to ask for it. And Frank is never around after Queenie's gone." Jenny's frown deepened as she gazed at him thoughtfully. "Any suggestions as to what's going on?"

Brad shrugged. "No, but I'd recommend we change the locks on the door."

Jenny slid off the corner of his desk. "We have a lot of employees walking through to talk with Pat or Esley, check schedules and pick up their pay. It's high time we paid attention to our own security."

Jenny had a niggling feeling as she walked back to her office. Her mind jumped to the memory of finding Norman in the office, just meandering in off the street at the end of the day. She remembered why she'd been so surprised to see him.

The building was old, mostly taken up with small offices, but the elderly caretaker was meticulous. He unlocked the entrance doors of the building at seven sharp every morning and locked them again at six at night. Jenny had keys, of course, to both the building entrance and their main office, as did Frank, Queenie and the managers. She didn't think even Alita had a key.

A person could always get out after the door was locked, but not in. Unless someone was going out just as Norman arrived and they let him in. She relaxed. But what about the times she felt her desk had been re-arranged? She kept her pens in a certain spot, and they'd been moved, papers appeared to be in a different order on her desk.

She shrugged. She must be getting antsy, nervous about expanding into a new area of security work just when she was leaving on vacation for two weeks. It was a big step. They should be careful, take their own security as seriously as they would take that of any client.

On the other hand, they could always assign Dave to investigate the office as one of his first jobs while she was away. Jenny laughed to herself and hurried back to her office.

CHAPTER SEVEN

Jordie watched Jenny walk around the kitchen in her housecoat, feet bare, making coffee and teasing him the way she always did. Her toes were pink from the chilly tile floor. Occasionally he caught a glimpse of leg, and his reaction was almost painful. She stood on the carpet just inside the dining room and curled her toes in the pile to warm them. He wanted to sit her on his thigh and warm them with his hands.

He sighed as she came toward him with that easy, loose-limbed grace that was distinctly hers. He must have spent half his life watching Jenny. Even when she was thirteen she'd already had a rounded womanly look that sent his fifteen-year-old heart racing.

His stepfather would lecture him about making Jenny miserable, hurting her feelings when he made fun of her. She would cry and Neal consoled her on his knee, assuring her that Jordie hadn't meant it, all the while giving Jordie stern looks above her bowed head. He'd feel remorseful and promise himself he wouldn't tease any more, but he liked to spend time around her and the teasing just came naturally.

She and his sister Harry played together all the time, girl stuff. And he couldn't resist breaking in to disturb things, just to get her attention. Sometimes the two of them would gang up on him and pin him down. He remembered once she'd actually given him a bloody nose, and then stood there horrified as it dripped down his face. He'd pretended it didn't hurt, secretly mortified that a girl had beaten him.

As the years passed, Jordie teased less and spent more time with his friends. And when he wasn't looking, Jenny grew up. He went off to college and when he came home, Jenny was engaged to Bobby MacDougall, of all men. Jordie had never liked him, a fast-talker who loved the girls. And Jordie had discovered to his chagrin that he'd always expected to marry Jenny himself. He'd never told her that. He'd just assumed she would be there, waiting while he finished college and got started in business. She should have known that they belonged together.

He'd been devastated, breaking down and sobbing at one point. His stepfather had advised that he tell Jenny how he felt.

"Give her the chance to know," he'd counselled. "She deserves the choice. She may find that she feels the same way about you. They aren't married yet, son. It's just that she's known you her whole life and still thinks of you as a cousin, even though you're no blood relation. This thing with Bobby MacDougall seems to have blown up pretty suddenly. Maybe she needs to think twice about it."

But Jordie had been in despair and said nothing. That was his first mistake. Now he sat in her kitchen, regretting it with his whole heart.

~*~*~*~

Dave Powers leaned back in his chair and rubbed his eyes. He'd been working long hours since he started with Sentinel Security. It wasn't exactly what he'd envisaged as early retirement. He'd imagined a part-time job, doing security somewhere and having time to fish or golf. He hadn't thought he'd be the head of a new department in a fast growing company.

Oh well, carpe diem, as they say. When this was offered, he'd jumped at it. Jenny said things would calm down once the department was established and personnel were in place, and he had enough experience to know that was true. This didn't carry the pressure of police work. There wasn't the stress involved, the danger, physical and otherwise. And the clients took what he could deliver. They didn't throw it back at him and demand more. He'd find his pace and do as much or as little as he wanted.

He shook his head ruefully and looked down at the dossier in front of him. He was a little uncomfortable with this deal. It was awkward, having one partner in the company telling him to do a job, and instructing him to keep it confidential from the other one. But ultimately Frank was the boss, what he said carried the most weight. So Dave had accepted the situation, albeit with reservations.

He'd had to take Esley Moro into his confidence. One man couldn't do this alone, and Frank had approved that. He trusted Esley from their long and close association. So the two of them were working on this file, and he hoped to hell when it finally came to light, which it was bound to do, Jenny didn't fire him over it. She'd be steaming mad if she discovered secrets within her own company.

CHAPTER EIGHT

J enny and Isabelle got off the plane to blinding sunlight. The white buildings and blue roofs were so overwhelming, Jenny couldn't open her eyes. No bloody wonder. She hadn't seen daylight for days. No walks, no runs, no fresh air for a solid week before they left.

She'd been dealing with last minute details at work, and more problems seemed to pop up every time she raised her head. She complained to Isabelle that she really couldn't leave. No one would look after the things that came up while she was away. Isabelle had immediately called Frank, who arrived in her office the day before the trip was scheduled with Brad in tow.

He had blustered around the room. "Jenny, don't think for one minute that we can't manage without you!"

She had the grace to blush in discomfort. Her gaze slid back and forth between Frank's aggressive, slightly red countenance and Brad's uncomfortable, but still sober expression.

"Furthermore," he continued, "Brad here, your alter ego, will keep his finger on the pulse and report every minute detail the instant you land on Canadian soil again. Won't you, Brad?" Frank gave him a little shove with his heavy elbow.

Brad grinned and nodded. "Jenny, you haven't left anything to chance. Dave Powers is totally focused on getting his resource people trained." He threw his hands up. "And besides, I'm here to help."

Jenny huffed a sigh and leaned back in her chair. "You're right. I'm just being a jerk. I know you managed without me before. But give me a *little* credit. The company *is* somewhat larger." She gave Frank a pointed look.

Frank gave her one back. "You were right the first time, Jenny, you're just being a jerk."

Brad suppressed a grin and backed cautiously toward the door as the boss continued, "Now go home and get packed. Isabelle deserves better than to have you grouchy on the flight. She's invested a lot of energy in prying you loose from your moorings, Lord knows why."

She gave him a sour look.

Jenny didn't go home right then, but she did load Brad up with more lists, instructions and reminders until he hunched his shoulders defensively when he saw her bearing down with a determined look and sheaves of paper in her hands.

~*~*~*~

Jenny lay in a rocky cove, the shade still and welcome in the late afternoon heat. Her skin was just beginning to turn a golden brown. Her hair seemed to have a life of its own in this climate, and swung around her head like a chestnut halo. She felt like a different woman, light-hearted and light limbed.

Their first week had been heavenly, once Jenny stopped fretting about what disasters might be happening back home. That took up the whole first day.

Isabelle was patient. She listened to the non-stop tirade with half an ear, interrupting now and then to point out the boats in the bay, the sharp sunny images, the lovely heat. She'd been to this island before and knew the best places to eat, the best places to shop, and where to hire a boat to take them on excursions through the glassy water.

Jenny couldn't believe she'd enjoyed herself so. They hadn't done much. She'd spent hours walking or lying on the beach, splashing in and out of the sparkling water, meandering along the narrow goat path the locals called a road. She kept one ear cocked for the interminable motorcycles that roared past, startling her and leaving clouds of white dust in their wake.

She felt as if she were living in limbo. Isabelle was more goal-oriented and had continued her exercise program, swimming for an hour, running for an hour, leaving her friend to linger where she would. Jenny felt her internal spring slowly unwind. She was no longer driven to phone the office, find out the latest minor event, or fill her time with purposeful, productive activity. She felt no urge to rise early and plan the day. The day was capable of planning itself.

At the beginning of the second week, Isabelle went for three days to a northern island to visit friends who were vacationing there. Jenny was on her own, and two weeks ago she would have gone into a tail spin at the very thought of all that time on her hands. Now she waved Isabelle off with a lazy smile and told her to take her time. She'd be fine.

She looked forward to being alone. She could do anything at all without consulting someone else or worrying that they might not want to do the same things. She couldn't remember the last time she'd been entirely by herself. Marriage with Bobby had been busy, he sometimes left town for several days at a time. But the kids were always there, babies who were totally lovable and totally dependent.

A tour bus had arrived in the village that morning. Aiden, the desk clerk, told her around the cigarette that perpetually hung from one corner of his mouth, that a new bus arrived every Monday loaded with visitors. And it left an hour later with people who had completed their stay. She'd be going out on the next Monday bus. She felt an unexpectedly sharp pang at the thought. She'd just gotten here.

The locals were so forgiving as she bumbled along, the typical tourist, probably asking typical questions. But there was never any hint that she wasn't as welcome as family, that they didn't have the time to spend enlightening her or directing her, or answering her requests.

She knew it wasn't fairy land. If she lived here she'd soon discover there were tensions on this island too, fights within families, unemployment, all the same old problems as back home. But she didn't see it, and it was such a relief to live on the surface for now.

Stretching luxuriously, she propped her back against a rock and stuffed a towel behind her head. The stones creating this little cove gleamed black in the strong light, and rose in ragged heaps up the beach. The beautiful white sand glittered down to the clear turquoise water. It made her think of pictures from the Bible she'd seen as a child, the sea so flat and blue, little waves lapping at the sandy shoreline.

Nothing could be more unlike the sea around Vancouver Island in winter, where great tidal surges roared in and out bringing piles of giant logs, boom sticks, lumps of tangled kelp. The mist flung up from the ocean and down from the clouds formed a haze that the winter sun struggled to penetrate. And the rain formed some part of every day. It was either raining, about to rain, or had just rained.

Here, the light had a completely different quality, so bright as to blind her. It reflected back from the pale sand, the shell paths, the sandy tracks, the white plastered buildings. It gave a surreal quality to the air, made her feel as if she were in a world not quite tangible. She felt far removed from her need to control work or battle her anger.

She sighed contentedly and swung her gaze around her private spot. A pair of sandalled feet came into view and she looked up, startled, to discover she had company. He stood in open shirt and khaki shorts, a beach mat over one shoulder, his back to her. He held his broad shoulders stiffly, one arm raised to shade his eyes from the glare as he looked out over the water watching a fish boat working its nets, the same boat Jenny had been watching earlier. His legs were muscled and tanned, covered in fine curly hair, an outdoorsman perhaps.

When he turned to face her, her suspicions seemed confirmed. His face was wide and weathered, deep creases from squinting against the sun bracketing dark brown eyes, brows heavy and low in a sun-forced frown. His hair was light brown and wavy, sun-streaked and a bit shaggy.

"Is this your cove, or do you mind sharing?" he asked. His voice was gravelly, as if he hadn't used it yet today. His brows rose in question and she could see his eyes were large, shaded by heavy lids.

Jenny shrugged and grinned. "It's not mine, I suspect a few people have discovered it before me. Although it's been very private all week. You're welcome to a spot, did you just come in on the bus?"

He nodded and bent down to spread his mat. "And you?"

"I came last week," said Jenny. "I'll be going out on that bus next week."

"Ah, yes, two weeks." He seemed to unbend stiffly by degrees as he sat on the mat and stretched out his legs. His breath came out in a huge gust. "Yes, it is heaven, isn't it? I haven't been here for years. I had forgotten how enchanted it is."

He lay back on the mat and heaved another sigh as if from the bottom of his chest. Then he closed his eyes and slept. Jenny watched him, on and off, as she watched the sea.

He had a guarded look about him, even in sleep. His arms lay at his sides, but the hands were not completely relaxed, the fingers curling from time to time. His mouth worked, tightening, then relaxing only to tighten again, sometimes with an accompanying frown. *Maybe just worn out. Kind of like me on my first week here.*

As the sun lowered she rose and left him there, carrying her mat back to the inn, walking across the shaded patio. She didn't see him at dinner, although the dining room was filled with new faces, a lot of the ones she had begun to recognize having disappeared.

CHAPTER NINE

But the next afternoon when Jenny was back in her cove after a wonderful morning on a walking tour, his presence was already apparent. His mat was spread in some shade, a shirt and book discarded in the sand. Jenny spotted a head out in the water. Presently the head disappeared, then reappeared nearer the shore.

He came slowly up the beach, barely panting from the swim and flopped down to dry. He grinned when he saw her. "Here I am again, hogging your beach. I figured I'd save it for you from the new arrivals." He looked so innocent, his brows quirked, water dripping down his face and forming rivulets on his chest.

Jenny laughed. They talked between swims and snoozing in the sun. His name was Greg, and he was from Seattle. Yes, he knew all about the rainy winters, the pervasive mist that defined the west coast, the shrouded light, the perpetual restlessness and sometimes overwhelming violence of the Pacific Ocean.

He'd been to Greece before as a youth, backpacking with friends. They had camped then. This time he was treating himself to a real bed with a roof over his head and meals in restaurants. He grinned derisively as he said this.

Isabelle came back from her visit to the northern island and by the time she returned, Jenny knew that Greg worked in an architectural firm in Seattle, downtown glass-walled offices, high profile powerful clients, and had been married for fourteen years. The marriage was rocky. There was one child, a twelve-year-old boy. His wife wanted to divorce but couldn't seem to bring herself to make the break.

The tension, a combination of work and home life, had gotten to the point where he thought he would either quit both his marriage and his career and walk away from it all, or take a more drastic step. He'd actually contemplated driving off the bridge one night on his way home from work.

"And that's when I decided that life was not so serious as to relieve myself of it entirely." As he said this, he frowned at his toes as if they offended him. "Thus the trip to Greece. I should be able to unwind enough in two weeks to at least be able to think logically again. I was on automatic pilot, performing by rote. Point me to it and I'll look after it."

Greg paused, grimacing as he stared ahead sightlessly at the clear twinkling sea under a cloudless sky. "Amazing, isn't it? We live in a society with one of the highest standards of living in the world, we have wonderful houses full of every gadget and appliance imaginable. Our children are intelligent and healthy, get the best education possible. We can afford to send them to university and still buy a new car every couple of years. And one day, driving home, you feel like driving off the bridge." His voice was bitter and laced with irony.

They were sharing a mat, facing out to sea, watching three local boys bobbing and playing in the water, tossing rocks and diving for them. Jenny squinted against the glare and adjusted her sunglasses. She swung her head to look at him. "Not so amazing. We're all capable of that. I forgot how to think for a while, myself. But I substituted rage. I was angry at everyone and everything."

She sifted the grainy white sand through her fingers and watched it form a pile beneath her hand. "I was so angry at my husband, for cheating me and the kids and then leaving us. The thing is, he'd already left us years before, but I didn't recognize it until much later. I was angry all the time and at everyone who crossed my path."

She drew a deep breath and risked a look at him. "I buried myself in work, and my kids just withdrew. They couldn't bear the heat of my focus. I wasn't angry at *them*, but I was angry *around* them. They couldn't even talk to me, I was so busy spouting off about something that had made me mad. I actually drove them away. I'm just now beginning to re-establish a relationship with my daughter."

Jenny wiped tears from under her glasses and faced out to sea again. "Maggie asked my mum to talk to me. To see if she could get me to actually listen. She's only eighteen. Isn't that something? She knew better than I did what needed to be done. I love that girl." Jenny stifled a sniff.

Greg put an arm around her and held her against his hot chest. Her head rested on his shoulder. "You're lovely, Jenny. And your daughter is lucky to have a mother who listens when she calls for help like that." He caressed her hair as he stared out to sea. "Lovely Jenny," he murmured.

~*~*~*~

Izzy had booked them on a boat cruise the next day to another island off to the southeast. They visited pottery works and local handicraft stalls. Jenny loved it all. She bought several large decorative pottery planters, knowing she'd have to have them carefully packaged for the plane trip home to get them back safely. But she could just imagine those lovely pots out in the summer sun on her patio, full of herbs and flowers. They would always remind her of this delightful land

There were some beautiful blown glass objects in greens and blues she knew Maggie would enjoy, and a shawl for her mother. Mum would probably never wear it, but the colours were so attractive she could see it spread across the foot of a bed or the back of a chair.

On the boat trip back, Jenny realized with a pang that they only had one day left before their flight home. She felt something like panic set in. *I'm not ready, I can't go back yet.* Not back to all that rage that seemed to fill her unexpectedly, to swell inside and seize a life of its own, robbing her of her children and friends, of peace of mind.

They trooped back through the patio of the inn, Izzy walking with her characteristic long-limbed grace, Jenny trailing behind reluctant that the day should end. Greg hailed her out of the shadows where he was seated at a table, a candle with a hurricane glass covering it casting a warm glow.

Jenny was delighted to see him and felt a small flutter in her heart. "Greg, there you are! Did you guard the cove today?"

He laughed in his husky voice. "I did, but to no avail. My mermaid didn't come."

Leaving Izzy to carry on alone, she sank down onto a chair beside him. "Oh, I'm sorry. But I had such a wonderful day. We cruised over to the next island. I got some lovely things for Maggie and my mom. And some huge pottery jars just for me."

Greg laughed, and leaning over, he grasped her cheek with gentle fingers. "Jenny, you're magnificent." He kissed her, his lips covering hers in a tender caress that immediately became more insistent. His warm hand slid around the back of her neck under her hair, pulling her toward him as he increased the pressure of his mouth.

She felt a stirring inside, powerful enough to throw her off balance. It had been so long, she'd nearly forgotten this visceral, physical response, this sudden rush of passion and longing. Her hands came up to brace against his chest, not to push away but to steady herself. She felt the mat of hair under his shirt, resilient to the touch. His chest was muscular, solid and warm beneath her palms.

He kissed her again, and a slow burn began, starting in her belly and uncurling along her nerves. When he paused for air, he was breathing heavily as he leaned his forehead against hers. "Oh, Jenny. This is probably a very foolish move. But I just want to take your hand and lead you off to somewhere private." He laughed ruefully.

Jenny rubbed her hands against his chest and studied his strong face with the wide cheekbones and honest, fearless eyes in the dim light. "Very foolish, Greg." She grasped his hand and stood. "Let's go."

He didn't hesitate. His room opened off the corridor on the main floor, facing the sea. The windows were open, the curtains flapped gently in the light breeze and the sound of slapping waves filled the room. But the ambiance was almost lost on them.

Greg hesitantly offered her a place on the couch and opened his fridge. "Would you like some wine? I have an Italian bottle here."

She laughed. "That would be nice. I'm not quite used to the Greek ones."

Sitting down beside her, Greg lifted his glass to clink with hers. "To new friends," he said.

She took a sip. It was lovely and she took another swallow.

Greg set his glass down. "Come here," he said.

As his mouth closed over hers, Jenny felt something loosen inside. Muscles she held tight slowly released as his mouth roamed to her throat. "Oh, Greg." She turned her head to give him access and felt the buttons on her blouse give under skilled fingers. When his hand wrapped around her, she let out a sigh. It felt good, it felt right.

But it felt like it should be Jordie holding her and caressing her breast. Jordie with the heavy-lidded eyes and watchful expression, the hot gaze. He was the one who cared for her, cared about her. He was the one who wasn't there when she was ready to marry.

Her breath caught in her throat at the sudden surge of anger as she pushed Greg's hand away. "Not now, please."

He pulled back slowly and looked into her eyes. "No? It feels pretty darned good."

Jenny nodded. "I know." She gave a little smile. "But I'm not ready for this. And maybe neither are you." She pulled the lapels of her blouse together. "I don't want to make another mistake. I've made enough in my life."

Greg sat up reluctantly and reached for his wine. "Yeah, I know the feeling."

CHAPTER TEN

I sabelle was just climbing into bed when Jenny bounced through the door to their room. Her eyes widened and she grinned but bit back any comment.

"Don't you say a word, Izzy," Jenny warned.

"I wasn't going to. I was just a little worried, but I saw you sit down with your friend and assumed you'd been abducted, so left it at that." Her mirth simmered just beneath the surface.

Jenny looked at her accusingly and then burst out laughing, Isabelle joining in merrily. As her laughter subsided, she drew a deep breath and braced herself against the door.

"Izzy, I'm not going back with you tomorrow," she announced. "I've decided to stay on for a while. I'll call Frank tomorrow morning to let him know. I'm sure things are fine back there." She looked bemused. "But I'm just not ready to face that again."

Isabelle's expression became sober as she listened. "Jenny, you don't know anything about this man. It's one thing to have a one-night stand kind of thing. I mean I don't recommend it, you can catch diseases." Her voice became louder as if to override any argument as Jenny raised her hands in defense.

"I'm serious. I know you've been under a terrible strain, and maybe this is just the thing to loosen you up. But you can't chuck everything for a fling around Greece with some guy who admits he has a wife and family back home. He could be very happily married, or his wife may think they're happily married and he just makes a practice…"

"Izzy! Isabelle!" Jenny talked through her words. "This isn't about Greg. I know, I kind of got carried away tonight, but I didn't lose all my common-sense."

Isabelle's brows rose, and Jenny smiled self-consciously, sinking down on the bed beside her friend. "This is about me. For the first time in years, I'm free. I don't have children here that need my attention. You don't know what a drain that is, being a mother every minute of the day."

Isabelle was silent as she took Jenny's hand and held it between both of hers.

Jenny looked at her, tears glimmering in her eyes. "I'm free."

Isabelle nodded.

"And," she continued, "I've been angry for so long, that it was eating me up inside. Maggie pointed that out and Jordie talked to me. He's a good friend, you know, Izzy, always there to look after me. Remember, even in high school he was fighting my battles. But when I moved back to the island, there he was mowing my lawn and getting me moved in."

She paused, and Isabelle continued to stroke the back of her hand in silence, waiting.

Finally, Isabelle said, "So, what does this mean, you not going back tomorrow? What are you going to do?"

"I feel like I have some work to do. I've just begun to let go of old hurts. It seems important to do this now, while I'm away from all the distractions back home. Greg's nice," Jenny blushed, "but he's not why I need to stay. I want to go up to Paris. Rob is supposed to be in France in a few days. I'd love to see him, he's been gone so long. He still has all those memories of me storming around, unable to listen. I really need to do this."

~*~*~*~

Jenny had such a vulnerable wistful expression that tears popped into Isabelle's eyes. Her old friend had always been feisty and assertive, and when she'd returned to Vancouver Island, Izzy had been astonished to see the changes time and a broken marriage had wrought.

Jenny was still assertive, even aggressive. But she wasn't the fun-loving girl Isabelle remembered. In fact, fun didn't seem to be part of her vocabulary. She was rigid in her responsibilities to her children and her job when she started with Frank at Acme Security.

Surprisingly, her new hairstyle had been the first recent sign of a chink in that armour. After that, Izzy hadn't been able to resist dragging her out to work on her wardrobe, encouraging her to experiment a little. If she'd been back home, Isabelle would have welcomed this change. But to leave her here was worrisome. On the other hand, for Jenny to open up like this was a mark that she'd been praying for.

When she voiced those very fears, Jenny flung her arms around the dancer's willowy form in a fierce hug. "Isabelle, it's alright. I'll be alright. But I want this time for me. I can get myself from here to Paris without losing my way or my money. Heck, I might even enjoy it."

In the end, Isabelle went down with Jenny for breakfast the next morning, joining Greg where he sat on the patio waiting for them. There were a few awkward moments, and Greg's face was red when he realized Jenny was leaving for Paris, but he braved it through. And when Isabelle left with Jenny on the bus that afternoon, she was more than a little reassured that her friend was strong enough to go on alone to find her son.

~*~*~*~

Jenny knew Isabelle wasn't happy with her decision, but Frank was an entirely different story. When she finally got through on the phone to the office, Queenie took her news in stride. She spoke to Brad, was quickly caught up on events and reassured that everything was under control.

However, Frank came on the phone and sounded like he was having an asthma attack. "But Jenny," he huffed into the phone, "we could barely drive you out of here when you were leaving, and now you want to stay longer? What's going on, are you alright? Let me talk to Isabelle."

Isabelle got on the phone and talked at length while Jenny paced up and down the airport walkway. Finally, she waved Jenny back and when she put the phone to her ear, she could still hear Frank puffing at the other end.

"Frank, what is the problem? All I'm telling you is I'll be a week later getting back. Queenie tells me everything's fine and Brad says things are in hand. Is there something they're not telling me?"

"No, no, nothing like that. Everything's good, Jenny."

"Well, I *will* come back. I'm not deserting you."

"I know," he said, "As a matter of fact, now that I've had time to think about it, it's a good idea. You'll come back rested and refreshed. We'll be all the happier to see you when you return."

Jenny hung up, a worried frown on her forehead. He'd still been breathing heavily when he signed off. Well, she'd check with the office again in a couple of days. Now she had a train to catch. She grinned at Izzy and hugged her goodbye.

CHAPTER ELEVEN

Frank placed the phone in its cradle and sat back, waiting for his breathing to return to normal. He could feel his heart pounding heavily in his chest under the crisp shirt that Alita sent out faithfully for laundering every week.

Jenny wasn't coming back! He didn't know why that news had taken him by the throat, why the alarm had flared in his head so suddenly. But he needed her right now. He needed her!

Gripping the arms of his new leather chair, he swivelled to look out the window, staring at the brick wall across the alley. He willed his heart to slow down, willed his breathing to come under control. He'd been counting on Jenny to apply her calm and creative mind to his problem, a problem that seemed to be growing in dimensions as time passed. He'd been relying on her to find a way out of this mess he'd gotten them into.

He was losing control. He never lost control, but this had been insidious from the beginning. Sucking him in, sucking him down before he recognized it for what it was.

He dropped his face into his hands, then slowly straightened. Jenny was good, but he was a match for these bastards, even without her. And she'd be home soon. He wouldn't panic. He knew he could beat them at their own game.

~*~*~*~

The next days were heavenly. Jenny's first stop was Athens. She took a bus to the top of the hill and strolled the Acropolis with its breathtaking views and stunning stonework, overwhelmed by the history of the place. She spent hours walking the museum and examining stone statues tipped at precarious angles in the dirt around the building. She had a lovely informal meal in an outdoor café in downtown Athens that evening, and watched couples strolling the streets in the dark as she thought of her encounter on the shores of that Greek island.

Greg had made her feel beautiful. He was a dear man and she'd found depths to him that she suspected she'd never seen in her husband of fourteen years. She felt intelligent and charming when she was with him, things she'd thought she lacked when her marriage failed. She'd soaked it up like a sponge, filling the void that had opened inside during the years since her marriage ended.

She rushed back to her room and cried her eyes out. When the sobs finally subsided, she realized she wasn't saying good-bye to Greg, but to Bobby. She'd been clinging to the image of her husband with some unnamed hope. Now she could let it go.

She spent the next day wandering the narrow crooked streets of Athens, pondering whether to buy a rug, where to eat lunch. As she walked the outcroppings of rock around the Parthenon other thoughts began to penetrate. Because it wasn't Bobby she longed for. It was Jordie. Cousin Jordie, who'd been such a good friend and huge tease growing up. Mature Jordie, the tall lean muscled businessman who looked after her without being asked. He just showed up.

Jenny had a sudden spurt of anger at him. It was so unexpected and forceful that she looked around in confusion at the rocky hill and took a seat on one of the old tilted stone benches. Where had that come from? Jordie had been a model neighbour ever since she moved back to Victoria.

So why was she mad at *him*?

She shook her head in mingled amazement and fury as the emotions swept over her, quaking with both rage and grief. He was there for her *now*, but he hadn't helped her before when she was in so much pain. Or even before that, when she was deciding to marry Bobby, where was Jordie *then*? She opened her mouth in agony, as she leaned forward over her knees, sobbing and hugging herself. She longed to grab his strong brown throat between her two hands and squeeze the life out of him, scratch her fingernails down his face, claw at him, pound his chest until she lost all strength.

Exhausted from the fierce attack, she lay on the bench and gazed at the light blue sky. A family counsellor had once told her, "emotions aren't rational. We can't explain them away. They don't have to make sense to be real. And as something real, they have to be accepted. They'll tell you a great deal about yourself if you let them."

Jenny relaxed, and the hurt began to ease. It would just take a little time to heal.

As the days passed, she felt like an emotional log-jam had been blasted away. She smiled, thinking that was a very West Coast analogy. She could thank both Isabelle and Greg for the progress, although she would hesitate to tell anyone about Greg's part in it.

~*~*~*~

She called Frank the night before she was leaving Athens and he sounded much better. "Have a drink on me in Paris," he said, "and give my love to Rob." His breathing sounded fine.

Then she called Jordie. There was no answer, and when the answering service kicked in Jenny didn't quite know what to say. She knew Linda would resent whatever message she left. So she simply said, "Hi, everyone, this is Jenny. I'm staying away a little longer than planned. Hope all is well and you don't mind looking after the cat."

As she rang off, she knew Jordie would call Queenie at the office if he wanted to know what was going on.

She flew to Italy, spent a few wonderful days in Florence, then caught a train that eventually deposited her in Paris. She'd almost given in to the temptation to fly but was thrilled that she hadn't. The train meandered, no straight-line journey this. The scenery was not to be missed, and the passengers just as entertaining.

She met a young German student who was returning from a language school in Italy. His great ambition was to become a translator for the United Nations, and he'd been perfecting his Italian accent and vocabulary. He was going back home for a quick visit and then planned to be off again, to London this time, to attend school there. His English was good, if slightly stilted. What Jenny found delightful was his overwhelming energy and enthusiasm. His English vocabulary was already larger than any young person she'd ever met back home, and he spoke so descriptively it was as if he'd digested a dictionary.

He was loaded down with what appeared to be all his worldly goods. When they debarked from the train in Paris, he struggled into the heavy straps of his towering backpack, picked up his suitcases and bags and simply stood there, immobile under the weight of all his luggage.

Jenny laughed until she nearly fell over. He grinned obligingly. She finally found a porter, and they both loaded their luggage onto his carts and set off. She left the young man at the taxi station, and last saw him arguing with the porter in what sounded like passable French about the best way to reach his destination.

Jenny checked into a little hotel on the left bank. The office and tiny lobby were on street level, like most of the small establishments in the area. She entered an elevator that would accommodate no more than one person and a single good-sized suitcase and found her room on the fourth floor. It overlooked the street and sported twin beds jammed into a tiny space, but still leaving room for a miniature balcony off the double windows.

Twin beds would work, if Rob managed to find her. The bathroom was almost as big as the bedroom with lovely black and white tiled walls and floor and double windows matching those in her room. She unpacked her things and set out to explore.

She found an internet coffee shop and sent messages to all the addresses she had for Rob and his friends. He already knew she'd be in Paris waiting for him.

Then she found a lovely sidewalk cafe and ordered an espresso. It was so strong she thought the spoon might melt. Next time she would just have coffee, but everyone should have espresso once at a sidewalk cafe in Paris. She watched the pedestrians flow by.

The air was fresh and slightly damp, the smell of the river permeating everything, wet, old, a little fishy. Pigeons rose and landed in flocks about her, making a whirring sound with their wings. They strolled hopefully under chairs and around the legs of the tables. She wrote a few postcards, pulling her sweater closer as she tried to adjust to the cooler weather.

The next day was spent wandering wherever her feet led her. She missed Jordie more than anyone, but not as much as she had feared. She was curiously at rest and comfortable with herself. She went to the Louvre, of course, and was totally astonished at the modern pyramid standing in the middle of the ancient palace courtyard, surrounded by buildings erected in the Sixteenth Century. Here was this Egyptian building formation built in the most modern style possible, all glass and steel, which led directly underground and was the main entrance to the famous heritage museum.

Even more astonishing, but in a different way, was when she found herself standing in front of the framed painting of the Mona Lisa. What a wonderful world, that she could come here and walk into this building to see a painting that she'd wondered about all her life. She watched the secret smile for the longest time, rooted to the spot.

Then she wandered on, through the long corridors of the old converted palace until her legs were too tired to take another step. She sat on a couch and watched the artists and students, set up with stool and easel in the wide halls, learning from the masters.

Wandering the streets along the Seine, she bought crepes from street vendors that were better than anything she'd had back home, went into churches whose names she didn't recognize. She found the Palais de Justice and walked around Sainte-Chapelle. Every gigantic stained glass window was different and each was more amazing than the last. The whole Bible was depicted in the enormous windows running entirely around the upper floor of the chapel. The colours were glorious and glowed darkly, greatly dimmed by time.

The people of the city were aloof and friendly by turns, and she enjoyed both, putting it down to the famously volatile French personality.

And then Rob arrived. He looked wonderful, tanned and lean, very self-assured and at the same time more open and vulnerable than she remembered. He gave her such a hug, and then another. He traipsed up to her room and deposited his heavy pack, taking up most of the space with his big shoes and clothing scattered around. She kicked his hiking boots out of her way and ruffled his hair.

He was hungry, of course. They took the edge off their appetites with a cheese and ham crepe from a street vendor, and searched for a local bistro recommended by their afternoon desk clerk at the hotel. Rob spoke a little French, which only infuriated the waiters. The server would pretend not to understand, or respond in stilted and haughty English. They did their best to hide their laughter.

CHAPTER TWELVE

The next day Jenny and her son caught the early train to Versailles to the beautiful palace of the Sun King, Louis XIV. Rob was eager to see it, having confided that he missed out on quite a bit in his travels because it was too expensive to pay the admission charges to many of the world-famous buildings and exhibits that he came upon. Jenny felt a twinge of regret for him, but gleaned from his comments that he was enjoying an entirely different view of the cultures he visited.

The Chateau was so lovely it literally took their breath away. In spite of the fact they had to inch their way through the rooms in a crush of people, the artistry, paintings and furnishings were absolutely stunning. Through much of it, they walked with their heads back, taking in the intricately decorated ceilings. Jenny started taking a hundred pictures, then finally put her camera in her bag and just soaked it up.

Outside the air was lovely and fresh. They took their picnic lunch down to the gardens and ate overlooking the Grand Canal. Strolling back up the garden avenues, Jenny could hear charming seventeenth century chamber music, and suddenly the lavish fountains erupted, water gushing in different formations all around them.

She could almost imagine she was there with Marie Antoinette, the music floating from discreetly placed orchestras around the grounds, people laughing softly and moving slowly up and down the walks in sumptuous dress, the fountains forming a lovely backdrop. It was entirely enchanting.

As they mounted the steps in the courtyard of the Chateau to get a better view of the gorgeous fountain of Latona, the wind shifted and a gust blew the water into the air. Jenny gasped and held her nose.

"Rob, look out!" The smell nearly knocked them over, and they ran, wiping the drops from their cheeks.

"Gee, Mum, you'd think they could at least use a bottle of bleach or something! I mean, it looks wonderful, but there's stuff *growing* in that water."

They laughed their way back to the train. "Well," she said, "at least we were lucky enough to be here on the day they turn the fountains on." Jenny sighed tiredly as they settled down in their rail car for the hour-long ride back into Paris.

She relaxed in her seat and looked over at her son. He was taller. He certainly seemed older. His face was longer, the strong jaw more pronounced. His beard was new, grown on his travels perhaps because it was easier than shaving. It curled in red-brown tendrils across his lower face, darker than his hair by several shades, and making him look like a young professor or a farm worker. How she'd missed him! He was mature and yet a child still in her eyes.

"How has your trip been, Rob? Has it been what you hoped? How are the people you're travelling with?"

"It's been great, Mum. Really fantastic." His eyes shone with enthusiasm amidst all that hair, and she smiled to herself.

"I started out with Michael, you remember, from school. But he got tangled up with a girl the first month and stayed on in London." There was a young man's disgust in his voice for a friend who would let a woman get in the way of his plans.

"So I headed across to Boulogne on a boat by myself and met a guy from Ontario, Pete, and we hooked up together. There are three of us now. We sometimes part and agree to meet again at a later date. Pete will get here tomorrow or the next day and wants to head down to southern France and Spain. I thought I'd go with him." There was a question in his eyes as he looked at her. *Is that enough time? Will we have had enough time?*

Jenny's heart turned over in her breast. But she smiled and took his hand. "Whatever plans you've made, I'll just fall in with them. This is your trip and I'm lucky to have been able to catch up with you and spend a few days." He grinned and squeezed her fingers, keeping her hand in his big-knuckled one.

"I've missed you dreadfully, Rob. It's very quiet at our house on holidays with just Maggie and me. She misses you too. We'll be glad to get you home, even for a short time."

She grew pensive as she prepared to wade into the conversation she knew she should have. "I've been hard to be with sometimes, I know. I've been full of anger. But I'm learning to enjoy life a bit." She smiled ruefully. "I don't want to get heavy, sweetie. But I'm changing and things will be a little easier when you come home. And I wanted to say that I wasn't angry with *you*, I was never angry with you."

He squeezed her hand again. "It's okay, Mum. I know all that." His voice cracked, and Jenny's eyes filled with tears as she smiled at her son, so much a man yet still a boy after all.

"That's the other thing you'll have to learn to put up with. I cry at the drop of a hat, but don't let it upset you. I quit really quick, too."

"Gosh," he said, his cheeks pink above his beard. "Don't cry here on the train, Mum." He looked around furtively. She laughed and punched his arm.

~*~*~*~

Jenny cried when she saw him off at the train station heading for Spain with his buddy. He was embarrassed but hugged her anyway, then came back and hugged her again. She smiled radiantly through her tears and assured him she was fine.

The next day she headed out of Paris, taking the train to Boulogne. She transferred to the hovercraft and settled in for the trip to Folkestone. She'd been in a quandary whether to take the Chunnel train, but decided to see the views even if it took more time. The crossing was swift but she was thrilled by the sight of the white cliffs of Dover approaching, and charmed by the small English fishing village at the foot of the cliffs. The train ride into London was an eye-opener. She'd never imagined that an island with the population that Britain boasted would still have miles of farms and fields, sheep dotting the grass as far as the eye could see.

Of course, the farms were small, the fields divided into what appeared to be miniature holdings by rock borders. She smiled when she thought of travelling across the Canadian prairies, never seeing a house, let alone a fence, for hours. Here it appeared that every inch of land was in use.

Now that she was nearing the end of her trip, she couldn't wait to be home. She missed everything, the wide spaces between towns, the misty weather, the high craggy mountains, Jordie, Frank, Queenie. As soon as she settled into her room near Piccadilly Circus she placed a call to Sentinel Security, waiting for half an hour before a connection was made.

Queenie answered. Yes, Frank was there, he'd been hoping she would call. Everything was fine, they were looking forward to her return and hearing all about her travels. Was she ready to come home and settle down for a while? That was a long two weeks she had been away, more like three or four, right?

Jenny laughed. Yes, she'd been away long enough. Couldn't wait to get back and dig into the work piled on her desk.

Frank finally came on the phone. Jenny thought his voice was weak. "Frank, are you alright? You don't sound so well. What's going on?"

"I'm fine, Jenny. Had a bit of a cold, haven't shaken it yet is all. Anyway." His voice came more firmly across the line. "So you're back here on Monday, I hear.

None too soon. I hope you've had a good trip. How was Rob? Did he catch up with you in Paris?"

"Yes, and he's great. He wants to travel another couple of months but is running low on funds. He'll be back sometime soon and says he's returning to university in the fall, so that's good to know. I wasn't sure if he would."

"Good, Jenny. Yes, yes."

She was alarmed. Frank sounded tired, bone weary. His voice had lost a lot of its usual vibrancy.

"Well, is there anything happening at the office I should know about? How is Dave doing with his new department, and how are Esley and Pat? Everything running smoothly?"

"Nice and smooth. No problems." Frank paused, as if for breath. "Dave has settled in just fine. We have a couple of big clients he's courting at the moment. Business clients, they want information on their competition. And there's a steady stream of the small stuff, marital, insurance and so on."

He stopped again, she waited.

"So that's about all. My, it'll be good to see you back here. Well," and his voice became more businesslike, "I guess I'd better let you go, being as how I'm paying for most of this call."

Jenny chuckled. "Okay, it's good to hear your voice. I'm looking forward to getting back. I want a nice big hug, just for being a good girl and coming home." With relief Jenny heard Frank's hearty laugh.

"And Frank? Could you put Queenie back on? I forgot to ask her something. Thanks."

Jenny frowned as she waited for Queenie to pick up the call.

"Hi, there," Queenie was back.

"Queenie, is Frank's door closed?"

"Yes, honey, it is. What's up?"

"Frank. He sounds tired, absolutely exhausted. Or else he isn't well. What's going on?"

"Well," Queenie drawled out the word, "I'm not sure exactly. I've been trying to figure it out myself. Alita was in the other day, and mentioned he was having fainting spells. But I haven't seen any sign of that. What he does look is worried, but the business is going fine. So I figure it's personal, you know? Maybe he's sick, or maybe he and Alita aren't getting along. She can be such a bitch."

"Queenie, when I first called two weeks ago, it sounded like he was having an asthma attack. He got all out of breath."

"Yes, I know. That was strange. I heard his voice get loud and I popped my head in to see if he wanted something. I think he just panicked for a minute, then he calmed down."

"That's what he said," Jenny replied. "He said *now that I've had time to think about it*."

"Well, don't worry. He's okay, his colour is good. He just looks stressed. And truly, things in the office are going smoothly. So, enjoy your journey home and we'll see you on Monday. Okay?"

"Thanks, Queenie." Jenny gave a big sigh. "What a jewel you are, see you next Monday." She rang off.

Poor Frank, he was such a decent guy. Well, if he was in trouble she'd do what she could for him when she got back. Probably just listening would help. When a person had problems in their marriage, there wasn't much an outsider could do for them. She should know.

CHAPTER THIRTEEN

London was lovely, wet but never dreary. She had one night, so went down to the ticket discount booth in Leicester Square to see what musicals still had seats available. Travelling by herself seemed to be a distinct advantage. There were single seats for just about anything. She had her pick of entertainment.

Miss Saigon was absolutely stunning. Jenny was enthralled with the poignant story, hurt when the characters hurt, and cried at the end. The pimp was such a talented performer she couldn't take her eyes off him. The role was similar to Joel Gray's in the movie version of *Cabaret*, and just as powerful.

It had such an effect that she walked down the street to her hotel room with tears on her cheeks. She sniffled her way to bed that night, and slept like a log, awaking refreshed and sunny. Nothing like a sad story and good cry to put her in a good mood.

Today she was going home! That's why she was so excited. She got into Vancouver too late Friday night to get over to the island. She'd booked a hotel room and invited Maggie to spend the night with her. Six months ago, she didn't think her daughter would have come, but now she sounded excited about the prospect. Jenny called from the Toronto airport stopover to confirm her arrival time and Maggie was waiting for her when she got off the plane into the balmy, damp mist of Vancouver.

Jenny took a huge breath and let it out slowly. Oh, the smell of the earth of home, there was nothing like it.

Maggie gave her such a hug, Jenny nearly dropped her case. So she dropped it anyway and hugged her back. They had a wonderful time, went for a swim in the hotel pool, had a drink in the bar, then went back to their room and changed into their pajamas. They chose a movie on the movie channel and ordered dinner from room service. They cuddled close in bed and chatted.

"Remember when we learned to ski, Mum?" Maggie said. "We skied in the back yard, didn't we, in Nelson?"

Jenny chuckled. "Yes, you were so funny. You were five and Rob was seven. You were covered with clothing from head to toe. You had your toque pulled down low and your turtle neck pulled up high, and both of them tucked into the edges of those big goggles you got for Christmas. So you just pointed your skis down the hill and did a snow plow."

"Yeah, that was so much fun." Maggie sighed.

Jenny looked at her curiously. "And do you remember swimming in the summer when it got so hot? We'd call Dad to meet us at the river after work, and then pack a picnic dinner and spend the afternoon down on the beach. You guys went in and out of the water for hours. Remember Horsey, the neighbour boy? He taught you two to swim. That kid was a natural in the water."

"Yeah, I remember! I thought he was so old, and really he was only a year ahead of me, he was just big for his age. And he did teach us, he'd take me out into the deeper water and hold me up and head for shore."

"Yes, he had a lot of patience, eh? Very kind, for a little guy. I had him in one of my classes when I was teaching at the elementary school. He was terrible in school, simply couldn't learn a thing, poor little fellow. He had no dad and his mum had real troubles. He came to school one day and told me the police had been at his house the night before because his mum tried to kill herself. Three strikes against him. No wonder he couldn't learn, he was too busy trying to survive. I wonder what ever happened to him?"

"He's at university, Mum. He's in my year and taking science courses, wants to be an engineer."

"You're joking!" Jenny looked at her daughter in astonishment. "How did you even know who he was?"

Maggie looked thoughtful. "Well, he's changed, but I can still see the same Horsey that we knew. And he knew me because I look like you." She slanted her mother a glance as she continued, "I noticed him watching me, and one day he came up to me in the cafeteria and sat down. He asked if I'd ever lived in Nelson, and when I said yes, he said I must be Mrs. MacDougall's daughter. I look so much like you, he would have known me anywhere."

Jenny's mouth rounded in an O of surprise. "He remembered how *I* looked? Isn't that strange."

"Not so strange, Mum. He said you were his teacher for two years."

"Well, that's true, I did have him for a couple of years. And he had a marvelous ability to do spatial visioning. He had the most amazing attention span for toys like Lego where he built with his hands. I'm sure he'll make an excellent engineer."

Maggie flopped over onto her stomach and looked down into her mother's face. "Mum, he said that you always thought he was brilliant, and that he could do anything he wanted. He never forgot that. His mum finally gave him up, and he lived with his aunt until he went off to university. He said it took him extra time to finish high school because of what happened at home and because school was hard. But he kept going because Mrs. MacDougall knew he could do it if he tried."

Jenny felt the tears pop into her eyes, and hugged her daughter. "Poor little guy! You never know, do you? You never know how what you say can affect others." She felt remorse for all the anger she'd unleashed in the presence of her children.

"I was so proud when he told me that, that my Mum had encouraged him when no one else saw his potential. He's really a nice guy, you know? Just like you said, about him teaching us to swim and how patient he was. I think he did it because he knew you'd be proud of him."

"Oh, Maggie, what a soft-hearted little thing you are. Why don't you invite Horsey home with you some weekend? I'd love to see him again."

Maggie nodded and snuggled in. "Are you eager to get back to work, and see Frank and Queenie and everyone? Oh, I forgot! Queenie called today. She was trying to find out where you would be, but I wasn't in when the call came and by the time I phoned her back the office was already closed."

"No problem, Mags. I'll call her tomorrow after I'm home. If something came up at the office, I can't do anything about it right now anyway."

They were silent for a minute, each thinking their own thoughts. Then Maggie squirmed. "Mum, do you hate Dad?"

Jenny stiffened and glanced at her sharply, then allowed herself to relax. "No, sweetie, I don't hate your Dad. I was very angry for a long time, but that just hurt us, eh?" Maggie gave a small nod. "Why do you ask?"

"Well, you never talk about him, except when you're angry. And he never calls us or sees us."

"I never talk about him because I don't want to say nasty things about your father, you don't deserve to hear that. And for a long time I couldn't think of anything good to say." She laughed and Maggie chuckled.

"I think I can talk about him now. I did quite a bit of work while I was away. It wasn't all fun. I had a lot of time to myself. So, what do you want to know?"

"Nothing much." Maggie was silent for a minute. "Just that at Christmas when I saw Dad, he said you wouldn't meet him and that you must hate him."

Ah, Jenny thought, the penny drops. "Well, if you recall, I hadn't heard from him in three years. But he didn't call to arrange to meet until Christmas Day and he wanted to see us on Boxing Day. I already had plans for the twenty-sixth. And right after that he left town. He could have called in advance if he wanted to make sure I was free to see him. You remember, I was at a concert that night."

Maggie nodded. "Yeah, that's what I told him. And I said if he gave us some notice next time, we could be sure to be available."

Jenny grinned to herself. "Anyway, I can talk about when you were little, we had some fun times with Dad. Remember when he took us hiking up Silver Mountain, and we got lost? And you and Rob decided we'd be eaten by bears before we were found?"

After her daughter fell asleep, Jenny lay thinking. The time difference was working against her, but she didn't mind. She could hear Maggie's even breathing, and feel her warmth against her side. She'd always been a cuddler. She was hot, and Jenny eased back the comforter on her other side to cool off.

Her heart swelled with emotion. She felt great. She'd had a wonderful visit with Rob, and now this gift of time with Maggie. She was getting her children back, after almost losing them to her own aggression and hurt. It was God's gift, and she prayed a *thank you* as she lay there.

Her mind leaped ahead to home, wondering if Jordie had looked after the yard and was still feeding the cat. She wanted to sit down with him and talk about her trip, about all her discoveries and adventures. Maybe not about Greg, but everything else.

She wanted him to know that she'd dealt with a lot of things while she was away, and now it would be different. Her breath grew erratic. She should be careful, because Jordie was married and she thought about him way too often and too intensely for just a *friendship*. But her thoughts of him made her aware how lonely her heart had become.

She eased to her side and turned her attention to the company. She couldn't wait to see Queenie and Brad. And catch up with Pat, Esley, see how Dave was faring. She wanted to have an afternoon to put her feet up on the desk and have a real chinwag with Frank, see for herself that he was alright, tell him about the changes she'd made. She drifted off to sleep, still making plans in her head.

CHAPTER FOURTEEN

Jenny staggered through her door and dumped the suitcases on the floor. She returned to the entrance and dragged in three boxes bound with tape, walking backwards down the hall. She was glad she'd just grabbed the airport bus instead of calling Jordie to come and collect her. He normally acted as her gardener, house-sitter and general handyman. She didn't want to ruin an already very good arrangement. Besides he had his business to run and didn't need to be her chauffeur as well. She felt a bump in her breathing as she thought of seeing him.

Slamming the door, she startled the cat into the living room and under the couch. "Oh, Gutsy, I'm sorry. You're really spooked, aren't you? It's been very quiet in here since I left, I'll bet."

Getting down on her knees, she crawled toward the couch. "Come on, come on, baby. Come to mummy."

She heard a chuckle behind her and jerked around in surprise, catching her arm under the couch. She fell over in a heap on the floor. "Jordie! You sneaked up on me," she squealed from her prone position. "Gutsy is frightened. Nobody's been here for weeks and she's spooked."

Jordie snorted and knelt down beside her. "I've been over here every day, and she's crawled all over me like I was a can of tuna. I've let her out to wander, she's even been over to visit at my place."

Jenny sat up. "She has? Why you little two-timer!" she shot at the cat, still hidden beneath the furniture, and jumped to her feet. "That's it then! No more sympathy. Do you think she's forgotten me?"

"Not if you feed her," Jordie replied, a suspiciously sober expression on his face. Jenny glared and walked back to bring her bags into the room.

He grinned and reached past her to grab her parcels. "So, how was your trip?"

She flopped down on a chair. "It was fantastic! I loved every minute of it." Resting her head against the back of the chair, she gazed fondly at him, humour shimmering in her eyes. He looked wonderful. His curly red hair was longer and more unruly than when she left. When he ran his fingers through it, it lost more of its arrangement. He looked trim, his wide shoulders and muscled arms giving an appearance of power, yet his body was lean, maybe too lean. *Had he lost weight?* She wasn't sure.

"And I'm ever so glad to be back. Thanks for looking after everything, Jordie. I hope it wasn't too much trouble. But I brought you something, sort of like a bribe. You're not too proud to be bribed, I hope."

She tugged at the tape on the nearest box and he leaned past her shoulder to cut it with his pocket knife, gently running the sharp blade down the secured flaps of the box. She looked around at him in surprise. "Are you a boy scout? Always prepared, and all that?"

He leered at her, "Try me, baby." His eyes held their familiar heated look touched with humour that she'd seen so often.

She felt warmth curl up her spine, but laughed it away and began hauling things out of the box. "Not on your life." she said lightly. "Okay, here it is." She heaved, dragging a heavy bundle onto her lap. "This wool blanket is for you, and there's something inside." She passed it carefully over to where he sat on the couch, an expectant, almost hesitant feeling in her chest. *Would he like it?*

Jordie looked bemused as he carefully unrolled the thick blanket. A heavy pottery figurine fell onto his lap. It was about two feet tall and made up of three figures entwined, a man with his arms around a woman seated beside him, both in turn with their arms around a young girl standing between the two adult figures. The glaze was a terra cotta clay wash that gave a warm earthy glow to the scene. He studied it for a long moment, and when he finally glanced up, Jenny could have sworn she saw the sheen of tears in his dark eyes.

"I hope you like it," she said anxiously, watching his face intently. "It's made by a well known Greek sculptor. It symbolizes hope, I think. Or comfort. Well, family, I guess. You've been very good to me and my kids, and I wanted to show you a little of how I... that is, we feel about you..."

She hastily glanced back down, unsure of his reaction. "The blanket is for you, too. I thought Linda might like it. The wool is top quality, and the design is elegant. I bought one each for the kids. I couldn't leave Rob's with him because he is still travelling, so..."

She stopped babbling. *Was he insulted by the statue?* Jordie didn't have any children, but when she saw the art work, it had such a powerful physical message to it that she had thought of him immediately. He was the kind of man who always looked after family, his long powerful arms reached out to surround those he cared for. He was so like his stepfather, Uncle Neal. She hoped he took it in the way she intended.

Jordie returned her look for a moment, his dark blue gaze intense, a series of emotions flickering there before he glanced down at the heavy statue on his knees. "Linda isn't here anymore, Jenny. She left."

"Left? When? Why, Jordie?" Jenny slowly sank off her chair onto her knees on the floor.

He shrugged. "Lots of reasons, I guess. Mostly, though, because I didn't love her very much. I couldn't love her, and it must have hurt a great deal." His voice sounded hoarse in the still room.

Jenny crawled her way across to kneel beside his crouched body on the sofa. She leaned against his legs and reached up to put her hands on his shoulders. "Oh, Jordie," she said, and pulled his head down as she saw the sorrow on his face. "Poor baby."

He wrapped his arms tightly around her waist, pressing his face against her. Jenny murmured, rubbing her hands up his arms, the bulky, sharp form of the family of clay caught between their bodies. She thought of the many times she had blubbered and cried on his shoulder, and all the time he had been hurting too, but never let on, never showed it. "Poor Jordie," she murmured again. "I'm so sorry."

He shook his head and she sat back on her heels, taking his thick fingers between her slender ones. "Tell me. What happened?"

Wearily he leaned against the back of the couch, the figurine still lying in his lap, cradled between his thighs. "It wasn't anything that happened. You know, it was an ongoing situation. Linda wasn't happy. Things never got any better. And I didn't have the patience that I should have had. We've been living separately in that house for years." His voice held a kind of weariness and despair that brought tears to her eyes.

She was silent. *They had been living separately?* There must be more to it, there always was when a marriage ended. Jordie would tell her what he felt safe in saying. She simply waited, but he said nothing more.

"Did my inheriting this house from Uncle Neal have anything to do with it?" she finally whispered.

He looked surprised and then embarrassed.

"It did, didn't it?" she persisted in a low voice. "Jordie, your sister told me that you all discussed it and agreed that I should have it, but I knew that my being here bothered Linda. She couldn't look at me. Did you ask *her* about whether I should have the house, whether she minded if Uncle Neal left it to me?"

Jordie sighed and looked resigned. "Jenny, it wasn't the house." His lips compressed in a tight line, deep grooves appearing in his cheeks.

Jenny knew that expression, she'd known Jordie too long not to be able to read him like an open book when he got that stubborn look on his face. Her own mouth tightened. "What if I signed it over to you? I can afford to now. Business has done well. I'm not in the fix I was in when I first moved here. Tell her that I've signed it over to you and…"

"No!" He startled her into shocked silence. "No," he said more quietly. "Believe me, Jenny. It wasn't the house. Just leave it."

The phone rang, and Jenny rubbed her hand across his heavy shoulders before getting up to answer it. "Queenie! Hi. Yes, Maggie told me last night that you tried to reach me, but it was too late to call you. No, I haven't even had time to get my messages from the answering machine. Oh….I see Jordie has written them all down here on a piece of paper."

Jenny paused, her attention diverted by two messages from Greg to call her at his Seattle office as soon as she got home. What kind of message had Greg left? she wondered giddily. *Hopefully not too personal.* She stole a peek at Jordie but he was examining the clay figurine in his lap, running a hand over the thin glaze. Her attention was drawn back to the phone. "You want to come over? Sure. I know, you want to see what I brought you," she teased. "Okay, I'll put the coffee on. Wonderful. See you then."

Putting the receiver down, she stared at the list of messages on the sheet of paper and felt a little uneasy, hoping Jordie hadn't heard something meant for her ears alone. She turned the pad of paper face down on the counter with a decisive gesture. "Queenie's on her way," she called. "I'll make coffee. I guess there's nothing to eat in the house."

She pulled the refrigerator door open. "Oh, Jordie, you sweetheart! Milk, cream, bread, eggs...Nanaimo bars! Holy cow, Queenie will have a heyday. She's a chocolate fiend."

Coming hesitantly back into the living room, she laid a hand on his shoulder. "Don't be too down," she said softly. "Don't give up hope. Maybe she'll come back." She lifted the blanket and began to fold it, gazing at him sadly.

"I like the blanket, Jenny. It's beautiful." His voice was gentle as he gazed up at her.

She felt her face light up. Holding the blanket against her body, she smoothed it tenderly with her hand. "It is, isn't it? I've never seen anything like it. I knew you'd love it. The designs are so delicate and subtle."

He nodded. "And I love the statue. It reminds me of you. Always with your arms around someone, even me." Tears formed in his eyes, but he rose from the sofa with an impatient movement.

Jenny laughed ruefully. "I bought it because it reminds me of *you*, Jordie. You always look after everyone. I know I've been a real drain on your time since I moved back here, yet you've been there for me. And for your sisters. You look after people. Luckily for you, I don't need you so much anymore. I won't be such a drain." She packed up her boxes and pulled them out of the way, not catching the look of determination that formed on Jordie's face.

CHAPTER FIFTEEN

The coffee had finished dripping by the time the doorbell rang and Queenie swept into the house. Her wavy blonde hair was combed straight back. Jenny didn't think she had ever seen it that way. Apparently she hadn't bothered to tease and spray it into its usual sweeping curls. But she'd taken the time to draw her eyebrows on and they were fixed into a straight line of concern high on her forehead. She looked pale.

Jenny rushed forward and pulled her into a hug. "I missed you. It's great to be home." Stepping back, she held Queenie's hands, pressing the ice cold fingers in her warm ones as she looked into her eyes.

"Jordie is here," she offered. "He brought Nanaimo bars. Let's sit at the dining room table. You're cold! The sun is shining right on that chair and it should warm you up in no time." She showed Queenie to an upholstered chair at the dining room table in the big bay window.

Queenie took a moment to catch her breath and Jordie helped her out of her cape as Jenny brought the coffee pot and poured into the mugs set out on the table.

"How was your trip, Jenny? You look lovely and tanned, very relaxed." Queenie's hoarse voice sounded strained.

"Yes, she does, doesn't she?" Jordie murmured. "I thought so too." His eyes held speculation and something else.

She shot him a dirty look to try to slow down his guesswork as to why that might be. "Behave yourself, Jordie. The trip was wonderful, Queenie. I can't wait to tell you all about it. Greece was fabulous, I'd go back in a minute. Florence was lovely, but I wasn't there nearly long enough. I saw Rob in Paris! Thank you for relaying messages to him. He's doing fine, he looks great. And he should be heading home soon. And I saw Maggie last night in Vancouver." Jenny sat down, one leg curled under her, a contented smile on her face as she beamed at her friends.

"Well," said Queenie, spreading her hands on the table as if to stop them from trembling. "I have news and it isn't as good as yours. I felt I had to come over and tell you right away. I'm glad you're here, Jordie. We may need your help."

She looked so serious Jenny felt a pang of alarm shoot through her chest. She took a deep breath. "What is it? Is something wrong at the office?" Her voice sounded thin and reedy even to her own ears.

Queenie met her gaze with a steady look. "Frank is dead. He died Friday morning. Two days ago, it seems like a week. Fell from the fourth floor of the parkade where he parks his car for the office. He didn't even get to work. Police don't suspect foul play."

Jenny gasped as a sheen of sweat broke out on her forehead. "No, Queenie! Frank dead? What do you mean, he fell? How could he? Those cement barricades are feet thick. Are you saying he jumped? He would never do that!" She leaped to her feet, and teetered there uncertainly, her chair tipping back before it righted itself. "Dead?" she said stupidly. "Are you sure? How can he be?" And she burst into tears.

Jordie rose beside her and wrapped his arms around her. She sobbed against his chest, her forehead resting against his shoulder, her hands clenched in his soft knit shirt.

She felt his voice rumble beneath her forehead. "Was it in the paper? I didn't see anything."

"No, not as far as I know." Queenie frowned. "I don't think they've decided what happened."

"So do *you* think he just fell?" he asked.

Jenny raised her head to find Queenie staring at them. "Funny, no one else has asked me that, Jordie."

Sighing, he laid his jaw against Jenny's temple, his beard tickling her skin. "It's alright," he murmured. "It's a shock, I know. At least he died quickly." He smoothed her hair back from her face with his big rough fingers. She clasped him to her with fierce strength as if to hold onto some stability as events rocketed out of her control.

"What a dreadful thing," she mumbled. Heaving a damp sigh, she let go of his shirt and moved over to her chair. "Tell me what happened, Queenie."

The secretary took a breath and blew it out. "Well, the police arrived at the office just after eight-thirty

Friday morning. Said they were looking for Frank Jensen. I told them he wasn't in yet. They wanted to know when he usually arrived. I said just after seven-thirty. He was always there when I got in at quarter to eight, but he was late today for some reason. Then they said his body had been found in the alley behind the parkade, apparently he'd fallen from one of the levels. They asked where he usually parked his car. I had to pull out the file and look it up. I could hardly read it...." Her voice broke, and she stopped for a moment, then plunged on. "I said he had a reserved space on the fourth floor, they confirmed that's where his car was parked."

She paused for breath again, her eyes tearing at the corners. "They sent someone over to tell Alita," she continued, her voice quavering. "She came down to the office, said he'd been having fainting spells and maybe that's why he fell."

Jenny swallowed audibly. "Did you know he'd been having fainting spells? Did he mention it to you?"

Queenie shook her head and her hair fell forward over her eyes. She swept it back with an impatient hand. "He never said that to me. He came to work every day. Didn't complain. But he had a lot of phone calls, and sometimes he'd come out of his office looking kind of haggard."

"How was Alita? What a terrible shock for her."

Queenie snorted, and then sniffed. "Cold as ice. She actually looked a little shaken, but she wasn't too broken up about it. When the police left, she went into Frank's office and closed the door. She was in there about two hours No noise, no nothing. It was eerie. We were all tiptoeing around."

Jenny nodded in sympathy. Jordie took her hand and held it in his, rubbing her fingers gently.

"So," Queenie continued, "then she suddenly flung the door open and came out. We all jumped. She started barking orders. Said she'd phoned for the locks to be changed. She said you were fired."

Jenny gasped and the heat rose and faded in her cheeks. "I'm fired? What is she doing? I own half the business!"

"Not half, Jenny, forty-five percent, right?" Jordie interrupted.

She turned her head slowly as if in a fog to face him and nodded. "Yes, that's right, forty-five percent."

"Then I guess she can fire you if she wants to," he continued. "She'll inherit Frank's controlling interest. You'll still own your shares, but she doesn't have to let you work there. She doesn't have to give you much say in how it's run."

Jenny's face crumpled as tears started again. Her hand was wrapped tightly around her coffee mug, her knuckles white, the coffee stone cold.

"That's not all," said Queenie urgently. "Brad was fired, too, I guess because he's your assistant. She made him leave right away. Couldn't even take time to say good-bye, just grab his coat and get out of there. She said everyone else would report to her. She took over Frank's office. Got a couple of the guys to rearrange the furniture. She took the plant table and plants from your office and the mirror from the back of your door."

CHAPTER SIXTEEN

Jenny looked ghostly. Her freckles stood out starkly on her face, tear tracks shining wetly down both cheeks. Jordie reached for her and wrapped an arm around her shoulders as Queenie continued. "So, I don't know what's going to happen. But there's something else." She lowered her voice and looked around. "Remember when you noticed the accounts were out? Too much money coming in?"

Jenny nodded. "Yes, I asked Frank about it and he said to check with you. I never got back to him."

Queenie shrugged, her eyes keen. "I thought there was something unusual. I kept looking back in the files, and everything balanced but I still didn't know what services we were providing for that money. Well, it's increased. There's well over six hundred thousand extra that Frank billed."

Jenny's eyes were huge in her pale face. "Good God! Six hundred thousand dollars. What does it mean?"

Jordie narrowed his eyes. "You're thinking Frank was into something illegal and they bumped him off."

Jenny flashed him a worried glance and teetered in her chair as if she was dizzy. He tightened his hold. "I think I'm going to be sick," she managed and hung her head.

He rubbed her arm and passed her a water glass.

Taking a sip, she set it down. "Don't you think it looks like that? If he wasn't having fainting spells..."

"We don't know that, Jenny."

"I know, but... well, Queenie says he was just worried." She sounded defensive and so vulnerable. Laying her head on the table, she groaned. "Why, oh why, did I go on vacation? I never should have gone."

Jordie hated the helpless feeling that rose in his chest. He patted her arm. "You don't have to worry, I'll look after you."

She sat up suddenly. "I knew he couldn't manage the company now it's grown so large." She was literally wringing her hands.

But Queenie stopped her with a look. "That isn't true, honey. The company perked along just fine. Frank had no problems at the company. I'm sure it was personal."

"Well, it still looks odd," she protested. "That money must have come from somewhere, and maybe they wanted it back."

"I don't know," said Jordie, rising and pacing the room. "If the money was illegal and Frank was trying to get access to it, he wouldn't have put it in the company accounts. First of all, he'd have to share with you, and then he'd have to explain it. Someone else might have been after it."

Jenny trembled in her chair.

He wanted to grab her up in his arms. Instead he turned to Queenie. "Look, we're all upset, and there may be a perfectly logical explanation. Maybe the invoices haven't come in yet for some major item, like outside contract services."

Queenie nodded reluctantly. "Maybe, we do that sometimes. But it's been building for months. You'd think something would have appeared by now. It would take a pretty big contract to take care of that much money."

"I can't believe that of Frank, anyway," Jenny interjected, her teeth chattering. "He was as honest as the day is long. Maybe there's some other explanation." She paused and gripped her hands together on the table top in front of her.

"Mind you, we may never know, if I'm fired and so is Brad. Queenie," Jenny turned to her friend, "you're the only one left who could try to find out. And you can bet that Alita will keep the purse strings tight. She was with Frank for his income, nothing more, I'm positive." She looked dejected.

The early spring sunshine flooded through the huge windows and slanted across the polished wood of the table, dust motes dancing in the glare. Jordie watched her move her coffee cup round and round, making damp circles on the smooth surface. She sighed, and tears leaked from her eyes. "If only he talked to me if he had a problem." More tears flowed down her face. It was breaking his heart.

Queenie sighed. "Well, that's about all. Oh, except I brought the files home on a drive, every file in the place. Brad helped me do a second complete backup on the computer, and I carted it all out in my handbag." She pointed to the huge bag sitting on the chair beside her, then reached over to pull it onto her lap and dig inside.

"I brought it with me. So maybe you can load it onto your computer, Jenny, and figure out what I can't. I can look up any hard copy that you want back at the office."

Jenny shifted tiredly and he stepped behind her to place his hands protectively on her shoulders. The way he saw it, she still needed him just as much as she ever had. And he'd do his level best to make sure she continued to need him, until maybe she'd begin to want him, too, the way he had wanted her for so long.

~*~*~*~

"One other thing," Queenie added, rousing herself. "Frank's lawyer phoned. Not Fred Flintstone, the fellow he uses for the company."

Jenny chuckled weakly. Fred Austin had always been Frank's lawyer. Queenie and Jenny nicknamed him Fred Flintstone for his ponderous girth, shabby clothes and seemingly less than necessary mental capabilities. Frank must have used his legal services because they'd been friends years ago, not because of his brilliance as legal counsel.

"A different law firm," Queenie said now. "His name is Ping. Mr. Ping said he has Frank's will, and he'd like to read it on Monday at two at his offices. He talked to Alita first and I guess he asked her and Norman to be there. Then he called back to the office, I recognized his voice, asked for you. So I told him you'd be back in town

Saturday. He wants you there. Two o'clock, the office is on Fort St. I'm to come, as well."

Jenny nodded and rose to get a piece of paper. She wrote a note to herself, and placed it on the counter then turned back to the table. "Well, it will never be the same, will it? Not for any of us. You were with Frank a long time."

"Twenty-two years," Queenie said, tears suddenly swimming in her eyes and charting tracks of black mascara down her cheeks. "And now that bitch of a wife of his is parading around the office, pawing through the stuff in his desk. I went in after she left yesterday and did a search but couldn't find any clue about that money, but there are those two locked drawers in his desk that I can't get into. Alita couldn't get into them either," she noted with satisfaction. "They're still locked. There might be something in there." She dried her eyes on the tissue Jenny passed her, and blotted her mascara.

"I don't know if I'll stay, Jenny. I don't know if I'll be able to bear it. Pat and I were talking, she's been there almost as long as I have. But it will likely be pretty awful working for Alita. She's vindictive. And she doesn't know what she's doing. She's never run a business and she certainly didn't spend any time in there with Frank to learn how to run this one." She sighed wetly.

"When's the funeral, Queenie? Has it been set yet? Alita can't prevent us from going to that." Jordie's voice was hard.

"I don't know yet, I don't think a date has been announced. We can watch the paper, I guess." She turned toward the door. "I'll be talking to you, Jenny, probably Monday."

Jenny promised and saw her to the door, then came back and slumped in her chair. Jordie had emptied her mug and poured fresh coffee for her. She sipped it, burning her lip, and set it back on the table, contenting herself with warming her cold hands around the heat of the cup.

"What do you think, Jordie? It's strange, isn't it? He falls from a parkade that he's been parking in for years. Just falls. I can't believe it."

She stared silently at the dark liquid that steamed in her mug. "You know, he was so good to me. I bought into that business for a song. When I see now what kind of money it brings in, I always think that I don't deserve this kind of payment. He did it for me because he liked me."

"And because of what you brought to the party," Jordie added. "He was a pretty decent guy, Jenny, but he was no philanthropist. You organized the business and managed it. It was earning more money even before you expanded, because you brought order to his chaos. Ask Queenie, ask any of them. Remember what Queenie used to work on, that old five-hundred-pound electric typewriter? It would have made a better boat anchor."

Jenny laughed. "She used to say exactly that." She looked at him with tear-filled eyes.

Jordie clasped her cold hand in his warm one. "I know, Jenny, I know." He pulled her back into his arms and held her tight as she cried.

CHAPTER SEVENTEEN

Jenny entered the offices of Ping, Murdoch and Co. on Monday afternoon and was immediately shown into a private room by the well dressed receptionist and asked to wait. The same woman returned to bring her a coffee, then closed the door firmly behind her as she left. Jenny was nervous. She'd worn her royal blue suit with the black pumps and matching handbag. Right now she needed to project a look of confidence and professionalism even if she didn't feel it.

She'd gone to the salon and had her hair cut this morning. She didn't want any chinks in her armour when she went in there today with Alita sitting across the desk.

Presently, Mr. Ping entered. He was a small dapper Oriental man in a very conservative and expensive charcoal gray three-piece suit that fit him like a glove. He was older, probably late sixties with iron-gray hair combed straight back. He approached with hand extended, his palm dry and soft in her clasp.

"I'm Paul Ping," he said. "Frank told me a great deal about you, Mrs. MacDougall. He was very proud to have you as a business partner and friend."

Jenny blushed and tears came immediately to her eyes.

"Yes," he said, "a terrible tragedy. Now, with regard to the reading of the will. I see the possibility of some difficulties this afternoon. I know there is high feeling between you and Mrs. Jensen." He made it more a statement than a question.

Jenny shrugged. "I haven't seen Alita since I got back, but the secretary told me that she fired me and my assistant on Friday after she was informed that Frank was dead. I haven't had time to decide what I should do about that. Alita has never been overly fond of me, but she's usually been civil." Jenny ignored the nudge of memory that immediately came to mind, when Alita had walked in on them with Frank's arm around her. She didn't need to drag up old history. She could afford to ignore the small stuff.

Mr. Ping nodded. "It's too bad she took that step. However, we'll simply have to proceed with what we have before us. Now, Mrs. Jensen and Mr. Suffron are waiting in the boardroom down the hall. Queenie Short is there, as well as Pat Rooke and Esley Moro. Just to prepare you, I'll read the minor bequests first, and then the employees can leave. Then I'll read the rest of the will with only you, Alita Jensen and Norman Suffron present. Now, if you would come with me."

He rose and escorted Jenny down the hall. When he opened the boardroom door, the murmur of voices within immediately became an uncomfortable silence.

Mr. Ping ushered Jenny ahead of him to a chair at the long mahogany table. She was on his right facing Alita on the other side of the dark polished surface. Norman sat beside his mother. The others were ranged around the other end in a tight group. Tension was palpable in the heavy air.

Alita looked as well put together as she always did, every hair in place, her matching black silk suit and scarf. Only her face showed signs of the strain she must be feeling beneath the carefully applied layer of makeup. Her gaze passed over Jenny as if she were invisible, as she smiled graciously at the lawyer. "I think we've waited long enough, Mr. Ping. Why Frank came to you with his will, I don't know. I must tell you our lawyers were equally surprised by this."

Mr. Ping nodded, ignoring the suggestion of some sort of legal impropriety. "Yes, it's time to get on with the business at hand. Mrs. Jensen, everyone, the will." He cleared his throat, assuming a formal tone. "The document is in two parts. I'll read the first part, and then ask the employees involved to step down the corridor to see my secretary. She'll need information from each of you."

He cleared his throat again. The will began with the usual declarations revoking any prior will, and stating that Frank was of sound mind. All debts of the estate were to be taken care of in the usual way. Then Mr. Ping got to the specific bequests. Each of Queenie, Pat and Esley were to receive a significantly large lump sum of cash and a particular item which Frank had wanted them to have.

Queenie got the old heavy typewriter, which Frank had had appraised. It was an antique and worth a fair amount. Queenie burst into tears. Esley was to have the huge oak desk that Jenny had bought out of the paper for Frank. Esley beamed, his face beet red. Pat was to get the artist's original pastoral painting on his office wall, she'd always admired it. Tears flowed quietly down Pat's cheeks.

Alita's face had gone paper white and her lips crimped beneath the pink lipstick outlined on her mouth at the loss of the desk. Then her mouth opened with an audible sound when she heard the painting was to go to Pat. Jenny glanced across to see Norman murmur a soothing word in her ear. He held her elbow firmly in his hand.

Mr. Ping directed the employees down the hall to see his secretary. Jenny rose and gave each of them a hug in turn as they walked past her chair. She hadn't had a chance to even greet them since she heard the news of Frank's death and she tried to make up for that, whispering words of encouragement and promises to come by the office tomorrow to visit.

Alita's sculptured features formed a disgruntled scowl as she turned to address the lawyer. "Mr. Ping, this is highly irregular. Jenny is an employee, not family. She certainly shouldn't be here now, the rest of the will is confidential and highly personal to myself and my son." Her brows rose in an imperious gesture.

"Yes, Mrs. Jensen, you are at least partially right. She's not family. But as well as being an employee, she's also Mr. Jensen's business partner. And the contents of the will are not confidential, they'll be filed in court for probate and as such become public documents." Ping seemed unperturbed by the animosity directed his way from that side of the table. He gathered the sheets in front of him and organized them on the table, tapping the edges with his fingertips.

"Now, if I could have your attention please, the rest of the will reads as follows." Mr. Ping began again to read. "To Norman I leave his car. That Jaguar is a lovely thing, bought on loan, for which I signed as guarantor. Since Norman has never made any payments on it, I instruct the estate to pay off the remainder owing and Norman shall receive his car without debt attached. That is all you shall have, Norman. I have paid your expenses for years, and bailed you out for the last time. You're on your own."

Norman gave a shadow of a grin and gripped his mother's arm more tightly. Alita was pale, her face expressionless.

Mr. Ping continued. Jenny was to receive a painting by Frank's first wife Joanie. It hung in his office and he had been very fond of it. Jenny had admired it often. In addition, Frank left ten shares of the company to her, with thanks for her hard work. The balance of his estate was to go to his wife, Alita. She would get the house and cars, his investment funds and other assets that were listed. And she was to receive the rest of Frank's shares in Sentinel Securities Group Inc.

Alita's smile was smug, her face finally relaxed as she gazed across at Jenny. "So," she said, her voice icy, "that is all you will ever get from us. You'll have your shares of Sentinel Security Group and that is all. You're fired and I tell you this formally now, although I'm confident Queenie has already informed you. I control the company. You will, of course, receive your share of the earnings. However, you needn't bother coming into the office again, as your services are no longer required."

Norman gave a sick giggle. "No, Mother. That's not how it works. Jenny controls the company now." His expression was confused and somehow vulnerable. He smiled thinly across the table at Jenny as he continued, "She owned forty-five shares before, and Frank had fifty-five. Now Jenny has fifty-five and you have forty-five. Jenny's in control."

Mr. Ping nodded. "That's correct, Mrs. Jensen. You've received the bulk of the estate, and Jenny has received ten of Frank's shares in the company. Therefore, she holds the control. You still hold a substantial interest yourself, of course. And I understand that's a valuable asset, the company is quite healthy." Alita turned sickly white. Her skin tightened across her cheekbones, her mouth stretched wide in a soundless cry. Norman looked ill.

Mr. Ping turned to Jenny. "There is something else, Mrs. MacDougall…"

"No!" There was a scuffle and a scream from the other side of the table. Jenny looked up and Mr. Ping's head swung around sharply. Norman was trying to restrain his mother as she leaped from her chair, dragging him along with her own momentum. "No, no, no!" Alita's face had turned a dark florid colour, her rouged cheeks looking wretched against the fierce red on her skin, her eyes blazing as she tried to reach Jenny across the broad shiny surface of the boardroom table.

"Never," she shrieked. "Never! I'll kill you first. You bitch! You tricked him. You must have tricked him! He never meant you to control the business." She turned on Mr. Ping. "You cooked this up together, you and Jenny! I knew there was something fishy about this! I'll see you in court. I'll challenge the will. I'll have your license!"

She was breathing so heavily, she gasped for air. Norman pressed his fingers over her mouth, trying to halt the flow of words. He smiled a parody of a smile at Mr. Ping. "I apologize for my mother, she's not herself. Frank's death has upset her tremendously. They were very much in love. Come, Mother," and he pulled her toward the door.

Mr. Ping reached for her handbag and held it out to Norman. "Of course," he murmured. "Of course she's upset. I'll talk to you later."

Alita leaned heavily on Norman's arm, weeping softly as they left. She muttered to him under her breath and he shushed her as they passed through the doorway.

~*~*~*~

Jenny sank back in her chair, feeling physically drained. Mr. Ping closed the heavy oak door behind the pair, sending the room into silence again, and resumed his seat.

"Now, you're not to worry about the integrity of the will. Mr. Jensen left plenty of clear written instructions as to what he wanted done and why. We were very careful to cover ourselves in case of a challenge to the will by anyone."

Jenny's eyes widened. "You mean you thought it was likely there'd be trouble?"

Ping's sparse brows formed a frown and his voice showed faint surprise. "A man is entitled to leave his possessions as he sees fit. Mr. Jensen didn't want his wife to control the company, so he was careful to conduct his will in such a way that it couldn't be challenged. Now," he continued calmly, "here's an envelope that he wanted delivered to you once the will was read. I know he was very fond of you, Mrs. MacDougall. I'm sure he's explained everything in his letter. I'll leave you alone to read it. Please stay as long as you need to."

He stood and pushed his chair into place against the table. "I'd like you to call my secretary tomorrow and set up a time to come back in. We'll need you to sign some documents to formalize the share transfer and then everything can be forwarded to your corporate lawyers. Please feel free to call me or drop by if you have any questions, anything at all." Ping shook her hand and excused himself.

CHAPTER EIGHTEEN

Jenny looked around the deserted boardroom. It was deathly quiet. The thought made her shudder. *Bad choice of words.* But it was noticeably still after such a confrontational and ugly scene that had just played out here. Save for Mr. Ping's, the rest of the chairs were all askew and she had the strong urge to get up and set them straight around the table. Everything in her life seemed to be lop-sided. She realized she was breathing shallowly and forced herself to draw a deep breath, noting the thin film of dust on the tabletop. *Guess they didn't use the boardroom all that much.*

She stared at the pictures on the wall. They were lovely graceful prints of flowers, peaceful pathways, shaded gardens. Different from the usual fare at lawyers' offices. She tried to remember what had been on the walls when she and Bobby were signing their divorce papers in front of the local notary. Stiff diplomas. Old documents framed and sealed. Stern unforgiving visages of former partners.

Finally, she gazed down at the envelope in her hand. Her fingers trembled. Should she open it now or wait until she got home? She stared at it for a long moment, then gently moved her thumbnail along the edge to break the seal. Better to read it now. She might have questions for Mr. Ping.

The heavy envelope opened, letting the pages inside fall out onto her lap. Narrow sheets of paper from a steno pad. Frank always used a steno pad, he never *cottoned on* to a computer terminal. Everything he did was by hand. She recognized his cranky, eccentric scrawl across the lined pages, and her eyes immediately blurred with tears. She looked out the window, watching the watery outline of a seagull perched on the ledge pecking at the glass until her vision cleared.

Then she began to read. The letter was dated three months ago, just before Christmas.

Dearest Jenny, my dear, dear, Jenny,

The greeting at the head of the page caused her to sob and press her fingers to her mouth. There was something close to a physical pain in her chest. Taking deep breaths, she waited for calmness to return.

When you read this, of course, I will no longer be here. Such a funny thing, to think of dying. A person never imagines they will, of course. Me included. I have never felt better, my health is excellent.

But I'm seventy-four, and I need to take a few steps to get my affairs in order. And so I shall.

You will never know how you turned my life upside down when you joined Acme Security those few short years ago. You were tough and bitter, bad divorce I know. But underneath there was a feisty, caring, loving woman. And so beautiful, so very, very beautiful. Sometimes I wished I was thirty years younger. I wouldn't have let you get away.

At this, Jenny's eyes filled with tears again. She rustled around in her bag and came up with a handful of tissue, blowing her nose before she could read further.

As it was, the letter continued, *you became like a daughter to me. You know that Joanie and I could never have children. It was heartbreaking for her, and for me. But we loved each other and it was good. You would have loved her, too, Jenny, if you had been able to know her and I know she would have adored you.*

There is no love lost between you and Alita, and I can see that you two are like oil and water. But Alita was good to me in her own way. Norman was another story, however. He is rotten to the core. Stay away from him. I think he might even corrupt his own mother.

I am leaving you ten shares in Sentinel Security. The company is really what you have made it over the last few years. I want you to be able to do what you can with it. And I know you and Alita would never be able to agree on what that should be. So I leave a controlling interest to you. Alita is well cared for. She'll want for nothing, if she doesn't foolishly give it all to her son.

I know you'll carry on without me, and the company will prosper under your continued exuberant guidance. You'll look after the old timers for me, like Queenie, Pat, and Esley. You care as much about them as I do. And the new ones too. Dave's a good man, he's looking for a place to put down a few roots, and Brad is just getting into his stride. Look for big things from that boy."

Jenny sniffed again, touched by his caring for each one of his employees. She read on to the end.

So I leave you my love. Take care of those wonderful children of yours. Love them all you can. It will come back in spades. You've been a good mother, now just love them, that's all there is left to do.

And look after Jordie. His heart is empty and you could fill it up so nicely for him. Take care, my dear. I'll see you in heaven.

Her own heart stuttered at his mention of Jordie. She was afraid of her cousin and all the feelings he stirred up inside her, feelings she'd managed to suppress until now. Drying her eyes, she folded the letter carefully into her purse. She knew she'd want to read it again when she was calmer and could absorb all that Frank was telling her.

She stood and, legs trembling, steadied herself against the table. The low light from the window showed that it was getting late, dusk had fallen, the street lights were on. She walked out into the quiet of the hall and found the lawyer's office. His door was open and she peeped in, catching him seated at his desk.

"Mr. Ping," she said, "thank you for all your consideration today."

He looked up from his work and smiled. It transformed his face. "You're welcome, Ms. MacDougall. You're more than welcome. Call our office tomorrow and we'll set up an appointment for you."

She nodded.

~*~*~*~

Jenny walked into the Sentinel Security office trying to appear calm but her stomach was clenched in a tight knot beneath the silk waistband of her jade green skirt. She greeted Queenie, then looked around, her eyebrows raised. The secretary shook her head.

"Nary a glimpse of her, Jenny."

Brad appeared in the hall at the sound of her voice, Pat hovering at his shoulder. They all looked nervous and a little shaken. Jenny spread her hands and shook her head. "Has anyone heard from Alita? Does anyone know if she's coming in?" She was met with three heads shaking *no*.

"Then I don't know any more than you do," she said. "I control the company, that's the one thing we can rely on. I was at Mr. Ping's this morning. As I'm sure Queenie told you, Frank left me enough shares to give me a majority vote. So Alita can't come in and fire me or anyone else. Mr. Ping just finished the paperwork.

"I stopped at the bank on my way over, the accounts have been changed to my signature only. That may be awkward in the short term," she said to Queenie, "but it will have to do for the moment."

"Thank you all so much for showing up for work. I hope you'll feel as welcome here with me as you have with Frank. I really need you, each one of you." As a group they smiled and nodded.

She turned, then hesitated. "Well, now I just need to find an office to use and in a bit I'll let each one of you catch me up on what's been going on since I left."

She peered into Frank's office. The big oak desk, now Esley's, was still there along with the leather chair. She looked at Queenie for help.

"I moved your things back into your office, Jenny. I didn't want to leave it all torn apart like that."

"Okay. I'll just carry on from there. Thank you, Queenie. I know this has been very tough for you. Brad, the first thing you can do is order the locks changed on the office door again and on the security file room. No copies for now, just a key for me and one for Queenie. We'll work out a security system with everyone before we spread keys around. Then come see me." Brad swiftly moved off.

"I'll have time to see you this afternoon, Pat, if you're still going to be in." Pat nodded with a wavering smile and went back down the hall.

Jenny sat motionless at her desk, staring at its smooth shiny surface. Then she shifted in her chair so she could see down onto the street below. What needed her attention first? Security for the company before anything, security on all fronts. Could she even trust the bank?

There were several tellers there who were long-time acquaintances of Queenie and Frank. They were garrulous. She knew from the infrequent occasions when she'd taken in a deposit, they had talked about what Frank had done on the last deposit he made as well as about other people's accounts.

That meant they probably also talked about the Sentinel account to others. She didn't know if Alita knew these people, but Frank's personal account was at the same branch so his wife would be in there doing some banking of her own. They should change banks.

That settled, she drew a pad of paper across the desk and began to make a list. She'd look into a new security system for the front door to give them a record of who went in and out. What about the lawyer, Fred Flintstone? Fred Austin, who held the company records, had been a friend of Frank's for years. Could he be trusted?

On impulse she picked up the phone and put a call through to Austen's office. After a short wait she got him on the line. "Fred, I know it's a shock with Frank dead so suddenly." She allowed him to express his murmurs of sympathy, then ploughed on. "He was an old acquaintance of yours, I think."

His voice sounded cautious. "A friend, Jenny, a friend of long-standing. Yes, he'll be greatly missed. Greatly."

Jenny murmured her agreement, "So I was wondering how you feel being in the middle of what's going on, with Alita wanting control of the company." She let the silence hang for a second.

Fred stepped carefully into the breach. "Well, I know that Alita has a good share of the interest in that company, Jenny. Although you hold control apparently."

She remained silent, refusing to rise to the bait, so he continued, "I'm sure you ladies will come to some agreement. Frank wouldn't want you to fight. And, of course, Alita is a grieving widow, she has to be forgiven for any foolhardy move she might have made. You know she wouldn't mean any harm but she should have a say in how the company is run. And it can't be forgotten that Frank started that company, right from scratch, and Alita is his widow. It's important to keep this all in perspective, Jenny."

Jenny made a noncommittal response and slowly hung up the receiver. Then she called Mr. Ping's office. No, Mr. Ping didn't do corporate practice but his partner did. Why didn't the receptionist make an appointment, he could fit her in tomorrow.

Jenny began the painstaking process of re-organizing her work. She made appointments at two banks to discuss opening a commercial account. Then she arranged a meeting with the accountant to see where they stood financially so she'd have information the banks would need.

Now that everything rested on her shoulders, she began to doubt the business plan she and Frank had begun to put in place. Maybe it was too much, reaching too far, for a little security company like this one. Maybe she should pull in her horns. Without Frank to give her confidence, to guide the course from behind the scenes, she felt vulnerable.

She dismissed the extra money in the company. It belonged to someone, she would act as if it weren't there, sitting like an overgrown varmint in the bank account. The laugh of it was, the Sentinel accounts had never been healthier. They weren't even using their revolving line of credit because they had so much cash on hand. It was too ironic, yet she didn't feel like laughing. What if Frank died because of that money?

The list of appointments grew. And at the back of her mind the question continued to nag. Where did this extraordinary amount of money come from? There must be a trail. Money didn't just appear. There would have to be checks, bank drafts, deposits. She was starting to have nightmares about it.

CHAPTER NINETEEN

Jenny remembered walking by Queenie's desk one afternoon some months before her trip to Greece. She'd been riveted by what she saw and stopped short.

"Queenie, what is that?" she asked.

"What?" Queenie was head down, engrossed in paperwork on her desk.

"That!" She looked up to see Jenny's finger pointing at a stack of cash held together with an elastic and stuffed into the bank book on top of a pile of folders.

"The bank book?" Queenie raised her penciled brows. "The bank book," she repeated.

"No, no, the money. Where'd you get so much cash?"

"Oh, that. Mr. Mahendra. I get that twice a month." Her head fell back to concentrate on her work.

Jenny gingerly picked up the bank book and pulled out the cash. She began to flip through it. A quick count showed over four thousand dollars in twenties and larger bills.

"Do you know how much this is?" Jenny's voice was getting higher as she spoke.

Queenie's head came up slowly as she corrected a figure on the pad in front of her. She looked at Jenny and then at the bundle of bills, her expression blank. She looked back at Jenny. "How much? How much what?"

"How much cash there is here!" Jenny nearly stamped her foot.

"Of course, forty-five hundred dollars. I just made up the bank deposit." Her voice was the tone used to explain the obvious to a two-year-old child.

Jenny stared at her wordlessly. Queenie stared back. Her head was just going down again, when Jenny gripped her shoulder with vice-like fingers. Queenie winced.

"Sorry," she muttered. "But about this money, how would Mr. Mahendra get forty-five hundred dollars in cash? Why would he pay us in cash?"

"He always pays us in cash. Twice a month he pays us, twenty-two hundred and some dollars. Has done for years. He just got behind this month. Why?"

"That's five thousand dollars a month!"

"I know that, I can add." Queenie blinked and focused finally on what Jenny was saying. "You know that too. Mr. Mahendra's account is five thousand dollars a month, has been for close to eighteen months. Before that, I think it was forty-four hundred, or forty-five hundred. Something like that."

"Yes, I knew his account was that much. Why would he pay in cash?"

The secretary shrugged. "Frank says he hates banks. Doesn't use them. He cashes any cheque you give him. He's a big man, apparently he doesn't worry about being mugged." She smiled cynically.

Jenny's mouth was open. "That's a lot of money!"

Queenie snorted. "He's not the only one. We have others."

"Like who?" she shot back. "Who would pay their account in cash every month? He must be a drug dealer or something."

Queenie glanced through the deposit book. "Here we go, twenty-five hundred cash, twenty-eight hundred cash, fourteen hundred fifty cash, eight hundred twenty cash, it goes on and on. Most of the accounts aren't as big as Mahendra's, but lots of people use cash. Mostly older people, you know, who have a distrust of banks, or people who don't want their families to know they hired a guard, or whatever."

"Does he just send us a plain brown unmarked envelope?"

"No, he brings it in. Frank's usually here at seven in the morning and Hiro Mahendra drops by to chat for a few minutes, have a cup of coffee and pay his bill. Has done for years."

"I've never seen him."

"You're never in at seven in the morning. Face it." Queenie went back to her work.

~*~*~*~

Jenny returned to her list. As soon as she had a moment she'd ask Dave Powers to take a look at it, see what he thought. Meanwhile, she needed to make sure her company was secure, from Alita, from Norman, and anyone else who had designs on it.

She waited until late in the afternoon before putting a call through to Greg at his office in Seattle. She felt a tingle of pleasure at the thought of reconnecting with him. Their attraction to each other had flared like a brush fire but just as quickly extinguished in her heart. What was left was a fondness for the man. It had been almost a month since she'd spoken to him, since she'd left the Greek island that sunny morning, yet it seemed like much longer.

So much had happened since Greg hugged her tight before she jumped on the bus with Isabelle.

Even just the emotional time while alone on her trip seemed to distance her from the brief friendship they had in that idyllic setting. There, she had felt a weight lift from her shoulders with the realization that she didn't need to forever carry around the guilt from her broken marriage. That had changed her perspective on many other things.

The phone rang and rang but no answer. Glancing at her watch, she realized she had worked late again and Greg had probably long since left his office for home. Well, she'd just have to try again some other time.

~*~*~*~

Jordie was waiting on her patio when she got home, sitting in the dusk in an old wooden lawn chair, watching the clouds changing colour over the restless water. Jenny felt a quiver in her stomach at the sight of this tall lean redhead lounging with his big boots on her deck.

She invited him in for a bowl of soup. She wasn't as lonely as she might have been, with things so busy at work, but she'd changed. She was more open to him.

"You've got messages," he called from the kitchen where he'd gone to get the milk carton and more crackers. "The little light is calling you. Two important ones." He grinned as he set the food on the table.

"I'll get it." She leaped from her chair to reach across the counter and flick the button. The first message was for some charity that she'd never heard of. She raised her brows at Jordie. "Yeah, really important. I don't even know who

115

these people are." Then there was a beep and Greg's voice came on, the same deep familiar tones she remembered hearing on that beach in Greece.

"Jenny, this is Greg, I don't know if you're home yet, can't seem to reach you. Please call me at work, I'm in every day this week. Here's my number."

Jenny flicked the button off and walked into the kitchen, opening cupboard doors at random, trying to look absorbed in her search for the peanut butter. Jordie sat silent, watching her. When she slipped back into her chair, he took the proffered jar without comment and set it down on the table top.

"Who was that?" he asked.

"Just a friend." She looked into her soup and stirred it with her spoon, searching for mushrooms.

"Greg who? I don't remember a Greg." Jordie's whole attention was on her face, he made no pretense of eating.

Jenny looked away. "Greg's a friend from Seattle. You don't know all my friends, Jordie. He hasn't been here.... uh.... lately."

"Is he a boyfriend, or just a friend?"

She snickered, unwisely she realized as his face immediately darkened. "Grown women don't have boyfriends. They have friends, and they have lovers." She regretted the words the minute they left her tongue. *Why did she like to bait him like that?* She should know better.

His jaw clenched. "And which is Greg?" he said through his teeth.

She swung her head toward him. "None of your business." Heat washed up her body as waves of roaring anger rolled over her. *Damn him! Why the interrogation?* He wasn't her father, or even related. Always, always, Jordie looking over her shoulder, judging her actions, commenting on her decisions. There had to be an end to it!

"No, eh?"

She watched him rise slowly from his chair as unease settled in the pit of her stomach. Suddenly all the anger was gone, leaving her singularly defenseless.

He looked darkly dangerous, the blood heavy in his face. Walking softly around to her chair, he pulled it back. Jenny sat stiffly, uncertain whether to wait it out sitting down. She soon learned she was not to be given a choice. His big hand closed around her arm and dragged her up, his heated face looming into hers.

"Well, I'm making it my business." He glared, his dark blue eyes boring into hers. "I can't take any more," he muttered before his mouth slammed down on hers.

Jenny quaked in shock, her body trembling against his. His lips were hot and hard, slanting across hers in a demanding attack, ravenously devouring. His arms were vice-like, encircling her waist, one hand tangled in her hair. She tried to catch her breath, and his tongue seized the opportunity to plunge into her mouth in reckless invasion. His beard tickled her face and his moustache prickled against her cheek.

His breath was sweet, his body hard against her. Jenny felt a heady sense of perfection, as if she'd needled and baited him until he finally did what she'd always wanted him to do. She opened her mouth softly and his tongue instantly gentled its motion, stroking hers and enticing her to return the attention. She obliged, gliding the tip of her tongue across Jordie's lips and running it along the edges of his beautiful teeth, then teasing his tongue with hers.

A low groan emanated from his chest, vibrating against her breasts, and his hands clenched then fanned out feverishly over her body. He shifted his legs, spreading them to draw her within his protective stance. His breath was hot on her face, as his eyes had always been hot on her skin. Her hands crept up his chest and rubbed, then stole around his back to hold him tight.

Jordie lifted his head, struggling for breath as he searched her face with his gaze. "Jenny," he said, "My God!" His eyes were burning into hers, his face pale under the tan, pale and appalled. "Jenny, I don't know what to say. I'm… I'm sorry."

He let go of her and looked down at his hands in confusion, as if they were well-known and trusted friends who'd betrayed him. Raising his head, he didn't look at her, gazing instead over her shoulder toward the window, as if the ocean view was all-absorbing. "Damn." He was out the door before she could think of what to say, before she could stop him.

She looked at the kitchen counter, the stove with the soup pot still sitting there, the lid beside it on the counter. It looked so ordinary, yet everything had changed with that single event. Jordie, her best friend, her ally, her confidante, had become her would-be lover, the man she desired with her whole heart. And then he ran. She was rooted in shock.

CHAPTER TWENTY

Jenny walked into the offices of Ping, Murdoch and Company for the second time in a week, and sat down in the reception area. She didn't have long to wait. Her appointment was with Angus Murdoch, obviously the partner in the law firm. *Not another bloody Scot.* She looked around, hoping no one was listening to her quiet monologue.

I hope he doesn't talk with a brogue. Probably as pigheaded and stubborn as Jordie. The unexpected ferocity of her thoughts were all down to the events of last night. He'd been impossible. Sometimes she wondered what got into his head to be so demanding, so impatient. And then to kiss her, kiss her like *that.* She didn't know if she'd ever been kissed like that. She shook her head, not for the first time since he'd stormed out of her house leaving her stunned and bewildered.

Her attention was distracted by the receptionist pointing her in the direction of Mr. Murdoch's office. He was a strapping man, fortyish, sandy haired. Rising from behind his desk, he introduced himself with a great paw extended. His voice had no brogue but she detected a slight burr, and frowned. She was in no mood for this. She'd gotten very little sleep last night as it was.

Seating herself, she glared at him. "Where were you born, Mr. Murdoch?"

His bushy brows rose marginally. "In Canada, Mrs. MacDougall, and yourself?"

"It's just that I noticed you have a slight burr to your accent. It seems I am constantly surrounded by Scotsmen."

He was silent for a moment, a small grin on his lips, then commented, "Am I to take it that Mr. MacDougall is no longer on the scene?"

"That's right," she asserted, "and I'm thinking of going back to my maiden name."

"Which is?" he inquired.

"MacKay," she snapped.

He gave a shout of laughter. "Is this a matter of the pot calling the kettle black?"

Jenny grinned sheepishly. "Well," she said weakly, "I do seem to meet a number of stubborn Scotsmen wherever I turn. However," she relented, ready to concede the point, "I may be needing one this time. I think we have a battle on our hands."

She proceeded to fill him in on the share transfer for Sentinel Securities, Alita's actions on the day Frank died and later at the reading of the will. She didn't mention the extra funds. She knew there would be trouble over it, but didn't want to face it until she had to. She didn't want to even hint to her lawyer that she ran a company with stolen cash.

Angus nodded as she talked. "Paul told me most of this. Okay, so far so good. And what about your regular corporate lawyer? What exactly is the situation?"

Jenny decided to level with him. "I know you lawyers all know each other, and Victoria's a small town that way, but I have to say this in confidence. I don't trust him. He should be acting on my instructions and in the best interests of the company. He was an old pal of Frank's, but he seems to have loyalties elsewhere." Jenny clamped her lips shut.

Angus considered a moment. "You're right, Victoria can be a small town. And most of the lawyers know each other, as you say, at least to nod in passing. However, everything you say in this office, *everything* is confidential, Mrs. MacDougall. You don't have to worry that it might go further. I sometimes discuss things with my partners to get a different perspective, but it remains confidential to the office. Are you comfortable with that?"

At Jenny's nod he continued. "Fred Austin, wasn't it, the former corporate lawyer?" He made a note on the yellow pad in front of him. "Now, I gather you want me to take over the corporate work, the records book and so on."

"Well, yes," said Jenny slowly, "but more than that I need to know where I stand with a company that has a hostile shareholder holding a forty-five percent interest."

Murdoch's eyes narrowed as he leaned into the back of his chair, which creaked protestingly under his weight. Finally he smiled, resting his forearms on the littered desktop. "Well, it can be hell. A hostile shareholder can make your life miserable. The best scenario is for one of you to sell. If that's possible I'd recommend it. Do you want to stay in the company, or would you consider selling your interest?" He watched her with a steady gaze.

Jenny's gaze was just as level. "There is no way on God's green earth I'm going to sell my shares. I built this company to triple what it was when I joined Frank. And he left me ten percent of the shares for the express purpose of giving me a majority position. He knew I'd look after the long-term employees who've been so loyal. I won't turn my back on it for both of those reasons. Plus, its mine. I've invested a lot of myself in it. Alita won't just walk in and take that from me."

Angus nodded and made a few notes as she finished. Now he grinned engagingly. "Call me Angus. And may I call you Jenny?" At her smile, he added, "Good. I see I'm dealing with a stubborn Scot." Jenny returned his grin with a self-conscious chuckle.

Then his expression sobered. "I'm glad to hear such determination, because you're going to need it. Alita may take her share of the profits, give you a little bit of hassle at the annual general meeting and stay out of your way the rest of the time. That would be really good.

"On the other hand," and here he frowned and rummaged around in the bookcase behind him, "she may decide to fight every decision you make." His head was down as he searched for something, then he emerged triumphant and spun back to face Jenny. "Now, here is a little booklet on corporate law that you might find helpful. By the way, are you a director of the company?"

"Yes, Frank and I were both directors. Mr. Ping elected to leave Frank's directorship vacant until the next annual general meeting. But we appointed me president, as the only director left. Frank was president before he died." Jenny's eyes teared up and she rummaged in her purse for a hanky. "So we made Queenie secretary of the corporation. Mr. Ping said we had to have a separate person hold that position, but not necessarily a shareholder."

"Okay, and who has the corporate records?"

"Fred Austin."

"Well," Angus drew the word out slowly, "we better get them over here. You know the directors have the authority to manage a company. Being as you're the only director, you can delegate tasks to yourself and Queenie as officers of the corporation, but you're still responsible for the management. When it's time for the AGM, we can talk about how to keep control. But on most things a simple majority rules. That's why Frank left you the extra ten percent."

Jenny pursed her lips. "So if I don't rock the boat, I won't need her vote. Did that get you an 'A' at law school in the Corporate Law course?" she asked with a snicker.

He grinned back. "Not quite an A, but I don't want to discuss it, okay?"

She laughed and consulted the list she'd made. "I want to change banks, is that going to require a special resolution? Will I need Alita's consent?"

"No," Angus looked dubious, "but it depends on the bank. If they require personal guarantees from the shareholders, dollars to donuts Alita won't cooperate. If they don't, then you shouldn't have any problem. She's not a signatory on the account, is she?"

"Nope, Mr. Ping read the will just in time." *And the bank isn't likely to demand personal guarantees, not with an account balance like we've got.*

~*~*~*~

That afternoon she heard Bernie Olsinger's low-pitched voice in the reception area and her heart sank. She hadn't seen him since Frank's funeral, when he'd mentioned he would like to drop around and see if she needed any help. The last thing she wanted was Bernie parked in her office for a couple of hours, but as Frank had drilled into her, there probably wasn't a more important person to spend her time with.

Consequently, when Queenie brought him to her office door, Jenny rose with a warm smile. "Bernie, have a seat. How are you? Thanks for taking the time out of your busy schedule to drop by."

Queenie took his coffee order and Bernie made himself comfortable on the sofa. Jenny watched the cushions sag as he settled in.

"I know Frank would have been honoured that you were at his funeral," Jenny continued, "Thank you for that."

Bernie waved his big soft hands in protest. "No thanks necessary. He was a good friend of mine, Jenny, a very dear friend. Mrs. Jensen held up well, didn't she?"

She felt herself stiffen and tried to hide it. "Yes, she did fine. It must have been quite a strain for her. It was a nice funeral though, wasn't it?" Her smile grew misty.

The event had been held in the Catholic cathedral downtown. There was a bit of a battle with Alita about who would speak during the service, as she wanted only the priest to talk. But Jenny, with the support of the priest who had also been a friend of Frank's, had been adamant. Pat, Queenie and Esley had each worked for Frank for more than twenty years and they had put together a eulogy that Esley was to read. And other old friends had come out of the woodwork and into the office, people Jenny had never laid eyes on before, asking if they could say something. In the end Alita threw up her hands and let it happen.

Five people took the podium, and it had been wonderful. A whole spectrum of Frank's life was held up to his friends and family for admiration. Jenny was overwhelmed. She'd stood also, wanting to tell his old friends what a difference he'd made in her life.

She had been amazed at the number of people who attended the service, including Jordie who drove her there and stayed for support, which softened her heart even more. She'd only known Frank for three years, but thought she knew him pretty well. There were literally hundreds of people in the cathedral, many of whom came to the reception in the hall afterwards.

She met dozens of his old friends. Even people like Hiro Mahendra were there, that elusive client of Frank's. He clasped Jenny's hand in his large, rough, brown one and introduced himself. He made a simple comment about what a strong, straightforward, honest man Frank had been, and if she ran the business in the same way, she couldn't do better.

It was deeply moving. Since then, many of his friends and business acquaintances had dropped by the office. They talked about old times when they'd worked with him in logging, prospecting, security work, investing in some wild scheme or other that lost as much as it ever made.

Jenny started to make notes, gathering lists of names and histories, as she began to put together a picture of Frank that had much more depth than it ever had for her when he was still alive. It also gave her a huge number of contacts, from which business seemed to rise like steam.

Bernie cleared his throat and brought her back to the present. "Yes, it was a good funeral, as funerals go." He smiled, his small widely-spaced teeth winking. "I came to see how you're managing, Jenny. I know Frank would rely on me to help you out any way I can. I'd be happy to find personnel for you, a business manager, whatever you need."

Jenny found his eyes curiously flat. "No, no problems, Bernie. But that's very thoughtful. We already found our investigations manager, as Frank must have told you. It was a little earlier than we had planned, but he's working out very well. An ex-detective, RCMP actually." She shrugged. "I wasn't aware of just how much Frank did, until he wasn't here to do it any longer. We're all having to stretch a little to fill the big gap he left."

Jenny felt herself getting maudlin and blinked back the tears. "I still get kind of weepy when I talk about him, so you'll have to forgive me."

Bernie nodded, then smiled affably. "I actually have a fellow who's available, and he's very knowledgeable, worked for me years ago, then went with one of the big firms in Vancouver. He wants to come back to the Island, and I think he could be very helpful to you. Name's Schwartz, Adam Schwartz. You'll like him. He can do just about anything, even take over Frank's position if you like. He'd certainly help take the load off."

Jenny hesitated, then nodded. "I don't know if we can use him but thanks for thinking of us. If you want to send him in, I'd be glad to interview him."

Bernie heaved himself off the couch. "Okay, I'll do that. Just want to be of assistance any way I can. You call me, now, Jenny. Anything you need. I don't forget my friends."

CHAPTER TWENTY ONE

Jenny was home early for the first time in a week. She had so many decisions to make on a minute-by-minute basis about what was going on at Sentinel Security, yet she didn't feel ready to make most of them. Sometimes it all just seemed overwhelming. Frank had shouldered so much of the responsibility when he was there. They'd discussed all the major decisions, and she'd relied on his experience and level-headedness.

Without him, everyone was coming at her with questions and demands that interrupted her constantly, disturbing her train of thought and leaving her feeling ineffectual and frustrated.

Plus, she was out of the office so much with meetings and appointments that when she was there she never got anything done. Thank God for Queenie and the other managers. They'd all been in their jobs long enough to know the routine and what the likely answer was to many of their questions.

To top it off, she'd had a call from Angus Murdoch this morning. Alita had filed a challenge to Frank's will, as she'd threatened and it was to be heard in Chambers in the not too distant future. "That brings it on quicker than if she went for a trial," he told her. "Fred Austen must have instructions to get control of the company back into her hands as fast as possible. I haven't had time to look into it, but Paul's handling it and he tells me she doesn't have a chance. I believe him, he's the best." He rang off cheerfully but Jenny was left with a deep sense of foreboding.

Sighing, she set her briefcase down and hung her coat in the hall closet. She sneezed once, then again, and went into the kitchen looking for a tissue. She'd picked up a terrible cold and couldn't seem to shake it. Two days of sneezing and a runny nose, alternately shivering and sweating, aching sinuses that left her miserable.

She'd go for a walk. She couldn't breathe well enough to run, but the fresh air would perk her up. And she did her best thinking on a walk, she could go from tangent to tangent in her mind uninterrupted by phones or people.

She peeked next door hoping for some company but Jordie's house was dark as it had been most nights for the last week. She hadn't seen much of him since he'd kissed her right here in her kitchen. The memory made her shiver. That whole thing was up in the air, and she didn't know how to handle it. Jordie was her conundrum.

She bundled up warm, put on a hat and stuffed her pockets with tissue. The phone rang and she debated whether to let it go to message. It was getting dark outside. But she picked it up anyway and heard Greg's voice, sounding exasperated to be leaving yet another message.

"Greg! I'm here! I was just going out for a walk and arguing with myself about whether to get the phone."

He laughed, his big booming voice coming through the receiver to warm her.

"It's good to hear your voice," she said. "How have you been? I called your office a couple of times but I never seem to get to it until things simmer down for the day, and by then there's no one there. You certainly work civilized hours."

Her voice was wry and he chuckled again. "I wondered why I didn't hear from you. Yeah, we cut the phones off at four-thirty when the support staff go home. I'm still here though, as are most of us until later. Let me give you another number. It goes straight to my office, so if I'm working late you can get me. Have you got a cold?" His voice lowered and Jenny shivered with remembrance of another time when his voice had caressed her like that, in running commentary to his hands.

"Yeah, the shock to my system of coming home to this damp, windy place." She sniffed ineffectually.

"You must have stayed quite a bit longer in Europe. I've been back for a month, and I only now get through to you." He sounded plaintive.

"Well, I did stay a few weeks longer. And I'm not home from the office until later, Greg. So much has happened since I saw you, it feels like a lifetime away, those days on the sand in Greece."

His voice came back low and sure. "Not so long. It's very vivid in my mind." There was silence between them for a moment as they each thought of that shared time. "I'm planning a quick trip over to Victoria in a couple of weeks and hoped to see you." His tone was hoarse and thick with emotion.

"Greg, how are things with your wife? Has that situation changed, any hope for the future?"

He was silent for a moment. "I'll talk about that when I get there. Listen, one of the guys is coming, I have to go for a meeting. Can I call you later tonight? We can discuss my visit."

"I won't be home," Jenny blurted, her voice thin with nerves. "Here's my office number. Call me there tomorrow. We can talk then." As she hung up she wondered if he thought when they saw each other again they'd just pick up where they left off on that other island.

And now there was Jordie. Things had changed and they had something to work out between them. One more item to worry about although it was more nerves than worry. She gritted her aching teeth.

As she opened her patio doors, the wind gusted and pressed her back against the glass. She looked down the bank, noting the scrub bushes bent beneath the force of it, the ocean whipped to a light froth. Weather was brewing. She pulled her toque lower on her forehead.

Jogging lightly down the path, she stopped at the bottom. This was certainly a popular time of day to walk. Quite a few people were on the path, most strolling sedately, even if they had to lean into the wind. More were down on the sand throwing sticks for dogs wading eagerly into the waves to fetch them back.

She started off down the beach, skirting giant clumps of kelp piled in jumbled height by the high winter tides, long streamers trailing off the kelp heads across the sand. Her mother had made dolls of the kelp when she was a child. They'd picnic at the beach and Mum would use a kitchen knife to cut the head of kelp off the stalk leaving a sturdy stump attached. She would trim the streamers for hair and carve a minimal face into the thick smooth tan-brown bulb. Jenny and her sister played with them for hours, planting them in families in the sand and building sand houses around them.

She walked along feeling invigorated by the brisk wind whipping the waves into a frenzy, then headed up the path above as the water washed higher around her feet. The toes of her shoes were wet. She noted Armadillo Rock farther out in the bay, almost covered by the high water. Passing the park on her left, she saw the swings were empty, clanging and banging together in the wind.

The rocks out in the water glistened wetly in the late light. Gulls floated above in the wind, adjusting the angle of their wings to catch each turn of the air currents. Some seemed to hang in one spot like kites tethered to a string. A flock of ducks crowded noisily in the leeward curve of the bay, facing away from the wind and twittering amongst themselves.

Jenny got as far as Turkey Head before she felt the first drops of rain. The wind was blowing hard enough to threaten her footing on the rocks, but she stayed for a moment, pushing back against the force of the gale. She wished Jordie was with her. He'd love it as much as she did. The waves dashed on the rocks, splashing straight up into the air and coating her with fine spray. She loved the wildness of it, the surge of energy from weather like this.

Hopping up and down, she tried to shake off the feeling of being cornered. She pressed her lips firmly together and turning, headed home, pulling her hat lower around her ears and holding a tissue to her still dripping nose. Going back was faster with the wind at her back. The rain soon started in earnest, driving her to a slow jog up the path to her patio door. She was breathing heavily when she stumbled inside, sliding the door closed behind her. She collapsed into a chair to catch her breath and kick off her shoes. Her jacket dripped, her shoes and socks were soaked.

As she shrugged out of her wet things, the doorbell went. Her heart jumped in anticipation, Jordie must be home. Trailing down the hall in bare feet, she opened the front door to a gust of wind and rain. It was dark and she hastily flicked on the outside light to find Norman Suffron standing on her porch. She took an involuntary step backward.

CHAPTER TWENTY TWO

N orman," she said in alarm.

"Hi, Jenny, can I come in?" He hunched his shoulders against the rain.

She gave a tentative smile. "Of course. Please step inside. Isn't the weather foul? And it came on so quickly." She was rambling as her mind frantically whirled around the question of why he was here.

He stepped lightly into the hall and shrugged out of his wet jacket. Jenny hung it up to drip in the foyer and led him into the living room. She brought hastily brewed coffee and set it on the coffee table, all the time wondering, *what is he doing here?* She hadn't thought of Norman since the scene in Mr. Ping's boardroom, but she'd just heard from Angus about Alita's challenge to the will and was slightly alarmed at his sudden appearance in her house.

Norman had a distinctive worldly look, smooth, as if he were polished every morning. His pale hair was always perfect. Just coming out of the wind and rain tonight, he only had to run his hand through the strands for it to fall into place.

And his clothes. It was nothing garish, they weren't crisply starched and ironed, with telltale creases. More, they pressed smooth to his body, falling gracefully against him, fitting impeccably. It reflected his manners. *Covering what?* Something that Jenny didn't want to look at. He attracted and repelled her at the same time.

Norman smiled as if amused at the way she watched him. He put his cup down and clasped his manicured hands together in a meek gesture of appeal, his expression sincere. "I've wondered how you're managing and I just happened to be in the area. I hope it isn't too much of an intrusion." He didn't seem to expect an answer.

"To be honest, that scene in Mr. Ping's office when the will was read was difficult, but I can only plead shock and grief on the part of my mother. I hope you can forgive her." He paused for a second to give her an earnest look.

Jenny was searching for the right words to respond when he changed direction once again.

"But that isn't what I wanted to discuss." He looked down at his hands a moment, and when he looked up his expression had changed. The humility and earnestness were gone. Replacing it was a gaze of profound warmth and overt male interest.

Jenny was astounded, and totally convinced it was an act. Her heart reacted in alarm. She didn't welcome his attentions.

He stood and she rose, feeling forced to take a step backward against her chair. He gave her a quizzical smile. "Jenny, we haven't spent much time together, and I regret that. But you're a lovely woman and it certainly hasn't escaped my notice. I've always admired you a great deal." His

134

look became sizzling as it rested on her face and then on her breasts under her damp sweatshirt.

She involuntarily put her hand to her collar as her breath caught in her throat. She didn't believe for one minute that he was attracted to her, unless it was as a victim of assault. She doubted he had normal emotions, especially when it came to women. She was suddenly desperate to get him out of the house.

"Norman, that's very kind," she blurted awkwardly. "I know you and Alita have been under a lot of pressure." She was chagrined to hear her voice shake and cleared her throat in an attempt to disguise it, reaching for a tissue. "You'll have to excuse me, I have a dreadful cold but it was nice of you to drop by. Perhaps we'll be able to sort everything out after all. I certainly hope so."

She turned, hoping to show him the door. "Give Alita my good wishes, and assure her I'll always act in the best interests of the company." Her voice caught in her throat and she coughed. "I'm really not feeling well. Thanks for dropping by."

Norman gracefully stepped around the armchair behind which she hovered, placing his hands on her shoulders. Jenny had to tip her head back to keep him in her sight. He looked down at her with his dark intense eyes, so striking in contrast to his fair colouring. She could see her reflection in his curiously flat gaze. Her throat squeezed shut and her heart thumped unevenly.

"Jenny," he said. "I want to take you out to dinner. Not tonight of course. I can see you aren't well. But next week, perhaps. How about Friday? I could pick you up here around seven."

Jenny felt his breath on her face. It smelled of mints and something else. Then she realized it was his aftershave, that sweet overpowering scent, and she thought she might vomit. "Thank you," she managed, "But I have to say no. I'm very busy and I don't like to..."

He cut her off by placing his mouth firmly over hers. Panic rose up her throat and she started to struggle. His grip tightened, not enough to bruise, just enough to hold her in place.

Alarm shot through her system. *Should she scream? Who would hear her?* As his mouth became more insistent, she stood stock still in frenzied indecision when a loud banging came from the patio doors. Norman must have heard it at the same time. He released her, stepping back as he whipped around looking for the source. His expression was angry, quickly masked to become mere curiosity.

Jordie stepped through the sliding doors, rain dripping from his face and off his oilskin. He shook himself casually and unclipped his jacket.

"Hi, everyone. How're things?" His voice was friendly but his eyes showed as two narrow slits in his face, fixed firmly on Norman.

"Hi, Jordie," Jenny's voice cracked with relief. "Come in." She waved him forward with her hand and at the same time backed away from her guest. "Norman was just leaving," she said, risking a glance at him.

He turned to give her a slow appraising smile, his expression changing again, becoming a look of admiration tinged with lust. Revulsion rose in her throat.

"Yes, as a matter of fact, I was. Just leaving," he added. "I'll see you Friday at seven." He leaned forward and, before she could retreat, planted a quick possessive kiss on her cheek and moved down the hall. He went out the door, jacket in hand and she rushed to close it firmly behind him.

She stared blankly at Jordie as he approached across the carpet in his sock feet, his hair unruly and glistening dark red with rain. "Jenny, are you okay?" He placed his hands on her shoulders in the same spot Norman's had been but the effect was entirely different. Jordie's hands were gentle, they soothed her. She wasn't afraid of him because she knew she could trust anything he did. She leaned forward and rested her forehead on his hard chest, sniffing through her stuffed nose.

"Jenny, are you crying? Did he hurt you?" He lifted her face anxiously to gaze into her eyes.

She shook her head. "No, he just scared me. I don't know what he wanted, why he came."

Jordie took in a sharp breath. "Don't know what he wanted? It was pretty obvious what he wanted." His voice had a sharp sting to it. He pushed her away to look her in the face. "And you made a date with him." His cheeks flushed a dull red.

"I did not!" she said, jerking out of his grip. She rounded on him, a tissue clutched to her nose. "He asked me out to dinner and I said *no*, then he said he'd pick me up Friday at seven, just as if I'd said *yes*. I don't need you here beating on me too!" Tears rose in her eyes, and she tried to blow her nose.

He looked belligerently around for someone to blame for this fiasco. "I'd like to knock his teeth in."

Jenny shook her head resignedly. "I know, but you can't. Just hold me, Jordie. I was so scared." A tear fell onto her hand.

"Ah, baby." he murmured, pulling her into his arms. "I just laid it all onto you as if you could control the bastard." He lifted her head, noting her red-rimmed eyes and sore nose.

She nodded and he hugged her close. "It's okay," she murmured against his shirt.

"No, it's not. When I saw him with his hands on you, I just... I couldn't..." He paused to catch his breath. "I've been a little over-protective, I know. I'm off kilter, Jenny, there's a lot happening, and some of it seems out of my control. About the other night, I..."

"It's okay, Jordie. I understand. You've been under a lot of pressure." She looked up at him and he stilled momentarily, his expression open and hungry.

Then he blinked and the moment was gone. His eyes became shuttered as he pulled her gingerly back into his embrace. "Poor girl. What a bad cold you've got. Things are pretty hectic at work, right?" He rubbed her back and she sighed against him.

When she pulled away, he let her go. "Actually, I came over to invite you to dinner if you haven't already eaten. I've made a pot roast and it's ready to go."

Jenny felt her face light up like a beacon, even with her teary eyes and raw-looking nose. "I'd love it, Jordie. I don't have a thing in the house to eat."

"Well, come on then. Let's lock up here to keep any further intruders at bay. We can talk shop, I'll tell you how my business is doing, and you can tell me about yours."

She grinned. That sounded like the old Jordie, her friend and confidante.

His voice hardened. "And we'll talk security."

She hunched her shoulders and grabbed her coat off the back of the chair.

CHAPTER TWENTY THREE

Jenny pushed a piece of pot roast around her plate with a fork and struggled to breathe while she chewed. "And then there's the problem of that money." She paused to try to swallow.

Jordie frowned. "Yeah, what about that money? Where did it come from?"

Jenny shook her head and gave up trying to eat. She shoved her plate away and rested her elbows on the table. "I don't know. I haven't had time to sort the files and see what's there. I've been so busy interviewing banks, changing lawyers, signing cheques, directing traffic in the office. It's been hectic. But Queenie tells me Frank would hand her a cheque or some cash and tell her to deposit it and promise to give her the back-up paperwork later. Except he never gave it to her. She'd forget and when she did ask, he'd be vague and say, *not now* or *how do you expect me to remember after all this time?*"

"But if there was a cheque deposited, there'd have to be a name on the cheque."

"That's just it, some of them were cheques from Frank's own personal account. Then there were money orders, sometimes it was cash. When the cheque was from someone other than Frank, Queenie says it had some corporate name that was hand written. You know, like a counter cheque. She didn't make note of the account numbers." Jenny stared bleakly at the half eaten dinner.

"Was the roast that bad?"

Her head popped up. "No, no, it was delicious. I'm just having trouble eating and breathing at the same time, so I opted for breathing. Sorry, Jordie."

He laughed, showing strong white teeth in his dark red beard. "It was the look you were giving it, Jenny, like you were trying to kill it with a glare."

She smiled. "This thing is so weird. I still think Frank was honest. He never tried to cut corners with me, or with his customers. He was always more than fair with the staff. So I have to think that the money was from an honest source or Frank was hoodwinked into believing that it was."

She lifted her head to make her point. "And I can't help thinking that it's going to come back to haunt me. I mean, the best possible scenario is that Frank contracted to provide some heavy duty services that haven't been delivered yet. That means someone may show up claiming we breached a contract that I don't even know exists, or that we're bound to provide a lot of services that may be so expensive it will break the company. Who knows?"

"And the worst case scenario?" Jordie's eyes were steady on her face.

"Well, I'm trying not to imagine the worst case. That money belongs to someone. What would they be willing to do to get it back? Did Frank die because of it?" She glanced with dread around the room, finally resting her gaze on his face.

"Frank wasn't sick according to Queenie. He had a moment of panic over the phone when I told him I wasn't coming back with Izzy. Maybe he wanted to discuss this with me."

"Yeah, about that," Jordie interjected. "I've been meaning to ask. Why didn't you come back with Izzy?" Jordie's gaze was intense. "Did you meet someone over there?" It was as if he couldn't stop himself from asking.

Jenny waved his interruption away, thinking of Greg's phone call and his impending visit with a quaking heart. She accepted that Jordie was protective. Vestiges of their childhood perhaps, when he'd been the leader of the gang with Jenny and his sister Harry following along behind. But things had changed and she wasn't sure how. Their relationship seemed to be in flux and the unruly feeling in the pit of her stomach told her she was nervous about where he might want to go with it.

She pasted on a stern face. "Jordie, pay attention," she said, all business. "And then I called Frank's doctor to see if he had been to see him about a problem with vertigo. I told him it was an insurance issue. Guess what he told me?"

Jordie waited, obviously chastised for his impertinent question.

"Well, anyway," she continued when he remained silent, "he said Frank had been in for a checkup in March, about two weeks before he died. And everything was good. No problem with being dizzy, or short of breath. He did tell the doctor he'd been under a lot of pressure, but his business partner was returning soon and things should ease up then." Jenny's voice faltered and her throat became thick.

"I let him down, Jordie. I should have been here instead of gallivanting around Europe trying to come to grips with my divorce, which was ancient history anyway. I should have come home when he was so upset that I was extending my vacation. I should have..."

"*Should haves* are a waste of time," Jordie interrupted, his voice unexpectedly hard. "Don't indulge. I've done enough of that in my life to know. You did what you had to do." His tone softened. "And if Frank was into something that was over his head, that was his doing, not yours. Besides, you have an investigator on staff, Dave Powers. Use him. Find out where the money came from."

She shook her head. "Sounds easy, Jordie. But do you seriously think Alita is going to allow me access to Frank's personal accounts? I don't even want to tell her there's an irregularity in case she tries to show incompetence on my part to seize control of the company."

She was silent for a minute. "Actually, now that I think of it, Norman might be useful after all. If he decides he likes me, maybe I could get him to..."

"No! Not a chance. I know you're just saying that to annoy me," he added stonily as she giggled, "but don't even think of it. The man's a snake. Promise me, Jenny." His look was determined.

She nodded. "I was fooling, Jordie. We just got so serious there, I thought I'd give you a dig. Just for fun." He smiled at her, his fierce look turning tender, and Jenny didn't think for a minute that it was fake.

~*~*~*~

Isabelle's face twisted into a ferocious scowl as Jenny pirouetted slowly for the benefit of her audience of one. "Well, does the dress look okay or not?" She was wearing a dark green wool dress, nicely but severely cut. It kind of reminded her of her polyester days, except this was better quality and certainly a classier style. She'd matched it with her black pumps and clutch bag. But she stopped short at the expression on her friend's face. "What? Does it look awful? What's the matter, Izzy?"

"That man is sixty-five if he's a day! Why are you going out with him? You're thirty-eight years old, Jenny! You haven't hit retirement yet!"

Jenny's mouth fell open, then she closed it with a snap. "This isn't a date, you goof. He wants to talk business. He has a big account to transfer to our company, and he wants to talk money. Don't be silly. Now, how does the dress look? Attractive but businesslike, right?"

Izzy frowned, glanced at the dress and shrugged eloquently, her mouth pursed.

"Oh, Izzy, come on. Does it look alright, or not?"

"It looks fine. Very conservative. A business meeting or a funeral. And Mahendra is not interested in sending other business your way. Take my word for it. He's after your body, and who can blame him? But you should be looking for a younger man."

Jenny collapsed onto the bed, staring at her friend. "Izzy, what's gotten into you? Of course he's looking to talk business. He dropped by the office yesterday to pay his bill, like he used to every other week with Frank. And he said he had several friends with companies who need security services and he could send that work our way. Asked if I'd like to talk about it over dinner. What's wrong with that?" Jenny frowned in frustration. "Don't be so critical. He's a nice man, Frank did business with him for years. He's reliable, honest, well fairly honest, although he does always pay with cash, so I don't know about that, but a steady customer."

"And sixty-five years old."

"Lots of my clients are older than that. It's the older ones who get security conscious, and want alarms and guards and things. I'd be out of business if I refused to deal with anyone older than I am." Jenny chuckled at the idea.

Izzy sat on the bed beside her and gripped her head in her hands. "Here's what I think. I think he wants to date you. And I'll bet you a shopping trip to Seattle that he comes onto you tonight. Deal?"

Jenny stared, but slowly extended her hand. As they shook, she asked, "Do you really think so, Izzy? The thought never crossed my mind. Are you serious? Well, maybe..." She fell silent, contemplating the possibilities.

Finally, she raised her head. "You see, my mind doesn't work that way. I never see this coming. And when I want it to happen, it doesn't. As if I don't send out the right signals, or the other party doesn't pick them up. Hiro Mahendra, trying to date me?" She fell back onto the bed, her arms flung out in surrender. "Izzy, that's the funniest thing I've heard in years," and she succumbed to gales of laughter, rolling on the comforter. "He'd nee... he'd need an oxygen mask just to get it up!" she gasped. Izzy joined her laughter and they clung together, screaming until the tears rolled down their faces.

"Ahhh... That's funny." Jenny lay with her head on Izzy's arm and her hands flat on the bed. "Poor old Hiro. Now I'll have a terrible time keeping a straight face all through dinner. I'll be waiting for his pitch, instead of concentrating on business." She threw her hands in the air and made an effort to sit up.

"Omigod, I'm going to be late. Well, he'll wait, no doubt. Let me get this done up." She struggled off the bed and began to work on her belt. Izzy reached to help her.

"Jenny, why don't you go out with Jordie? I hear he's great in bed." Izzy tugged on the belt and pulled her friend around so she could see to buckle it.

Jenny's hands stilled. "Where did you hear that?" Her voice sounded muffled. "Linda certainly didn't confide that to you. Did she?"

"No, it wasn't Linda who told me."

"Well, what are you talking about, Izzy?"

"Oh, I just heard rumours about him. He's supposed to be a fantastic lover," she said lightly.

Jenny frowned. "Come on, Izzy, if you know something, spit it out."

"Well..." Isabelle was obviously having second thoughts about bringing the subject up. "I ran into Jordie and another woman one day, this was years ago. He looked a little embarrassed but he introduced me and we chatted for a minute. Then I met her again some months later, and I was curious, so..."

"Izzy, you didn't! You *asked* her if she slept with him?" Jenny sank down on the bed again, suddenly weak in the knees and not sure she wanted to hear what her friend might have to say.

"No! Give me a little credit. I just remembered myself to her and we began to talk. We ended up going for coffee. I ran into her a few more times after that, on purpose I might add. Eventually she told me she and Jordie had been seeing each other for a while. Not often, because he was married. But she said that he was a wonderful lover, patient and attentive, so even though she dated other guys, she still saw him. He was great in bed, the best she'd ever had. And I have to admit, from the look of her, she might have had a few." Izzy eyed her cautiously.

Jenny was hot, her cheeks flushed as she looked at her friend's elegant face. "Izzy, is that true? Jordie has a lover? I can't believe it! All the times I've railed away about Bobby and his cheating, and Jordie was listening to me, sympathizing."

"Jenny, you can't totally blame him. Linda was a very strange wife. I'll bet they didn't have sex. He always seemed to skirt around her, as if she was a cactus and he'd get jabbed if he got too close."

Jenny hesitated, then confided, "I know they didn't have sex, at least for a while. He told me they've lived separately for the last few years. She moved out without even leaving."

"Yikes. So he found someone who wanted to sleep with him." Izzy's voice became persuasive. "At least he kept his hormones working. Otherwise he would have frozen up, just like she did. And he'd be no use to any woman."

Jenny gave a short burst of laughter. "Well, we don't know for sure if he's of any use, do we? How long ago did you meet that woman?"

Izzy shrugged. "It doesn't matter. Just think about it, though. Someone's going to snap him up. He's very eligible. Financially well-off, good looking, virile. He's going to find himself a woman. Just don't wait too long, if you want to make a bid for him yourself."

Jenny frowned and shook her head. "I'm really going to be late, Izzy. Can you hand me my purse?" She took the clutch and went into the bathroom. Closing the door, she leaned on the counter, staring at herself in the mirror. *Did she want Jordie that way?* Her heart was pounding erratically and her palms were damp. The answer was obvious.

But did she have the nerve to put herself out there? *What if he turned her down?* It would be devastating. Her stomach lurched at the thought. But if she didn't, someone else would. As Isabelle had just pointed out, Jordie was a very attractive man. She couldn't wait too long.

There was a light rap on the door. "I'm going to go, Jenny,' her friend called. 'I'll be late myself, if I don't. So I'll be waiting for a report on tonight. I want to know what approach Mahendra takes, and I'll be looking forward to that shopping trip you promised me!"

Jenny forced a laugh through her tight throat. "Thanks. I'll see you later. Have a nice time."

CHAPTER TWENTY FOUR

Jenny sat in the restaurant toying with her fork and fighting off thoughts of Jordie with a lover. Hiro Mahendra was a nice man, but Izzy was absolutely right. He wasn't looking to send any business her way. He'd been delighted when she arrived, praised her appearance right down to her fingertips, and seated her with great courtliness at the table. His eyes sparkled. He was carefully dressed, every detail perfect, including the rather dated navy and silver ascot around his neck. He was now deep into the story of how his wife had died and the loneliness of the last few years. He'd continued with tales of his friendship with Frank, and how he held Jenny in the very highest esteem.

She tried to pull her attention back to the present. She wasn't interested in what he seemed about to offer, but the least he deserved was that she half-listen to what he had to say. Yet her mind was fixated on the image of Jordie in bed with another woman, writhing and plunging, his muscular back and buttocks flexing with his efforts, a sheen of sweat covering his skin, his mouth on her mouth, on her throat, on her breast. Jenny could hear their cries and murmurs, until she wanted to put her hands over her ears to shut it out.

She flung down her napkin. "Hiro, I've enjoyed myself, I really have. You've been very kind but I have a sudden headache. Please excuse me."

As she drove home, she wondered when Izzy would drag her down to Seattle for that shopping trip. Maybe Seattle wasn't the best idea, there was Greg... Life was just too damned complicated!

~*~*~*~

Jenny woke to the sound of the phone and reached groggily for the handset on her bedside table. "Hello?" Her voice was hoarse and she cleared her throat to try again. She was met with a ring tone in her ear. Had she just imagined it? She slammed the phone down and fell back onto the mattress.

The light was leaking in through the gap in her drapes and she checked the clock. Five forty-five. She lay there a minute in shock, stunned by the anger bubbling up inside at the nerve of someone for phoning her so early. Then she pulled the quilt up to her chin and huddled against the pillow. What was happening to her? She was becoming a shrew again, or worse. She stared with worried eyes at the closed curtains of her window.

Heaving herself out of bed, she crossed the room and pulled them back into their ties. The sun was low in the early morning sky, glistening off the remarkably still water below. Her neighbour Mrs. Boznik was out in the garden already, her crippled old body hunched over the flower beds, gnarled fingers finding tiny weeds and clearing them lovingly away. She hadn't realized Mrs. Boznik was about so early. But that made sense. The lights were usually out in her house by about eight o'clock at night.

The morning was absolutely glorious. Jenny's spirits lifted and she opened the casement window to lean out.

"Hello, Mrs. Boznik," she called. "Isn't the weather beautiful?"

Jenny saw her kerchiefed head pause and then the woman turned carefully, straining to see in spite of her bent back. She smiled, her face creasing into a maze of lines and wrinkles. "Yes, my dear, it's lovely. Just as God intended, I'm sure."

Jenny laughed. "I guess that's right. Your flowers look beautiful. That blue delphinium is absolutely gorgeous. It must be a double. If you have any extras, I'd be happy to have one. I've never seen anything like it."

Mrs. Boznik nodded happily. "I always collect the seeds. When I get them this fall, I'll save some for you. They grow so easily. Showy, aren't they?" She looked proudly at the display of flowers just bursting into bloom.

Jenny withdrew her head and turned back into her room, feeling much better about herself and the world in general. Not everything was out of kilter. Some things were still working the way they should. Now that she was up, she'd just have a lovely peaceful early stroll before the rest of the day broke in on her.

~*~*~*~

Jenny greeted Adam Schwartz in the reception room and brought him into her office. She gave him a seat at the pine table in the corner and took the chair opposite. Adam was a short stocky man, middle-aged, ruddy complexion with heavy lashings of broken veins across his nose and cheeks.

His face was hard and closed, difficult to read. She pulled a pad of paper across the table's polished surface.

"Bernie Olsinger gave me your name, Adam, so we're pleased to have the opportunity to talk with you and see if our needs and your experience can complement each other. Bernie didn't give me your resume, did you happen to bring one with you?"

Adam shook his head and leaned forward in the chair, resting his beefy forearms on the table top and clasping his thick fingers together. His wrists protruded without the benefit of shirtsleeves from the arms of his sports jacket, a dark nondescript garment, well-worn.

"I don't own such an item, Ma'am. Never have. But Bernie is as good as. He can give any kind of reference that you need. I've worked in this industry for years. I know it backwards and I know it forwards. I can run the whole show here if that's what you're looking for. This is a rough trade for a woman, if you get my drift." His eyes rested knowingly on her chest.

Her temperature rose by degrees under his open appraisal. Finally, she leaned forward, imitating his posture and partially protecting her breasts from his gaze. "Well, Adam," she began in what she hoped was a restrained tone of voice, "why don't you tell me where you worked last, and how it is you don't work there any longer."

His gaze flickered up with surprise.

"Uh, yeah. Fair question. Well, it's like this. I was working for Bernie here in Victoria years ago, and then he sent me to Vancouver to help open up some new operations. When he franchised them all, I left and went with the biggest security company in the city. Owned by a friend of mine,

Freddy White. Then White got bought out by a newcomer, guy by the name of Stouffer."

A light went on in her head. Wasn't that the guy whose license had been lifted a couple of months ago, some police investigation, a real hush-hush deal? She listened more closely.

"Stouffer kept me on, he could see I was the main character in the action, if you see what I mean, and that he needed me. But he went out of business so I'm looking for something over here. I kind of want to get back into the Victoria scene." Up to this point Adam recited his history as if it were a lesson learned at Mama's knee.

Now he got a little livelier and actually looked her in the eye. "So, you see, I have all the experience you need. Bernie told me your partner died a couple of months ago. Sorry, tough break. I heard of Frank Jensen. He was good." He paused, then added, "I can step right into his shoes where he left off. Take all the problems off your shoulders, you know? This is a hard business, especially for a woman."

Jenny suddenly thought of the little sign Queenie kept tacked to the note board behind her desk. It had a picture of an angry cat hissing over its shoulder, and the words beneath read: *I'm right out of estrogen, and I have a handgun. Any questions?* She wondered what Adam would say is she showed it to him. He probably wouldn't even get it.

Apart from the patronizing tone of this gentleman, Jenny didn't have a good feeling about the interview. She reached behind her for the phone, conscious that her action gave Adam an even better look at her chest, and asked for Queenie. When the secretary arrived Jenny told her to find Dave Powers and send him in with coffee for everyone.

~*~*~*~

152

By the time Dave arrived, a tray of cups in hand, Jenny's face was pink and her lips pressed tightly together. Dave sent her a questioning look but she just shook her head so he focused his attention on Adam Schwartz. It didn't take long to realize why Jenny looked like he might have to restrain her from wringing the man's neck. Schwartz never took his eyes off Jenny's breasts, and the more agitated she became the keener his gaze.

Dave made himself comfortable and took over what he thought of as the interrogation. When a man was looking for a job, and acted like a jerk during the interview, that's what it became. Plus, this guy was recommended by the fellow who held the business's license in his back pocket. He'd better measure up, or Dave would find out why.

Adam perked up with another man in the room and opened up under Dave's aggressive probing. By the time he left the office, they had a lot more information than they'd started with, and none of it good.

Adam had been Stouffer's right-hand man. The police began an investigation into Stouffer's operations about a year ago. They recommended lifting the security license and laying charges for breach of conditions. Even then no action was taken by the Ministry.

The police must have become frustrated, Dave filled that fact in between the lines of what Schwartz told them. It was after the story in the press made it public that the license was suspended, 'pending investigation of irregularities'. So far, no charges had been laid.

The interview came to a close. Within an hour, Dave reported that Adam Schwartz had a credit rating that made a scam artist look good. He had no bank account, but did have a string of debts, all outstanding. To add to that Dave found through a police source that although Adam had no criminal record, he did have a lengthy notation of 'brought in for questioning', 'associated with known criminals', and charges laid that were stayed by the prosecutor.

"This is not an honest man," commented Dave, leaning back in his chair. "Why would Olsinger suggest you hire him?"

Jenny's face had paled. "I never did like that guy, now I'm beginning to think I had good reason not to."

"Who, Bernie?"

"Yes. Have you met him?"

Dave frowned, meeting her gaze. "Once, in Frank's office. I gather he was an old friend."

"Yes, he was. Dave, do you know if Frank had a criminal record? I can't believe he did, if he managed to get a license to run a security company, but…"

He shook his head. "No, I checked before I hired on here. Nothing. You don't either." He grinned at her surprised expression. "A guy can't be too careful, and if the means are there to find out, you can't blame me for having a look."

Jenny looked smug. "You don't have one either. Believe me, Frank checked before we hired you. We wanted to make sure you didn't leave the RCMP under some kind of cloud."

Dave laughed outright. Sometimes Jenny was a lot of fun.

"Well, we don't want Adam anywhere near here. How do we do this so that Bernie's nose isn't out of joint?" She ran her fingernail along the edge of the desk, deep in thought.

"You just tell him the guy's scum and you have no intention of hiring him." Dave's jaw bulged.

She shook her head. "Bernie himself is scum. We want to be very careful to stay on his good side. That's where our security license resides, in the office just below his. You know that." She lifted her head. "I think I'll tell him that Adam Schwartz certainly had enough experience. At this point we don't have a spot for him. And I'll tell Adam the same thing. Nothing now, but maybe later."

She studied the scene out her window for a minute, her face sober. "But you know, Dave, there's something weird about this whole thing. Bernie can't seriously think we'd hire this guy and put him in charge of the company. So what did he hope to get out of it?"

Dave shrugged and got to his feet. It looked pretty straightforward to him. "Probably just likes to keep his fingers in everybody else's pie. Lots of guys are like that. Adam lost his job, Bernie wanted to find him one, and be seen doing you a favour at the same time. That way you're both in his debt."

"Maybe." Jenny looked thoughtful. "But I think it's odd that they each had the same line about how tough this business is, no place for a woman. They've obviously discussed it. It's almost as if there was an implied threat there." Jenny's brow furrowed in worry.

Dave snorted. "I can't see it. They're old school types, macho as hell. They probably thought if they pointed out how tough it is out there, you'd fold and decide to hire a guy to run the show."

Jenny's glare brought a chuckle.

"Don't let it get to you. Consider the source, after all. Not bright lights, either one of them."

She rose and grabbed her jacket. "That's not what Frank said. He thought Bernie was very bright. How else

155

does a franchise security company owner become the Assistant Deputy Minister for the Attorney General?"

Dave conceded the point and made a mental note to keep a watch on Adam Swartz.

CHAPTER TWENTY FIVE

Jenny picked up the pile of messages from the cubby on Queenie's desk and sifted through them with one hand as she carried her purse and briefcase into her office. She immediately spied one with Greg's name on it. He'd called around noon. The message read "Greg Houston, not at a phone, will call back."

Jenny involuntarily looked back at Queenie, wondering who she thought this was. She knew she was being ridiculous. Greg Houston could be anyone, a new client, a government agent. And why should she feel guilty?

Queenie gave her a puzzled look but she shook her head and disappeared into her office, closing the door firmly behind her. What if Greg just showed up here? What if he got loud and aggressive when she told him that he couldn't just pick up the traces of the relationship?

She shuddered. Life was too confusing! What felt good at the time, felt right on a sunny Greek island in the Mediterranean months ago, suddenly seemed ill-advised in the real world of families, jobs and commitments. She looked out her window but saw only that sunny beach, and the hazy light in Greg's room in the hotel. It *had* been wonderful. It *had* been right, at least for her. She wasn't breaking any commitments.

And it had been good for her, if fleeting. It had broken down some walls within, helped her to step out of a prison of rage and hurt. Everyone in her family had benefited. Her visit with Rob had been wonderful. Maggie was thrilled to come home to visit, and was looking forward to the summer at the house. Because Jenny could smile now, laugh and love, where before she'd been shut down.

But Greg was out of line to think he could come back here and pick up where they had left off or even carry it further than in Greece. Jenny straightened her back and her lips tightened. She wasn't going to get drawn into some affair with a man who was not only living in another country but had a wife and son at home. The fact that he was also ruggedly good-looking had her tightening her lips in resolve. Jordie was more than his equal in that department.

Greg had left a message on Jenny's phone, she found when she arrived home. He was in town on business today, and would call around to see her about nine. Jenny was not just determined now, she was in a panic. Nine o'clock! Jordie was always nosing around then to see that she was alright. What was she going to do? Her heart beat in her throat at the thought of any confrontation.

What confrontation? That was her more rational self. Jordie was her cousin and a friend, nothing more. And she could have other friends if she wished. Jenny listened to those rational internal comments, but she knew Jordie. And it wasn't going to be fun.

Well, so be it. She popped the rest of last night's casserole into the oven and threw on a pair of sweat pants.

Just enough time for a quick jog before dinner. The fresh air would clear her head, and she was going to need that.

~*~*~*~

When the doorbell rang, Jenny leaped from her chair. She was carefully dressed, not too casual but definitely flattering. Green was her best colour, and the soft cotton shirt was just the right shade. She combed her bangs back with her fingers one last time and opened the door.

Greg stood there, looking down at her with the same warm expression in his brown eyes that she'd first noticed on a beach in Greece. She felt a surge of excitement well up inside and walked into his arms. She hugged his broad back before pulling him into the hall. He looked tired, the lines down his cheeks and between his brows were more pronounced than when she last saw him.

She seated him on the sofa, plied him with wine, crackers and paté and settled beside him to catch up. As they talked she realized she'd missed him. He was someone she felt comfortable with, comfortable enough to discuss events in her life that she didn't tell just anyone.

Things were not going well with Greg. His wife was finally taking the initiative on a divorce and she wanted custody of their son, limited access for the father, extensive child-support, and the house. Greg was suddenly looking at a future where he might be without his son except every second Saturday afternoon, and with astronomical maintenance payments. His face was an unhealthy gray under the tan that still lingered on his skin.

As they talked, Jenny realized the sexual attraction was gone. It might have been a product of the freedom of the place and the pressing need within her own body to explode out of its shell and make contact in a very basic and life-affirming way.

Greg was still Greg, but he was a friend, and a friend who was in trouble. Suddenly her nervousness was gone. If Jordie called around, that was alright. She could introduce these two men of whom she was very fond and hope that they would come to like each other as much as she liked them.

Jenny talked a little but mostly listened. There was so much going on in her life that she couldn't casually say, "Oh, by the way, Frank died while I was gone, left me a controlling interest in the business, a wife who is fighting me in court, and an unexplained bank balance. Would you care for more wine?"

Finally, she reached up to kiss his cheek. "It's good to see you, I'm glad you came. I work tomorrow but if you're still in town later in the day, we can spend some time together. Right now I'm beat."

A tapping on the glass doors caused her to glance up to see Jordie silhouetted against the night sky. She smiled and crossed the room to slide the glass back.

"Where have you been? I missed you tonight." She hugged him and giggled to herself. Here she was with two burly men in her living room. She felt the stiff way he held himself as he cautiously returned her embrace. She drew back to look up at his face.

'Jordie! Where's your moustache?" She gaped in amazement. "You shaved it off! My God!"

He grinned at her shock, and she recognized him again, his white teeth gleaming against his tanned face. Except only the upper slopes of his cheeks were brown, the lower half of his face looked pale. She ran her palm experimentally down his cheek. The skin was smooth.

"You've had a beard ever since you came back from college." He looked so much younger. His eyes appeared larger, dark blue and intense in his strong featured face.

Greg cleared his throat and Jenny jumped. "Oh, I'm sorry. Jordie this is my friend, Greg Houston, from Seattle. Greg, this is Jordie Cochrane. Jordie's my cousin and lives next door. It's a long story." Her smile widened as she finished the introductions. The men nodded and eyed each other like tomcats circling the barnyard.

She sighed. Why were men always so territorial? Drawing Jordie into the living room, she seated him in an armchair and brought another glass of wine. "Greg's in Victoria on business, and he's staying in town tonight." She gave Jordie a hard look. "He has to go back tomorrow. We were just getting caught up."

Her cousin seemed to relax, and Greg gave her a pointed look before turning back to answer a question. The men cautiously entered the conversation as she felt herself flagging. It was getting late, but the other two seemed determined to out-wait each other.

In desperation she finally stood, stifling a huge yawn. "Sorry, guys, but I can't stay awake. I'll have to either throw you out or abandon you to finish the evening on your own."

Greg immediately leaped to his feet in embarrassment. "Sorry, Jenny. I should have noticed. I don't want to wear out my welcome."

Jordie got to his feet as well. "You just go to bed Jenny. I'll lock up."

She made a face. What was he trying to do, tell Greg that he lived here, for heaven's sake?

Greg gave her a parting hug and moved toward the door.

"I'll take off then." Jordie headed reluctantly for the back where his boots warmed on the carpet. "Nice to meet you, Greg. Have a good trip back to Seattle. Bye, Jenny," he added, "see you tomorrow."

~*~*~*~

Jenny got home the next evening and threw her briefcase into a chair. She was bone tired. She'd played telephone tag with half a dozen people during the day and was dismayed to find six messages on her machine when she got home. She pulled a diet soda out of the fridge. Taking it with her, she opened the glass doors and flopped down into a lounge chair on her deck.

Ahh, it was nice out here. The sun was hazy today, creating a halo effect around everything and giving a feeling of surrealism. Her body relaxed, bone by bone, muscle by tense muscle as she let her eyes wander the rocks and sand below. She sighed deeply and pressed her head against the cushion.

Jordie woke her when he laid his hand on her shoulder. "Dinner's ready, sweetheart, if you're hungry," he said, his voice incredibly gentle.

CHAPTER TWENTY SIX

L ate the next afternoon, Jenny remembered the locked drawers in Frank's desk. Most of the staff was gone, just Brad left poring over papers at his desk.

She leaned in his doorway. "What was the name of that company you called to change the locks? I can't seem to pick the lock on Frank's desk, nor can Dave, so I need a locksmith to open it for me."

Brad reached for the phone. "I'll give them a call. Do you want them tonight?"

"As soon as they can get here."

She strolled into the reception area and over to Frank's door. His office sat vacant for now, the door usually closed. None of them wanted to disturb it. She peeked inside.

It was starting to get dusty. The plant by the window was still green, obviously Queenie watered it. The room was pretty well as he had left it.

She sat down at the desk, Esley's desk, and rocked back and forth in the huge brown leather chair, running her hands over the polished oak surface before her. It was time to move on. Time to empty the desk of Frank's things, and let Esley move the magnificent piece of oak furniture out of here.

Her fingertips rubbed over the drawer that Frank had kept locked, instinctively finding the gouge marks where someone had tried to break into it. It looked like the work of a small screwdriver or lady's nail file. She'd bet any money Alita had spent at least part of her time in here the day Frank died trying to force the drawer open.

She fingered the brass base to the old desk lamp, snapping it on and sending a glow of light over the desk's surface. She touched the smooth face of the great chunk of dark green jade, collecting a little pile of dust on the tip of her finger. Frank once told her he found the rock in the interior of British Columbia when he was prospecting for the summer with a friend.

She smiled. There wasn't much Frank hadn't done. Her first impression of him had been fairly accurate. Frank had been a logger as a young man, working in the rain forest up Island, operating a donkey engine. Before that, he had told her many times, he was a choker, running cables from the donkey engine around logs before the operator dragged them up. He talked about what it was like when a line snapped. He had seen accidents in the woods, men lashed to ribbons by the snaking cables. He showed her a scar running down the outside of his shin where a line had cut him open from knee to ankle.

There was a gold-finish pen set. Jenny didn't know if it had had any special significance. She did know that the pens had never worked. Three postcards from her were propped against them, all sent while she was still in Greece.

Brad poked his head in. "They can come first thing tomorrow morning, about eight o'clock."

Jenny nodded. "Thanks, Brad."

"I'm gone now, Jenny. Are you ready to leave, too?"

She nodded again. "Yes, I guess it's time." They locked up together, and Jenny headed off through pouring rain to her car. The parkade had passed its afternoon rush, although there were still a few people walking along the parking levels, coats dripping, heads down. She threw her wet briefcase into the passenger seat of the Mustang and buckled herself in. The car didn't respond to the key in the ignition, and Jenny checked to make sure the transmission was in park. She tried again. No response.

"Damn!" She slammed the heels of her palms against the steering wheel in total frustration. "What is going on? I'm so *sick* of this! Nothing is working. Nothing!"

She looked around. Not a soul to be seen. Popping the hood, she climbed out. Everything looked okay, but what did she know? Who to call? She fingered her phone uncertainly. Well, the car was probably safe here for the night.

When she bought the convertible a year or more ago, she'd fallen in love with it at first sight. It was a dull silver-gold colour called titanium, with a black convertible top and black leather seats. That little car had given her a lot of fun and never a moment's problem. Until now.

She'd call a cab, and have a mechanic look at it tomorrow. Hauling her briefcase and purse out, she locked the door.

By the time the taxi approached her house, it was over an hour later and very dark. They ran into road construction near her street and the driver began a detour that would take her a long way out of her way, but Jenny had had enough. She paid and climbed out. The rain wasn't that bad, she was already wet and it was only two blocks to home.

It was dark as she walked up her road. Darker than usual. Neither of the two streetlights near her house seemed to be working. She could still dimly see her way along the sidewalk, and trudged on. Passing Jordie's house, she noted a couple of lights on at the back. He must be home.

As she gazed ahead, a shadow shifted in the gloom of the bushes beside her doorway. Startled, she stalled on the sidewalk.

Was she imagining things? Everything had gone wrong and now she was jumpy. Besides, it was simply too dark to see. *And wouldn't her porch light have turned on?* It was on a motion sensor, and if anyone was there they would have tripped the light.

Then she spotted a car farther down the block near the dead-end. It was moving slowly towards her and that's why she'd noticed it. The headlights were off.

Jenny turned around and walked swiftly up the path to Jordie's front door, praying he was there. Stepping into the portico, she frantically rang the bell while watching her house. Someone moved in the bush by her front door, then promptly melted back into the shadows. She pushed the doorbell again with desperate fingers and held it down, rattling the locked knob with her other hand.

A light went on in the entrance and Jenny heard the lock snick back. When the door opened, she stepped right into Jordie's arms, pushing him backward and slamming the door behind her.

"Whoa," he said, but his arms grabbed her tightly almost as if by reflex and held her close. "You don't have to ask for a hug, sweetheart, I'll be happy to volunteer," he said, humour and surprise mingling in his voice. "But you're pretty wet. Did you get caught in the rain?"

"There's someone at my door," said Jenny, her voice muffled against his flannel shirt. She pulled back an inch so she could look up at him.

"What do you mean? Where?" He pushed her aside with one hand and yanked the door open.

Jenny clung to his arm and leaned to peer around his big body. "Right there." She pointed toward her front step. "There was someone in the shadows by the rhododendron bushes when I came down the sidewalk."

Jordie pressed her behind him protectively and ran down the steps in his sock feet, sprinting onto the sidewalk. Jenny was after him like a shot. "Jordie!" Then she stifled her protests, her hand against her mouth. She didn't need to alert the guy lurking there.

Jordie stood on her walk, staring around in the gloom as Jenny puffed up behind him. The bush beside her doorway was empty, as was the porch and step. Turning slowly, she searched the darkness for the figure of a man or any sign of the car she'd seen creeping down the street toward her.

Jordie didn't wait. He sprinted around the side of the house, crashing through the rhododendron. She shivered, looking up at her porch light. It hadn't turned on. Finally, he reappeared around the other side of the yard and came toward her. "Come back to my place, Jenny."

Jordie peeled his wet socks off and left them in a heap at the entrance. Then he locked the door behind them and ushered her into the hall.

"Who was it?" he asked. "Did you recognize them?"

She took a deep breath, trying to calm her shaking voice. "I couldn't tell. They were standing in the shadows, right in the bush. Then I saw a car coming slowly down the street with its lights off. I just panicked and rang your doorbell."

Jordie's eyes were black with concern. Raindrops sparkled in his eyelashes, and glittered darkly in his red hair. A light spatter of rain wet the shoulders of his red flannel shirt. He enfolded her icy hands in his big warm ones and anxiously searched her eyes.

"I didn't imagine it!"

"I didn't say you did." His voice was soothing as he continued to massage her hands. "Why are you so wet? Where's your car?"

"It wouldn't start. Something wrong with the battery. Not even a click. So I took a cab, but I got out two blocks over because of the road construction and walked the rest of the way."

Jordie looked confused. "What road construction?"

"Down on Dallas Road, two blocks from here." Her voice rose in exasperation and alarm. "There were signs. You couldn't have missed it!"

Jordie paused, then turned out the lights and stood at the window, contemplating the dark street. "There's something very odd here, Jenny. There's road construction on Dallas Road, two blocks from here, with a detour? I came home at five and there wasn't any detour."

"I'm not joking! I know a detour when I see one and so did my taxi driver. There were red markers closing off the road for a block and a half as I walked down here." Her face set in a belligerent expression, her eyes blazing.

Jordie stared at her again. "Jenny, I'm telling you, there's something going on. There was no road construction when I came home. And," he gestured out the window, "these street lights were working yesterday. I know because when I got home, your cat was out. I had to run around to catch her. Then," he continued through her protests, "your car doesn't start. If it was the battery, you would probably have noticed that it was getting low before it actually gave out on you. And it would have made a noise when you tried to start the car, even if it wasn't strong enough to turn the engine over."

She felt sick as his words began to hit home. "What are you driving at, Jordie? Spell it out."

"We should call the city to find out if there's road construction scheduled for Dallas Road, and get a mechanic over to check out your car right now, before someone has a chance to work on it, if they haven't already."

Jenny reached for the phone with a shaky hand. "I want to call Dave."

CHAPTER TWENTY SEVEN

Later that night, Jenny was stretched out on Jordie's couch wearing his bulky housecoat over a pair of over-sized pyjamas, woolly socks slouched on her feet. She'd been running her fingers through her hair and the bangs stuck out like quills on a porcupine.

Her investigator Dave Powers was perched opposite her on an overstuffed chair, his feet crossed at the ankles.

Jordie's house was designed similar to hers, with the living space at the back overlooking the ocean. Double-paned French doors were closed against the wind and rain, but still showed glimpses of the warning light from the lighthouse on Trial Island, and the running lights on cargo ships heading out to the Strait of Juan de Fuca.

He walked over to plop down on the floor at her feet as she finished saying, "So, we don't know yet how the streetlights went out, but we do know that the road construction signs were not there at five o'clock, were there when I came along, and are now gone again. Did you talk to that taxi driver, Dave?" Her forehead wrinkled in concern.

He shook his head. "No, but I'm waiting for his call. The cops say they had a complaint from a resident that their driveway was blocked by construction signs. When the police arrived to investigate, all the markers, lights, everything had been removed."

She nodded, and Jordie butted in. "I just got a call from the mechanic. It was the battery cable on her car, placed so it looked normal but wasn't connecting. He said there were fresh marks on the terminal where the cable had been pried off. I don't like this." He narrowed his eyes.

"It looks suspicious, alright." Dave said, carefully avoiding Jenny's gaze. "If we accept that the car was tampered with, and add in the road block, it seems obvious she was being forced to walk the last bit to her door. Then the streetlights are out. Let's face it, streetlights go out all the time, or kids shoot them out, throw rocks at them."

"Okay, forget the lights. Say they went out on their own." Jordie waved his hand impatiently at Dave's pedantic reasoning. "It still looks bad. Jenny sees someone by her door, and a car approaches with its lights off."

Dave shrugged, seemingly unconvinced.

Jenny's voice flashed into the silence. "Plus we have the fact that my motion light isn't working. It was working last night. You don't have to play silly bugger, Dave. Try to take this seriously." Her voice rippled with sarcasm, and the investigator flushed darkly.

Jordie watched her pull herself upright on the couch. "Sorry. This has shaken me up. Frank died in what seem to be suspicious circumstances. I have a hostile business partner who said she'd do anything to ensure I don't get control of the company. Norman is coming onto me, when I know there's something else behind his actions."

When she paused to catch her breath, both men seemed ready to protest that last statement, but she rushed on, "Then my car might have been tampered with, and there was a road construction setup that was a fake from what the police say. I saw a figure outside my door, I'm positive. When he moved he was visible against the bushes. As far as the car without lights, it was clearly moving, although I couldn't see who was in it."

Dave nodded, made a mark in his notepad and put it down. "I believe you, Jenny. I think we should put a couple of men on Mrs. Jensen, find out what she's up to. Will you authorize that?"

Something in Jordie's gut eased at the plan. He wouldn't be the only one taking Jenny's protection seriously.

~*~*~*~

When they were alone, Jordie began gathering coffee mugs. "I think you should stay here tonight. You can go home in the morning and get what you need for work. Those guys might decide to give it another try."

She thought of protesting, but felt too warm and cozy to stir. Her hair had finally dried on its own, although probably looked frightful. "Okay, Jordie, if you say so." She gave a mighty yawn, and spoke around it. "I can sleep right here. I just need a blanket."

"No, you take the bed. I'll throw a sleeping bag on the spare mattress in the other room."

Jenny objected weakly, but he ignored her so she ambled after him into the main bedroom while he checked the bed and added a blanket. The room was dominated by a huge bed with an oak frame, the giant spindles on the four corners turned in lathe-work designs. The wood was dark with age and the marks of many hands. The head board and foot board were carved in an intricate pattern centred on a giant thistle flower.

"This was your dad's bed, Jordie! I didn't know you still had it." Jenny turned to him in amazed delight to see such a reminder of her childhood.

Jordie glanced up and nodded. "It was the only antique left in the house. The girls decided I should keep it. It was made for his father back in Scotland. He was such a tall man apparently, he needed his bed custom made to accommodate his height. I guess Dad brought it out with him when he came to Canada."

"I know, he told us that story. He had this bed in his bedroom at the other house, he and Auntie Harriet. We'd crawl in with them on Sunday mornings when we were little. Do you remember?"

Jordie laughed. "Yeah, I remember. You and Harriet, both squealing when Dad tickled you. Then he'd finally boot you out so he could get dressed."

Jenny giggled. "That's right. He never wore anything to bed. We always had to stay on Auntie Harriet's side. She would say, "Now, Neal, they'll get too excited." And of course, that's exactly what we wanted."

Jenny's gaze turned teasing as she looked at him. "So where are your pyjamas, Jordie? Don't tell me you sleep naked, too."

"Like a good Scot," he answered over his shoulder as he gathered some things from the top of the dresser. "A Scot never feels the cold. That's why they didn't wear anything under those kilts. Besides, you've got my only pair."

He grinned fleetingly as he turned to her, his hands full. "You should be alright, the sheets are fresh. If you need anything, I'll be right down the hall. Just call me."

She looked at him for a second, then put her arms around his waist, raised on her toes and kissed his freshly shaved cheek. "Thank you, Jordie. I'll be fine. Sleep well."

Jenny lay in bed and stared around the room in the dim light. This was the bedroom from the marriage of Jordie and Linda. Nothing very feminine about it. Linda must have taken everything that softened the room from the bare bones it now contained.

She nestled under the covers. It was comfy, must be a new mattress on the old frame. There were blinds but no curtains on the long windows. Functional, and plain. One picture on the wall, a lovely watercolour of the rainforest somewhere up the coast, solitary in its loneliness.

The oak dresser that matched the bed frame occupied one corner as if it were a giant pillar holding up the wall. It was like a wardrobe, the doors opening closet-like on the top, two huge drawers in the bottom. She remembered they had hidden in it as children. There was a smaller dresser that must have been Linda's, the top clean of clutter, slightly dusty. Kind of like Frank's desk. So many changes.

She pulled the quilt higher as the wind howled around the house to the faint echo of the ocean surging below. Now that she'd calmed down from her earlier fright and hashed out the day's events with the two men, she was exhausted. A general lassitude stole over her, and she rolled to her side, bunching the pillow and burying her face in it. She noticed a faint odour, a mixture of cologne or soap and something else, something infinitely Jordie.

She knew that scent so well. Thoughts flitted through her mind dreamily, Jordie holding her while she cried about Frank, while she cried about Bobby, while she cried about...

Poor Jordie, his shirt was habitually soaked. She giggled to herself, the sound echoing hollowly in the bare room.

He was just there, like a fixture, a permanent part of her world. She thought vaguely of the terrible anger she'd felt toward him while sitting on the beach in Greece, as if he'd let her down. Mentally, she shrugged and cuddled lower in the bed. She was too tired to sort it out. The last conscious thought she had was of Jordie sleeping naked in this great big bed.

~*~*~*~

Jordie woke in the night. Had he heard something? Was it Jenny calling him? He waited for his eyes to pick out the room's unfamiliar night shapes in the dark, while he strained to hear. Slowly he crawled out of the sleeping bag and walked softly down the silent hall to the bedroom door where she slept. The door was slightly ajar and he pushed it just enough to peer inside.

She was curled in a ball under the covers, her head poking out of the top showing a halo of dark curls. Her face appeared like a pale patch against the quilt.

His heart seemed to lurch in his chest with a physical pull. Jenny, in his home, sleeping in his bed. He wanted nothing more than to crawl in beside her and pull the quilt around them both. He wanted to hold her through the night, for his own comfort as much as hers.

He could smell her, a faint spicy woman scent that he always noticed. Like when they danced Christmas Eve at her place, that waltz. She'd been wearing a fantastic green dress and he couldn't take his eyes off her. He'd just started having fun, then Dave danced with her. He remembered that helpless feeling of being eaten up with jealousy and knowing he had no right.

Grimacing, he pulled the door closed. Things had changed, Linda was gone. But there were other unresolved issues that weighed heavily, to the point where he wished he could just lay them before her and take his chances, flaws and all. The waiting, the suspense was killing him by inches.

On the one hand it seemed too soon to make a move. On the other, there were a lot of guys sniffing around. He was a little more at ease about Dave, who didn't show any overt personal interest in his boss. That was reassuring. And then there was Norman Suffron. He was handsome, a woman could have her head turned. The hair stood on the back of his neck at the thought. He itched to wrap his hands around that well groomed throat and squeeze.

And who the hell was Greg, calling her ever since her trip to Greece? Jordie clenched his fists.

He walked down the hall to the family room and over to the windows. The wind had died down in the early hours. The bushes stopped banging against the house, and the broom on the hill below was waving lightly, not laying against the ground like it did under the force of the storm.

It was still raining, drops bouncing on the sundeck. The ocean below appeared deceptively calm. He glanced toward Jenny's house, but could see nothing out of the ordinary. On top of these men sniffing around, there was a real threat of danger. She was at risk, he could feel it.

Well, she'd have to cooperate. She could phone him when she left the office and he'd be here waiting for her. That would solve one problem. But the larger one was if they tried to break into her house. If she wouldn't stay here, he could camp out at her place. Of course, that would be difficult. He'd be hard pressed to keep his hands to himself.

She could have some of her own men stake out the house but he didn't like that idea much either. That would mean Dave and maybe some others spending the night with her. Not something he was anxious to see.

He'd tackle her in the morning. She wasn't going to like it, so damned independent she hated being told what to do. She'd always been like that, stubborn as hell! But he was determined that she'd listen to him this time.

CHAPTER TWENTY EIGHT

J enny thanked the locksmith and returned to Frank's desk. She'd had nightmares recently about what might be in this drawer. Sometimes in her dream the drawer was empty, the dark unfinished oak boards visible in the depths when she pulled it slowly open. Sometimes it was overflowing with something that was pushing to escape, creeping over the lip of the drawer, a type of white foam, slimy and glowing.

Now all she had to do was tug on the handle. She sat in the great brown leather chair and braced her knee against the desk as she pulled. It opened easily, gliding on its slides without sound. It was deep and wide, probably a filing drawer, with wood partitions at intervals along its length.

There were some file folders in the bottom, with several objects stacked on top. She pulled out a picture frame and turned it over. A woman's face stared back at her, no one she had ever seen before. Her light brown hair waved back from her face and was piled in a bun on the top of her head. She smiled into the camera, her eyes slightly closed against a strong sun. In a round firm hand was written 'To Frank, my only love' in the lower corner.

This must be Joanie. The wife he loved. She was beautiful. Not the way Alita was beautiful, in that carefully manicured fashion with every hair coloured and in place, expensive clothes and enough makeup to cover any flaw.

No, this woman was comfortable in her own skin, confident in his love. Her face glowed with it, her flowered blouse draped attractively over her throat. Her smile was warm, loving and carefree. Jenny smiled back. As she set the photo on the desk, she was pleased to know in her heart that Frank had been well loved and had loved well in return.

As she bent to retrieve the folders she felt a little frisson of wariness, like a voyeur going through Frank's things. It had to be done. Normally Alita would be the logical person to take the personal items but this was cold hard business, and she couldn't risk the luxury of handing the task over to anyone else.

Some photos fell out of the top folder and she picked them up off the floor and laid them on his desk. Then she laughed out loud. Here was a picture of Jenny sitting at her desk, with her tongue poking out at the photographer, her hair in a lopsided bun at the back of her head. There was a picture of Queenie, must have been before Jenny was hired. She was backcombing her hair and looked startled to be caught by the camera. There were a few pictures of people Jenny didn't know, and then a selection of shots from the various Christmas parties over the years. There was even one of Jenny and Pat jiving at the last one.

She opened the file to find a selection of cards to Frank. Birthday cards, a few lines dropped here and there, a postcard from Japan with a picture of Mount Fuji on it. Jenny leafed through the memorabilia, then set it aside.

The next folder held papers written in Frank's cramped hand. They appeared to be copies of a business plan, maybe when he started the company. The edges were yellowed and brittle. There was also a copy of her plan when she'd proposed the expansion. It made her proud to see the two documents together like that.

There were other things, sheets of numbers, perhaps projected cash flows, yearly budgets, some income tax returns.

That was all. Jenny looked on the back of the last folder and then into the depths of the drawer. There were a few bits of paper, nothing of interest. Then she spotted a square black shape in the bottom and reached in to pull out a small book, like a diary. As she flipped through the pages she saw notations under different dates and numbers penciled in. She frowned. Slipping it into her jacket pocket, she returned the photos to their folder. She had a feeling if she compared these notes to the questionable bank entries she may find a close connection between the two.

Picking up the piece of dark jade from the desk top, she held it in her hand, hefting it lightly. It could sit on her desk, like it had sat on his, reminding her to be solid, to remember the value of her relationship with her clients, because as Frank was so fond of saying, 'without the clients, we might as well not be in business.'

She used to chuckle to herself when he said it, it was so obvious. But now with everything resting on her suddenly frail shoulders, she felt in danger of forgetting the client. Her eyes were off the ball, because she was entrenched in a kind of warfare that was side-tracking her.

~*~*~*~

Queenie poked her nose around the corner of her office door and Jenny held up her hand to stall her as she talked into the phone. "Thanks, Bernie, I appreciate... I'll certainly keep that in mind. Thanks again. Yes, I'll keep in touch." She lowered the receiver, then snapped it into the cradle.

"Oh, that man irks me. 'Never give up Bernie' must be his nickname." Jenny pressed her fists together under her chin and glanced at the secretary standing in front of her desk.

Queenie held out a letter. "Well, this will irk you a little more."

Jenny snatched it and flattened it on her desk. "Special Licenses Branch. Yikes, not bad news, I hope." She was silent for minute, then raised puzzled eyes to Queenie. "They want to review our license? What does that mean? Because the owner has left the company they want to review our license. Well, I was an owner before Frank left, and I've been on the license for three years. Esley and Pat have been on much longer than that. Call Angus Murdoch, and fax him a copy. I'm going to talk to Special Licenses. This Mr. Dilworth better have a good reason for what he's doing."

Two hours later Jenny sat in Dilworth's office as he shuffled papers on his desk. She'd been there for forty-five minutes. "What I need, Mr. Dilworth, is a copy of the regulations regarding the licensing of security agents. As far as I'm aware, this is highly irregular. Frank was licensed for years, as were Pat Rooke and Esley Moro. I've been on the license for three years. Because Frank is no longer listed doesn't change that fact, does it?"

He had the grace to flush. Jenny thought she might have liked him under different circumstances. He wasn't the sneaky varmint of a bureaucrat she'd envisioned as she stomped her way across town. He had an open honest face and was distinctly uncomfortable with the situation.

Finally, he pulled her file out of the mess on his desk and opened it. "No, that doesn't change the fact that you're already on the license."

"And that license is valid, right?" she pursued.

"Yes, it's valid. I'm simply reviewing because the owner died. We're very careful about these licenses, Ms. MacDougall. We screen all applicants thoroughly."

"And I'm glad you do," Jenny interrupted briskly. "It maintains a pretty high standard in the industry. However, only one of the owners died. You don't need to screen me. I've been screened. These licenses are an ongoing right. My business is constructed on the strength of it. Subject to wrongful activity by the holder, the license remains valid. Are you alleging wrongful activity?" Her tone was brusque.

"No! No, no. Nothing like that. It is merely a review, as I said." Dilworth was now very red and beginning to sweat.

"Is it routine to scrutinize, or 'review' these licenses if a partner dies in these businesses?"

"Uh, well, I have done it before. Oh, certainly, it's not unheard of."

"But it's not routine, is it?" Jenny persisted.

"Well, not routine, exactly." He was cornered and he knew it. He stared miserably at the file in front of him.

"And who decides if a review should occur?"

He looked at her reluctantly. "Normally, it would be me or one of my fellow officers." He clamped his lips together.

"So who decided this time?" she demanded.

"Well, it's not just our judgment that counts, you know. We do have bosses." He laughed weakly.

Jenny grabbed the file and pulled it firmly from his reluctant fingers. "Really, Ms. MacDougall," he protested, "that file is highly confidential."

"Yes, and it's about my license. I have the right to know what and who I'm dealing with." She flipped the top page and read a memo to Dilworth, instructing him to conduct a review of her license. It was signed by a Ms. Kramer. "Who is Ms. Kramer?"

Dilworth took the file back and closed it firmly. "She's the area manager. Her office is in Vancouver. I can give you the number if you wish," he offered reluctantly. He dragged a sheet of paper forward and began to write.

"Thank you." Jenny sat back to think. She took the sheet containing the number and looked at him speculatively. "Just what does this review consist of, and how long will it take? What is the result of such action?"

He was back on firm ground, and his voice lowered with conviction as he answered. "It takes anywhere from three to six weeks, depending how much cooperation we get from you and what evidence surfaces. It consists of similar procedures to those taken when issuing a new license. The result of a review could be a decision to take action in one of three or four ways." He ticked them off on his fingers. "Continue the license as is, recommend actions be taken within a specified time or risk suspension, suspend the license pending recommended actions being taken by the licensee, or cancel the license altogether. The last measure is very rare and only when illegal activities have been found. Usually we recommend charges be laid if that's the case."

Jenny's breath seemed caught in her throat. "Mr. Dilworth, you're threatening the existence of my business. We've done nothing wrong. I don't understand this."

Dilworth steepled his fingers in front of his lips. "I don't see any cause for worry, Ms. MacDougall. You've been one of my case files since just before your name went on the license. I don't see anything that would warrant a review, let alone a suspension." He smiled, friendly this time. "I'll need your cooperation, of course. But I'm sure you'll be able to satisfy any concerns that arise."

Jenny rose and shook his hand. "Thank you, Mr. Dilworth. I'm sorry if I was abrupt. I was quite rattled by the letter. You can count on me and my staff to be as helpful as possible."

She left with a disquieting feeling. She definitely needed Mr. Dilworth on her side. But she also needed to find out why Ms. Kramer was ordering a review in the first place.

~*~*~*~

That night Jenny slammed her door and dropped her briefcase in the hall with a heavy thud. She walked haltingly into the kitchen and set her purse on a chair, staring at the black windows. Glints of the ocean showed far below, partly obscured by the reflection of the light in the front hall. Her head pounded.

Leaning over the counter, she pressed her forehead in her hands. Ah, what a headache! It had been building all day, till she could hardly see. Aspirin hadn't touched it. She opened her cupboard and pulled down a vial of painkillers, shaking them out into her hand. Maybe a few more of the stronger ones would do the trick.

She downed the pills and peeled her coat off, throwing it in the general direction of a chair in the dining room with a weak gesture of her arm. It landed in a heap on the carpet and she left it where it lay.

She was so confused these days, there were so many things to do, leads to explore, details to fuss over, so many threats to her business. She pressed her palms against her temples and sighed. Maybe if she took a walk.

Jordie had phoned to say he'd be late getting home so she was on her own. She couldn't jog, not with this pounding in her head. But she hadn't taken the time to get out for days. No walking, no running, no fresh air.

On the other hand, she should just plop those discs into her computer and go over the accounts and receivables one more time. The booklet she found in Frank's drawer had proved to match most of the suspect deposits. But that only told her that Frank had known about them. It didn't tell her what they were for. There could be something that she'd missed.

And she needed to talk to Maggie, hadn't heard from her for over a week. She'd also missed lunch, feeling too nauseous to think of food.

Her head pounded anew. Okay. One thing at a time.

CHAPTER TWENTY NINE

Jenny emerged from her bedroom, old jogging pants and sweatshirt hurriedly donned. Maybe a windbreaker, it might be colder than it looked. Grabbing her runners, she yanked them on, pausing to give her head time to calm its increased hammering.

As she tightened her shoelace, it parted in her hand. "Damn!" Tears sprang to her eyes. Nothing could go right! She didn't have another pair of laces. *Now what?*

She'd wear her hiking boots. They had hard soles with a good tread and laced up the ankle. And she wasn't going to be doing any running anyway.

Consoled, she set out, boots tightly laced, windbreaker zipped against the late spring wind. She stepped out her glass doors and off the sun deck onto the trail. Following the broad path down to the walkway below, her eyes adjusted to the dark and she picked out the beginnings of the sandy beach off to her right. The ocean flashed beside her, high tide driving the sea relentlessly up and over the sand. Logs and kelp were piled at the high water mark, waiting for the scavengers who warmed their houses with the free fuel and fertilized their gardens with the rich seaweed.

Moving carefully, she tried not to jar her tender head. Even her eyes hurt. She became distracted by the soft seething of the water near her feet and the glitter of a few pale stars overhead. Breathing deeply, she pulled in the salty damp air, letting the tension drain from her neck and shoulders.

Her head began to clear and she smiled faintly in the dark. This was like a tonic, the walking and the sea. Increasing her pace, she jogged slowly up the stairs at the end of the beach and went briskly down the paved path at the edge of the park. She stopped, then headed back to use the restroom before she went further.

Was that a sound behind her? She glanced around, but could see nothing in the gloom. The ocean made such a roar it was hard to pick out different noises. There were others out walking, it wasn't that late.

She moved off the path across the grass to the restroom. Tugging the door open, she felt her way to a cubicle in the jet black. She peeled off her gloves and felt for a pocket to tuck them away, then pushed into the nearest stall and flipped down her pants. Yikes! It was too cold to bare her bum for long. She was just tugging her jogging pants up when the door to the cubicle smashed open, hitting her in the face and banging her sharply back against the toilet.

Jenny reeled from the blow, connecting her spine painfully with the toilet tank. Her eyes ran with tears, her nose must be bleeding. She saw stars and flashes of light behind her eyelids, then was overcome by a tall body, long arms, longer legs. Someone wearing heavy clothing engulfed her in a bear hug and crushed her battered face into the front of a woolly coat. She screamed, managing only to produce a thin muffled sound. The arms tightened, smashing her back against the wall. The toilet between her legs prevented her from getting any purchase with her flailing boots.

She dragged in a breath to scream again and a gloved hand clamped over her mouth, suffocating her and banging her bruised nose. Her eyes and nose streamed again from the renewed pain.

She clawed wildly as she silently fought her assailant. She felt for his head in the dark. It was totally covered, only eye and mouth holes. He must be wearing a balaclava. Her fingers dug into the holes and clawed cruelly at the nameless face. She heard a heavy grunt and was rammed against the tank again. The blow to her spine nearly paralyzed her, her attacker's weight adding to the impact. He was breathing heavily, panting in her ear.

Jenny thought she might black out at any moment, the fear and pain were so intense. White hot anger surged over her like a roiling blanket, shooting adrenaline through her brain and into her limbs. She wasn't going to faint like a little girl! She might not get another chance to save herself, and no one was within hearing distance to help. She would fight to the last.

Finding the holes in the head covering, she scratched and clawed with all her strength, digging and gouging, going for the eyes. The man staggered back, a groan escaping the muffled mask.

She panted, her mind spinning wildly. A vague thought was trying to leap to the surface, some spark of recognition. Then his feet scraped on the concrete floor as he lunged for her. She was ready. She fell back, sitting on the toilet and lashing out with her heavy boots. She must have caught him in a vulnerable spot because he staggered. Her back was braced against the toilet tank as she kicked high, then low, feeling her blows connect.

She panted, focussed on keeping her attacker at bay, when that struggling thought burst through like a blow to the brain. The smell of cologne. She'd recognize it anywhere, that sweet cloying scent.

"Norman!" she shrieked. "Norman! You bastard!"

Her attacker stalled as if he'd been shot. The door of the cubicle swung wildly as it hit the wall with a bang. Boots thudded on concrete, then the outer door slammed back on its hinges. Silence.

The only sound was her own sobbing as she struggled for breath. She sat until her breathing calmed, the pain slowly receding to a dull pervasive ache. Staggering to her feet, she held onto the cubicle door with both hands to steady herself, still gasping with rage and fear.

She ran her hand gingerly over her face. It was wet and tasted salty as she passed her tongue over her swollen mouth. Creeping across the floor, she planted her feet soundlessly. She was still panting when she reached the exterior door, willing her frantic breathing to calm as she listened for the sound of anyone outside.

What if he was waiting for her? What if he came back in here? That second thought propelled her through the door and into the dark under the overhang of the roof. Her eyes strained, catching the flash of light reflected back from the ocean as it rolled out past the grassy serge. The pain in her back staggered her but only for a moment.

Moving her head from side to side, she listened. Nothing. Far away came the barking of a dog, it's owner's answering whistle. She pushed away from the building, moving cautiously over the grass to the concrete path and the stairs leading down to the beach.

There were heavy bushes there and she hesitated in an agony of indecision. Then she heard voices and turned cautiously to see a couple walking toward her through the gloom. She waited until they were close before stepping out in front and preceding them along the trail.

Her legs shook and she staggered, holding her arms tightly wrapped around her body, willing herself to keep going. She'd be safe, if she could just get home. Jordie would help her.

The path up the cliff was in front of her and she leaned forward as she climbed. Her battered hands walked up the steep incline as her breath came in gasps. She looked up to see the lights blazing in her house. She paused, agitated.

Had she really turned on all those lights? Her mind seemed fogged. Crouching at the brow of the hill, she ducked lower as she saw movement in her dining room. Oh God, no! Had Norman gotten here first, waiting for her to walk back into his grasp? Sweat beaded on her forehead and ran down her temples. She felt light-headed and faint.

Twisting her neck, she stared at Jordie's house next door as her mind ran in circles like a gerbil in a cage. But only one light was on over there, no movement visible through the windows. Jordie was probably not home. Her breath caught in her throat, then burst out in a sob. *No!* She cast around wildly, seeking safety.

Just then her sliding glass doors opened and a man stepped out onto the sun deck. Jenny cringed on her knees against the side of the hill. She saw curly hair and broad shoulders silhouetted against the back light. "Jenny?" a hoarse, familiar voice called. "Are you there?"

"Jordie!" she sobbed. "Over here." Her throat was raw from screaming and her voice came out in a whispery thread.

His head turned toward the path. "Hello?" he called again. She stood unsteadily and took a step toward him. He was on her in a bound. "What in hell are you thinking, going out at night, walking by yourself?" He gripped her arm with strong fingers and firmly escorted her onto the sun deck.

"I got delayed at the store so I came over to see if you made it back alright. You were nowhere to be seen, your door unlocked, lights on. You know things are…" His voice trailed off as they stepped into the light.

"Jenny!" His eyes darkened, staring at her face. He half dragged, half carried her through the doors and into the kitchen. "My God! What happened?"

Blood dripped steadily from her nose. More blood covered the front of her jacket. Her hair was matted at her temple. But her eyes must have scared him the most, wild and starting from her head.

Her lip was swollen and bruised, the skin broken. She put her hands up to her face and saw the blood and mud caked on the knuckles and under her nails. She leaned against him gasping but unable to speak.

"Were you raped? What happened? Who…" He made a move to go to the door as if to see who had done this, but she grabbed him with her battered hands, gripping his shirt with superhuman strength. Panting, she shook her head. "No," she muttered. "No."

He stood there holding her gently, trying to feel for broken bones, waiting for her to speak. Finally, he led her over to the sofa and sat her down. He brought a glass of water, a towel, the telephone and sat down himself, pulling her onto his lap. He mopped at her face gently. With urging she took a sip of water, most of it spilling down her front, her lip tender and misshapen against the glass.

Jordie rocked her for a minute in his arms, then dialled 911.

~*~*~*~

When the police had finished, Jordie left her ensconced in an overstuffed armchair with a blanket and rose to make coffee. Dave Powers hitched his chair forward and leaned his elbows on his thighs. He was dressed casually, a pair of rugby pants and a turtleneck sweater. They'd obviously caught him off guard. But his demeanour was the same as usual, all business.

"Dave, it's time to get serious." Jenny spoke painfully around her swollen lip. "No more fooling around. I don't want you to keep information from me because you don't want to worry me. We have to be smart about this. It's getting far too dangerous now."

Dave's eyes sparkled. "Jenny, you're amazing. Most women would be weeping hysterically by now." He grimaced, then shifted in the chair. "You really should head in to the hospital, though. Get some medical attention and let them take all the samples and tests to ensure we can pin this on the guy when we catch him."

She nodded. "I'm going to, don't worry, just give me a minute and a cup of coffee." She tried to smile, her mouth moving awkwardly. Jordie's heart turned over painfully in his chest. The marks on her face were pitiful to see, and he was afraid of what else had been done to her. He'd had a look at her back before the police arrived, and was appalled at the bruising and broken skin down her spine. She looked like a war victim. He could hardly see for the red blanket of rage that engulfed him. He tried to contain it, his shoulders shaking from the effort. He passed a second cup to Dave and steadied Jenny's hand.

"I only filled it halfway," he said. "It'll be hard to drink with that lip. We should be leaving for the hospital soon, anyway."

Jenny nodded, her attention back on her investigator. "I know you and Esley have been worrying some problems around between you. I'm sure it was Frank's idea and I have to admit I turned a blind eye because I've been so busy with other priorities."

Dave looked startled.

"Yes, I knew," she said. "And I won't put up with it. I want to know everything that's going on. I demand that of all my employees. If I don't get that kind of cooperation from people who work for me, I have to let them go. I'm sure you understand, Dave."

She paused to let that sink in. The investigator blinked and Jordie smiled to himself. Here was Jenny, curled up under a blanket with her face scratched and swollen, still in shock from a violent physical attack, and she was letting her ex-RCMP detective know that she'd fire him in a minute if she didn't get his full cooperation. The thought struck him that this side of his employer might come as a distinct shock to Dave Powers.

"Now," she continued, "I have a few things I want you to know before we leave. I imagine the hospital visit will take the rest of the night."

Dave nodded. "Yes, ma'am, it usually takes a good six or eight hours depending on who's available to do the work."

"Okay, well, here we go." She grinned awkwardly and Dave grinned back, seduced into relaxing. "I'm pretty sure I know who the man was that attacked me. And I didn't tell the police for a couple of reasons. They might have dismissed what I said because it was so dark. At the same time, they could ruin our advantage if they blunder ahead, convinced that I don't know what I'm talking about."

She had Dave's complete attention. "It was Norman Suffron, Alita Jensen's son."

Dave's face reflected his shock and doubt. "How can you be sure? You said it was pitch dark in there, and he didn't speak."

"I recognized his cologne. Norman wears a very distinctive sweet-smelling scent. The first time I noticed it he came into the office after hours and surprised me. It's very strong. That doesn't mean he's the only man to wear that cologne but it's distinctive."

Dave nodded at her last comment. "Are you sure you remember accurately?"

"He was right here in this house, not more than two weeks ago. I had a cold, yet I could still smell that scent."

"Okay." Dave's attention focused on her.

"Tonight when I realized who it was, I shouted his name. He froze as if he'd been shot. Then he ran." Tears gathered in her throat and she stopped speaking for a moment.

Jordie reached a hand to pat her knee under the blanket.

"And I scratched him up good," she spoke slowly around her tight raw throat.

"Didn't you say he had a balaclava on?"

"Yes," she whispered, "I stuck my fingers inside the holes in the mask and clawed him as hard as I could. That's where all the blood under my nails is from."

"That's enough, Dave, she's had enough." Jordie put his hands on her shoulders. "We've got to get you to the hospital, Jenny. You might have more injuries than you think."

Dave sat back, his eyes gleaming. "The blood and tissue samples from your hands can link Norman directly to the attack. This is excellent."

"Okay, I'm coming. Dave," she said over Jordie's shoulder as he bent over her arranging the blanket, "I want you and Esley to find Norman and get a look at him. If it was him, the marks will be all over his face. He may be lying low, but you've got to find him and get photos. Then we can call the police. And I want a meeting with you and Esley tomorrow morning. Well, maybe tomorrow afternoon. I'll fill you in on the rest of what I know," at which Dave's brows climbed his forehead, "and you can fill me in on everything you have. I mean everything."

His brows lowered again at her grim tone, but he grinned and saluted. "Yes, ma'am," he said.

Jordie's chest swelled with pride as he carried her to the car.

CHAPTER THIRTY

J ordie tucked her into bed and adjusted the covers. Pushing her hair off her damp forehead, he sat down on the side of the mattress to take her hand and hold it in his. Her eyes were closed. At the hospital they had given her something to make her sleepy and she'd only roused enough on the trip home to make her way into the house from the truck at his urging.

He'd managed to get most of her clothes off her and a nightie over her head. Not that she had been wearing much. After hours of examinations, interrogations from police and medical staff, he had simply slipped her shirt over her head, pulled up her rugby pants and wrapped her in the blanket for the short trip home. Not exactly how he imagined getting a chance to see her naked.

Rising, he snapped the lamp off and did a complete tour of the house, checking the windows and doors, the basement. Then he turned off the lights and watched from the darkness to see if there was any movement outside.

Walking back down the hall, he lay fully clothed on the bed in Margaret's old room. He shifted and turned, finally rising to remove his shirt and jeans, crawling back under the blanket.

Sometime later he woke with a start. There was a strange noise, like a kitten mewling. He raised his head and listened. Nothing. Then it came again. He padded out his door and stepped into Jenny's bedroom. It was louder here, like a child crying.

In the early gray of dawn, she was hunched under the quilt, her hands clutching the pillow in a death grip, her eyes tightly shut. The pillow was wet with tears as were her scratched cheeks. Jordie knelt by the bed and rubbed her back and shoulders tenderly, talking softly. The noise stopped and her hands relaxed on the pillow. He knelt there till his knees were sore.

But when he started back down the hall, the sound came again. He stopped mid-stride, turned and went back into the room. Sitting on the bed, he stroked her hair, then lifted the quilt and slid in, careful not to jar her or touch her bruises. Gingerly he reached to settle his arm across her waist, placing his hand over her clenched fingers, massaging them until they relaxed their fierce grip on the pillow.

Jenny curled one fist trustingly into his and moved her bum back against his warmth. He relaxed on the sheet, sighing to himself. This was what he wanted, Jenny in his arms, Jenny in his bed. It may not be exactly the set of circumstances he'd imagined, but he'd take what he could get. Her bottom pressed against his groin, and he pushed back a little, feeling the material of his shorts rub against her silky bare skin where her nightie had hiked up. Rubbed just enough to start a reaction he didn't need right now. He concentrated on cuddling, making her feel safe.

~*~*~*~

Jenny tried to open her eyes, but they didn't cooperate. She stifled a groan. Everything hurt. Then she became aware of a heavy weight across her waist, and heat down her back. She shifted and felt legs rough with hair rubbing against hers. An arm stretched under her neck and along the edge of the pillow. It was thick and muscular, golden-red hairs curling riotously right down to the wrist and across the back of the hand. Big fingers curled laxly. She recognized Jordie's signet ring.

She lifted her hand to move his arm and a shot of pain rippled down her back. She moaned. The arm tightened, moved up to pull her closer against the warm body behind her.

"Shhh, it's okay," Jordie's voice grumbled near her ear. He rubbed his hand warmly wherever he could reach, across the tops of her breasts and curling in toward her neck. "It's okay," he said again, then a moment later the arm went limp.

Jenny dozed and woke again, finally pushing him away to roll onto her back. She tried to stretch, moving slowly. Everything had stiffened in the night. *What time was it?* She squinted toward the window, and saw bright daylight shafting through the gap in the curtains. Rolling her head sideways, she looked directly into midnight blue eyes, heavily fringed with red-brown lashes.

"How are you, sweetie?" Jordie's voice was no more than a growl. He cleared his throat and tried again. "How do you feel?"

"Not great." Just talking hurt her lip, but putting her hand up to feel the sore place made her muscles scream in protest.

Jordie leaned up on an elbow to hover over her. "Poor little thing. Look at this." His finger touched a place below

198

her eye where her skin felt scraped raw. He leaned closer and placed a tender kiss on the spot. She didn't move and he was encouraged to place more kisses on abrasions and bruises across her face, ending finally at the side of her mouth where her lip was split. She winced and he drew in his breath sharply.

"Aw, I'm sorry." His eyes were dark pools of concern looming above her.

"Jordie," she whispered, "What are you doing?"

He smiled crookedly. "I was just trying to make it feel better. Mmm," he said consideringly, looking her over for more bruises. He leaned down and planted one on her nose.

She giggled, and he grinned at her. She had never seen him like this, relaxed and open. Not since they were still children. She examined the sandy coloured bristles covering his jaw, the bracket of dimples either side of his mouth. The way his lower lip was fuller than the upper one. The aggressive look of his wide high cheekbones. She was glad he had shaved that beard off. Now she could see his expression.

He watched her watching him. "What do you think?" he said.

She blinked and then tried to smile around her sore lip. "I'm wondering what you're doing in my bed. I mean we are cousins, after all."

He shook his head and raised his hand to run his fingers through her hair, pulling it back from her face. In so doing, he uncovered a scrape beside her right temple. He leaned to give it a tiny kiss, pressing his lips gently to her skin.

"We're not cousins, you know that, Jenny. I'm no relation to you, except through marriage, am I?" His eyes rested lightly on her face, but Jenny could feel the tension rising in him.

"No, I guess not. But you've always been my cousin from the time we were kids. I don't want to lose you now." Her eyes filled with sudden tears.

Jordie pulled her close and rocked her softly. "You won't lose me, sweetheart. Not ever. It's okay. You can cry if you need to." His hands stroked and soothed as he murmured against her hair.

"Well, why are you in my bed?" she muttered, sniffing against his chest, the curly hair tickling her cheek.

"Do you mean to say, it wasn't as wonderful for you as it was for me?"

Jenny pulled back to stare at his grinning face. "You jerk," she choked, laughing.

"I'm sorry, I couldn't resist." He took a breath. "I'm here because you were having nightmares, and every time I left the room you started crying. I was freezing to death, so I finally crawled in."

"Oh," she whispered on a sigh. "I'm glad you did. I slept well, I was even warm, which I haven't been since Frank died. It's been one shock after another."

"I know. You've had a lot to deal with." They lay there quietly for a while.

"You know," Jordie broke the silence, "When you mentioned Armadillo Rock last night, I didn't know what you were talking about. You said you met a couple at the top of the stairs near Armadillo Rock and walked back in front of them."

She nodded against his arm.

"Well," he continued, "I'd forgotten about that rock. We named it, remember?"

She looked at his curiously. "No, it was always called that."

He shook his head stubbornly. "Dad took us to Mexico when I was about nine, and I saw an armadillo for the first time. It was such a funny looking little animal, I was really taken with it."

She lay against his shoulder, listening quietly.

"Then that summer we were swimming in the bay, you and I and Harry."

"And Douglas," she added.

"Yes, probably your brother Douglas too. We were sitting on the rock. I told you about armadillos and how this rock looked just like that little animal only much bigger, with its rounded back and parallel grooves cut into it. We called it Armadillo Rock after that."

She laughed, a shaky sound. "Yeah, I remember. We swam a lot in the bay, didn't we? Now, I think I'd turn blue if I even put my feet in, but then we didn't care."

Jordie was quiet for a moment. "Do you remember something else about that rock?" His eyes looked intently into hers.

She stared back warily as memory stirred.

"We swam out to the rock the summer I turned sixteen. We didn't spend so much time together then. But we were swimming in the bay that day. You were so pretty, you had a new swimsuit, and your hair was up in a ponytail to keep it out of your face when you swam."

Jenny sighed, a smile on her mouth. "How can you remember all that, Jordie?"

His expression was serious. "You'd grown, your legs were long and slim and your little breasts were round under the suit."

Jenny went still in his arms, as a warning sounded in her head.

"I noticed," he continued. "At sixteen, there isn't much you don't notice about girls. We were sitting on Armadillo Rock, sunning ourselves to get warm again from our swim, and I put my arms around you and kissed you." The darkened look of memory dawned in his eyes. "You were furious. You slapped me right in the face and then dove back into the water and swam for shore. Why did you run?"

"I was frightened." Jenny's voice was low. "You'd always been my playmate, one of the cousins. But when you kissed me, that changed everything." She put her head back to look at him. "You suddenly seemed so much older and I'd always felt safe with you, but then you changed the rules."

"Ah, Jenny. I'd been wanting to do that for so long, and I thought you were old enough. Mum and Dad were like that all the time and I used to wonder what it would feel like. Just to have my own girl and hold her." He sighed into her hair and nuzzled the side of her head. "Innocent dreams, eh? We were just kids."

Her eyes closed and a tear seeped from the corner. At length she pulled away and sat up, using her nightie to wipe her eyes.

"What is it, Jenny?"

"Nothing. I'm just vulnerable right now, I guess." Her voice changed to humorous. "I hope you have some clothes on under there." She glanced pointedly at his bare chest.

"Not a stitch." His expression became teasing as he slowly pulled the sheet down with one hand, moving it lower across his abdomen.

"Jordie! What...?" When the waistband of his briefs came into view, her gaze flew back to his face. "You brat!" She gave his chest a weak slap and shifted her feet onto the floor, groaning with the effort.

He leaned to give her a hand up. "I think you have some messages. I heard the phone go a couple of times."

"Okay." She stood hesitantly, then staggered over to pick up her housecoat from the chair near the door before disappearing into the bathroom.

~*~*~*~

Jenny looked into the mirror, wondering how to wash her face without inflicting more pain. She examined the scratches on her cheeks, the bruise below her eye, the scrape at her temple. Then her gaze turned inward.

Talking about Armadillo Rock had opened a door that had been long closed. She remembered those golden days of childhood. They'd run around in a pack, a pack of cousins.

Gingerly, she held a warm facecloth to her skin as she looked back. She'd spent weeks at Uncle Neal's place. They swam in the bay, caught crabs with an old trap that he fixed up for them. They had a little row boat that held three kids and the crab trap. They would ferry it into the middle of the bay and drop it, it's buoy on the surface of the water to mark the spot. Once it had floated several miles down the bay, and they discovered they'd put too short a rope on it. When the tide came in, the float lifted the trap off the bottom and carried it away.

Jordie had been the leader. He was older than the others, all except her brother Douglas. But Douglas was a reader, and didn't always come along. So Jordie ran the show, although at times the girls ganged up on him. Then they'd set him back on his ear for a bit, before they all went back to normal.

Aunt Harriet used to call them for lunch with a big whistle she kept on a nail by the door. She fed them outside under the old tree in the back yard. They'd flop down on a blanket, the dogs lying panting beside them, and wolf down sandwiches, fruit and anything else she handed out. She used to laughingly say it was like feeding birds or a pack of wild animals.

Sometimes Jordie's mum would pack them a picnic lunch and they'd climb around the rocks and visit nearby bays, or head for the park. It had been a wonderful time, an ideal, carefree childhood. Jenny gently wiped her eyes and wrung the cloth out. Her hand stilled, resting on the counter.

Yes, she remembered when Jordie kissed her. She'd been shocked, and furious. He'd spoiled the easy comfortable relationship they had. Like any girl going on fourteen, she'd had thoughts of boys, and she admired Jordie tremendously. In her eyes, he was always so mature. There wasn't anything he couldn't do. Uncle Neal often complimented his step-son, saying how smart he was, that he could turn his hand to anything.

When Jordie kissed her, she hadn't been ready. So she slapped his face and ran like a jack rabbit.

After that, Jordie spent more of his time with his friends and Jenny lost her hero. It would have happened anyway, he was already pulling away. But when he went away to college, she was heartbroken. She hung around Uncle Neal's house, helping Aunt Harriet with her baking, hoping for news of Jordie.

When he did come back, he'd seemed so much older, taller than Uncle Neal, his shoulders broad, a new knowing look in his eyes. And she was engaged to Bobby MacDougall.

She felt that wall of anger well up again like a suffocating blanket. That unreasonable, illogical rage that she had first identified on the beach in Greece. It was like a freak wave coming out of nowhere that threatened to drag her out to sea. She shook, her battered hands trembling as they crushed the towel between them.

Anger at Jordie, for leaving her undefended. Anger at Bobby for being who he was, a weasel and a liar. Anger at Frank for leaving her to sort out this mess. Anger at Alita, that cold bitch for all she'd done to Frank and was now doing to her. Anger at Norman, the smooth bastard!

Rage washed over her like a tsunami coming up the beach. Her mouth opened in a cry of despair as she crumpled against the wall. Warm arms wrapped around her and a furry chest pressed against her face. Strong hands propelled her through the doorway and back onto her bed. Big fingers threaded through her hair, and a low gravelly voice murmured near her ear, soothing and calming her frantically beating heart.

"Why, Jordie? Why did you do it?" she cried low in her throat.

"Why did I kiss you? Because I loved you, Jenny. I wanted to hold you and kiss you. It was innocent."

"But why did you leave?" she sobbed. "You never came back. You left me for Bobby." Her voice rose in a wail. His arms tightened reflexively.

"It was a mistake, Jenny." His voice was a low growl of anguish. "I made a mistake and I've regretted it every day of my life since. You weren't ready when I left, and you grew up so fast, you were more than ready when I came back. I felt you were my girl, you were always my girl. But you forgot me while I was gone."

Jenny's sobs slowed. "I didn't forget you. I just didn't know. You never said, never wrote. I thought you were gone for good."

She snuggled closer to his body heat. "I'm so tired, Jordie. I've never been so tired in my life."

"I know, sweetie. Just go to sleep. You can't go in to work today. I'll call Queenie and look after things. You just rest." Her eyes closed and she was sleeping before he finished speaking.

CHAPTER THIRTY ONE

D
ave settled into the seat of Brad's car and pulled the wool blanket across his legs. He wasn't too old for this work, but he was usually a hell of a lot more prepared than he'd been in the old days when he did surveillance. He used to rely on adrenaline to keep him awake.

Now he used other techniques. He pushed the button on the radio and started the music. He would play it at a low volume for ten minutes than turn it off for twenty. That way he stayed alert. The camera was lying next to him on the seat, the infra red lens placed carefully beside it. A thermos of coffee and bag of sandwiches rested on the floor. He was ready.

He'd roused Esley from bed after he left Jenny's house the night before and they met at the office to refine their plan. Esley was remarkably good at this stuff, a real backup man. His job was to knock on Norman's door. You never knew, some of these guys were really stupid. He might just open the door and they'd have him. If it was him.

Norman wasn't at his townhouse, so they drove past Frank and Alita's home on Christmas Hill. His Jaguar was in the drive parked beside Alita's BMW. Dave stopped around the corner and climbed out to speak to Esley through his car window. They arranged their strategy, then Esley drove up the long drive to knock on the door. When there was no answer he pushed the doorbell again, and after a long wait, Alita appeared, dressed in a negligee as if ready for bed.

No, Norman was not there. What did he want with Norman? Yes, that was his car, but her son had been out of town for a few days. Alita had driven him to the ferry and brought his car back to her house. Where had he gone? That was certainly no one's business.

Esley walked back to his car, Alita's attention still riveted on him as he backed down the drive. Then the door closed and the outside light went out. The house was too high to see into from the road. Dave climbed through the neighbour's yard in the dark. There were lights on in Alita's windows. He stood on the patio out of line of sight, peering through the gap in the drapes into the family room. He remembered the layout of the house from the staff Christmas party. This room led straight into the hall which branched off into the front room and led to the kitchen on the other side of the house. The stairs up to the bedrooms also came off that hall.

There was light in the kitchen window, but all Dave could see from the yard were the tops of the cabinets. He waited. When his legs became stiff from standing so long, he moved silently from one foot to the other as his back began to ache.

Finally, he saw a shadow in the hallway, and a hand reached around the door jamb. It was definitely a masculine hand, and the shoulder was higher than Alita's would have been. As he watched, the fingers brushed the wall searching for the switch and flicked it off. It went pitch black.

Now he was pretty sure there was a man in there. Whether it was Norman or not was still in question. If not Norman, then Alita moved pretty fast for a recent widow. Frank had only been dead, how long, a month at most?

Dave climbed silently off the patio and backed down the hill, keeping in the shadow of a line of shrubs, his eyes searching the house for activity. Several minutes later another light went on upstairs. He studied the silhouette of the building. The second floor was built up into the roof, the windows cut as dormers into the roofline. It would be easier to get up there from the back, where the porch railing gave him something to stand on. There was also less likelihood of being heard climbing his way up. The bedroom lights were at the front of the house.

He called Esley to tell him his new plan and warn him to keep an eye out. Then he proceeded to scramble his way onto the porch railing and over the gutters onto the roof. He crawled silently around to the front, wincing as the shingles cut into his knees. The first window was Alita's. He stole softly to the casement and crouched down to peer through the corner of the glass. Naked to the waist, she was sitting up in bed, filing her nails under the light from the lamp on her night table.

Jeez, he always felt like such a sleaze when he did this work, not that it bothered him nearly as much as it used to. Now he saw it as the price people paid for being in the wrong business, associating with the wrong people. She had a pretty nice set, considering. Good old Frank, she had to have something to offer, after all. Wonder if he knew he was marrying a poison pill?

He sidled past the window keeping low, placing his feet carefully to avoid sound, the slight scrape of gravel under his shoes from the asphalt shingles barely audible.

The next window was dark. The third window was lit, showing an empty bedroom, well lived in. Books lying around, a corner table with papers strewn across it. Then the door opened and Norman walked in. He was bare to the waist as well, pyjamas covering his lower half. And the sight was just as interesting. His face looked fine to Dave, and his heart sank. Jenny would be upset. This wasn't as straightforward as she thought.

Shutting the door, Norman advanced into the room. As he sat on the bed, he turned and suddenly Dave saw the devastation on the other side of his face. His eye was covered with some kind of surgical dressing and scratches marched down his cheek like tire tracks. They looked swollen and angry. There was another bandage on the side of his jaw.

When he turned on his bedside lamp, Dave got a closer look. He didn't know if the camera would take a good picture from this range but he'd take some anyway. However, the pictures would probably be inadmissible, taken illegally while climbing on the suspect's roof and peeping into his bedroom windows without a warrant. Dave's lip curled in disgust at the gymnastics done in court to protect the rights of guilty people. He stayed where he was until the light went out. By that time his knees were stiff and he knew every scratch and mole on Norman's face.

~*~*~*~

Carefully, Jenny climbed down from Jordie's truck and adjusted her skirt. She'd worn a bright cotton and silk wrap-around this morning, a green and gold print that seemed to match the glorious sunny weather. She hoped it would brighten her mood.

She'd lost the whole day yesterday. By the time she awoke it had been late afternoon. She'd been so weepy, Jordie had bundled her into a quilt and taken her outside to sit on a lounge chair and look at the ocean. He made some phone calls, brought her coffee and a sandwich, and sat beside her saying nothing. He held her hand for a bit, pointing out the seagulls as they hung on the wind. The ocean grumbled below, a low murmur beneath the sound of the birds and the occasional putt-putt of a fish boat moving through the water.

Then he filled her in on the situation at work. Queenie said everything was under control, not to worry. She had some cheques to be signed by the end of the week, and she could bring them by the house if needed. Brad said everything was under control. He'd scheduled a meeting with Dave, Esley and Jenny for tomorrow afternoon, but that could be put off for a day or two, or they could do it at her place. Dave said everything was under control. They all sent their love.

Jenny started to smile as the litany of calls and well-wishers grew. Everything must be going okay, they all said so. Jordie grinned and squeezed her fingers reassuringly. They had a quiet supper and Jenny took a leisurely bath. She came out to find Jordie standing on the sundeck in his sock feet, looking at the ocean.

When he turned, his eyes held a strange expression of hunger and hurt. He lowered his lids, and when he raised them again she saw the same old Jordie, that hot look in his eyes as they rested on her face. He glanced away.

"I've been thinking about your patio here. What would you think of a hot tub in that corner?"

"A hot tub?" she said blankly.

"Yeah, you know. A hot tub, Jacuzzi."

"Umm," Her mind stalled.

"I know, it's kind of off today's topic. But, look over here." He walked to the end of the sundeck. She followed. "You don't seem to have anything growing here."

She looked dumbly at the spot. "A hot tub? You mean where everyone takes all their clothes off and drinks beer?"

Jordie threw back his head and laughed. It was a wonderful sound, coming from deep in his belly.

She gave a slow grin.

"Don't you want to take all your clothes off and drink beer?" He was choking on his words between bursts of laughter.

"Wellll..."

He peered at her in the gloom of the early evening. "Hot tubs are great, you can look up at the stars and the sky. The jets relax your muscles. It'll warm you up when you're cold. What do you think? I carry them at the store and this spot would be perfect. We'll just build a little more deck out around it."

She shook her head. "I don't know," she said dubiously. "I never thought about it."

He put his arm gently around her shoulders and led her into the house. "Too many decisions, and not enough energy, right? Come on, I'll tuck you into bed and I'll sleep in Margaret's room. We should give her a call, let her know what happened."

Jenny shook her head. "No, I don't want to tell her until Norman's caught. I don't want her to worry, just going into exams. Anyway, she'll be home soon, a couple of weeks now." Her voice had lifted at the thought.

Now she straightened her dress and turned to close Jordie's truck door.

"I'll be at the office," he called. "Call me when you're ready to head home. Promise?"

Jenny nodded. He'd brow beaten her, there was no other way to describe it. He was going to drive her to work, pick her up, stay at her house. Her mind refused to grapple with this. It was like he was taking over her life, except she knew there was a good reason.

Shifting her briefcase into her other hand, she walked up the steps into the building. Queenie greeted her as she came off the elevator, looking her face over carefully. "Poor thing. This has gone too far. But you've done a good job with the makeup. I can hardly tell. Come on, I've got fresh coffee, and nearly everyone's here. Dave and Brad want to see you first. There's a pile of messages on your desk, but these are the most important."

Jenny grabbed the yellow slips from Queenie's hand and went into her office, dropping her case on the table. The top slip was from Bernie Olsinger. There were two from Angus Murdoch, several from the bank accounts manager, one from Adam Schwartz and another from Greg Houston in Seattle. Jenny sighed.

Just then the phone rang. It was Schwartz. Bernie had suggested that he call. He thought there might be an opening for him in the firm. He was certainly ready to take over. And this was a rough trade for a woman.

Jenny took a deep breath, assured him nothing had changed and his name was at the top of the list should a position open up.

She gritted her teeth. Did Bernie know she'd been attacked? The very thought made her shudder. What kind of asshole would continue this kind of pressure? Unless that was his tactic, to seize an opportunity to get his guy into her company while she was feeling vulnerable. She'd better deal with this head on, it didn't seem like it would go away.

She called Bernie's office but found he was in Vancouver today. She left a message, then called Angus. As the call was put through, she saw Brad and Dave coming down the hall and waved them in.

Angus reported the bank had contacted him because they had a request from Fred Austin, acting on behalf of Alita Jensen, to get copies of the bank records. He'd advised the bank to deny access without a court order, but he'd quickly received notice that Austin was launching a derivative action to investigate Jenny's salary and salaries paid to the department managers. Jenny gasped in outrage and stood, knocking her chair backward on its wheels.

"That's ridiculous, Angus. Our salaries are the same as they were before Frank died. In fact, they're probably on the low side. Frank was always careful."

"It's okay, Jenny. That's good to hear, at any rate, so we don't need to worry about the actual content of this. But Austin is, as usual, out to lunch. He's bringing the wrong action." Murdoch's hearty laugh came over the phone. "We'll go ahead and defend, asking for punitive damages for a ridiculous waste of the court's time."

"Okay. What about the bank?"

"The bank can't show anyone those records without a court order. However, you do have an annual general meeting coming up, so you'll have to disclose your financial statements to Alita then."

"That's no problem. Just keep them off our back for the moment. One other thing, Angus."

"Okay, shoot."

"We're under a lot of pressure from Bernie Olsinger. He was a friend of Frank's and for some reason he's pressuring us to hire one of his hand-picked guys to work in the company."

"I take it you don't want this guy?" Murdoch's voice lowered to an antagonistic growl.

Jenny grinned. "No, he's crawled right out from under a rock. The problem is, Bernie has our license under his jurisdiction and we're getting static about it. Queenie faxed you the letter last week."

"Ah, gotcha. Okay, I'll look into the regulations and get back to you. Meantime, hang tight. And don't forget Chambers tomorrow at ten for the challenge to the will."

"I haven't forgotten," said Jenny. "It's on my list. Along with about a thousand other things. This had better go as smoothly as Paul says it will."

Jenny hung up and turned to see her small crew seated around the pine table in the corner, their eyes pinned on her.

"Hi, Jenny," Brad's voice was cheerful. "You look great, I can see the bruises but you still look great." He grinned and she smiled back. He had loosened up over the past months, letting a little more personality show behind that serious demeanour. And he was becoming more indispensable all the time.

She took her place at the table where a pad of paper and pen were already set for her, presumably by her assistant.

Dave eyed her keenly and became immediately businesslike. "Do you want to start with that phone call? What's going on there?"

Jenny jotted a few things down on the pad before her. "Okay, but where's Esley?"

"He's sleeping," said Dave. "He worked last night and will be in later this afternoon. I'll tell you about it in a minute."

Jenny levelled a gaze at the group. "Everything I'm about to say is confidential. It has to stay within this room. I'm sure that didn't need to be said, but I wanted it on the table. Okay," she settled into her chair and squared the pad against the edge of the table with her fingers as she talked.

"Let's start a few months back, before Frank died. There was extra money in the company bank account. I noticed it before Christmas."

As she talked, Dave's brows shot up and Jenny shook her head. "This isn't irregular the way a cop would look at it. Frank had a lot of long time clients, and some of them paid cash. They did business on a handshake. He carried it all in his head. We had a few arguments about it but he was stubborn as they come." Her voice choked and tears popped into her eyes. She still couldn't talk about him without crying. She cleared her throat and Brad shuffled his sheaf of notes awkwardly.

"Anyway, that's how it was. So when I began to notice that there was too much money..."

"How much are we talking about?" Dave interrupted.

"Mmmm, about a hundred and fifty thousand when I first became aware of it."

Brad whistled.

Dave's eyes never left her face. "What did Frank say?"

Jenny shifted around to see him better, her neck still stiff. "He didn't explain. Some was cash, some checks and a few money orders. We have a lot of cash clients."

"Yeah, I know. I've done work for some of them since I started here." Dave was doodling on his paper, then put his pen down. "Go on."

"Frank didn't think it was a problem, but promised to sit down with Queenie and sort it out. Not like it was a big issue. I'd be more worried if we were a hundred and fifty thousand short. However, now it's officially a problem. We're more than seven hundred thousand dollars over what we've logged this year." She waited for that to sink in.

Brad was pale, Dave's eyes had narrowed as he gazed out the window. "Yes, that's significant." His tone belied the understatement of his words. "I think we may have found the source of most of our problems."

Jenny nodded, her eyes lighting up at the wryness of his voice. "Definitely significant. The extra money stopped coming in when Frank died. The cash flow has gone back to normal. So, we have this money." Her eyes flooded, but she continued resolutely onward. "Then there's Frank's death." A tear leaked down her cheek and she brushed it away. "Then we have Alita launching a challenge to the will, and Norman comes to my house."

"Well, be realistic." Dave had a little smile on his face. "You're a very attractive woman. And Norman isn't blind."

Jenny flashed him a look. "Don't give me that old line. Norman has never had any interest in me."

Dave looked down at his papers and became busy making doodle marks on the cover of the folder.

"Do you know anything about his travels?"

He glanced up and nodded. "I do. But the last item on your list is that Norman attacked you two nights ago." His matter of fact voice brought them all back to attention. "We got a good look at him, Jenny. Norman's car was in the drive at Jensen's, and Alita told Esley he was out of town. So we staked out the house. I managed to get a good look at his face. The skin was ripped to shreds. You did a real number on him." He beamed his admiration.

"Anyway, I made notes, tried for photos. Esley stayed there the rest of the night. I covered it yesterday, and Esley came back for the night shift last night and saw him leave the house. We got a picture of him with the infra-red lens just as he came out Alita's front door. Still had a bandage over his eye, but the other scratches and gouges were clear to see."

Jenny's face went pale. "Good." She felt nauseous at the news and took a deep breath, pressing her hand against her stomach. "Uh, where do we go from here? Well." She took another breath, "We have Bernie Olsinger sitting on us, applying pressure to hire Adam Schwartz. And Schwartz has the gall to phone this morning, said Bernie told him there might be an opening. Bernie must be aware of what's happened."

Brad added, "We have a review about to happen regarding our security license."

Dave nodded, but everyone's head turned at Jenny's next words. "Murdoch just told me Alita is trying to get access to the bank account."

Dave gave a low whistle. "She must know about that money. If she was really worried about the company's financial position she would have demanded the bank records be shown in court."

Jenny shrugged. "Anyway, it's your turn Dave. What have you and Esley been working on besides what I've given you?"

He flushed. Jenny kept her gaze steady as the blood rose in his face. "Frank gave me an assignment the minute I started work here. He wanted me to investigate Norman and keep it top secret." He looked slightly abashed at her glare. "I'm sorry. I felt pretty uncomfortable with it, and so did Esley when I finally asked him for help. But Frank swore us to secrecy. He especially wanted to know where Norman got his money.

"After a bit I began to see a pattern in Norman's activities. He made a trip about twice a month. It was hard to tell what his real destination was. No through flights past Seattle. He has excellent instincts, never left boarding passes lying around, no ticket stubs. I even got access to his bank account at one point, but he must have been using cash."

Jenny's eyebrows rose. "If you got at his bank account, can Alita get access to the bank account of the company?"

"Probably," he grinned. "But not legally. I used an old contact from police days and swore not to tell a soul. Next I followed Norman to Seattle. Found a ticket agent who remembered him. She told me he flew in every two or three weeks, went on to the southern US or Mexico. Wherever they had a charter flight going with cheap sell-off seats. Sometimes Mazatlán, or Puerto Vallarta, San Diego. Always on the west coast."

Jenny was riveted. "He always looks like he has a tan. Have you noticed that?"

"He's not down there for the tan, Jenny!" Dave's voice was sharp with impatience.

"I know that."

He shot her an irritated look.

"His father is part Mexican," she added. "He may have family down there."

Dave made a note. "I wasn't aware of that. I'll check it out."

"Anything else?" Jenny looked at Brad. He cleared his throat and opened a folder. "I've gone through the accounts over a two-year period. There are fourteen clients of Frank's that have no contract. These are fairly long term, all of them for more than two years. But they have a pattern of how they pay, how much they pay, and when they pay. Here it is." He placed copies in front of the others.

Then he pulled out a second sheet. "So what that leaves are two lists: one of deposits for services of one-time events, and the other of deposits without apparent corresponding services." Brad spoke with his head down, concentrating on the sheets of information. "Then," and here he looked up, his face tense, "there are a bunch of things that look odd. For instance, services billed to us for a six-month period by one specific person, Mr. J. Donne. Then Mr. Donne disappears and a new contractor appears, a John Dane, for about two months, then he's gone and a P. Downs starts billing us. There are lots of money orders, and lump sums of cash. It's a mess."

There was silence as they studied the sheets. "I'll go over these with you, Brad." Jenny lifted her head to smile at him. "Let me spend a bit of time on them first. You've done a great job."

She glanced at Dave. "By the way, where did Norman go last night? Shouldn't we be calling the police now that we've identified him as the guy who attacked me?"

"Only if we can get full police cooperation." Dave was all business again, arranging the papers before him into an organized pile. "We want to let Norman lead us to further information. And he won't if the police come calling. He'll either deny everything or bolt like a jackrabbit. Either event won't tell us what we want to know.

"As it is, Jenny, you have to take every precaution for your own safety. Norman left town last night, flew out on the last flight to Vancouver, then Vancouver to Bellingham, Washington State. But we don't know where he travelled from there or how long he'll be gone. Nor do we know when he's coming back. Besides, you saw at least *two* men the other night, one by your door and one driving a car, so Norman may have left someone else behind for us to worry about."

Jenny's shoulders hunched. She fidgeted with the pen. "You sound like Jordie. If you guys had your way, I'd be a prisoner. Surely the police can help with that," she added hopefully.

"Yes. But it's just common-sense. You can't go to the parkade alone, or stay in the office after everyone has gone. You can't be home alone. In other words, you need a bodyguard. Now Esley and I can take turns but it will slow down the investigation."

"Well, I want the police called. Dave, I'll leave that to you. You know who to talk to."

"Okay. Let me do that and I'll call Jordie. Between him and the cops, I'm sure we can work something out."

"Don't bother," Jenny muttered. "He's already laid down the rules, He has a new cellular phone as of yesterday, and I have to report in hourly." Her voice was sour.

"Good!" Brad and Dave spoke simultaneously, then broke into matching smiles. Brad continued, his face deadly earnest, "It's good, Jenny. We can't have anything like this happen again. We should at least be able to protect you if we're any kind of security company." He flushed, embarrassed at his emotional outburst.

Jenny used her fingers to cross her heart. "Okay, you guys. I'll behave, I promise. Jordie will pay for it though. Someone should."

They all grinned.

CHAPTER THIRTY TWO

Saturday, Jordie rose early and went into the kitchen to start the coffee. Jenny must still be sleeping, there was no sound from her room. He made a phone call to confirm his plans for the day and grabbed a bowl of cereal, eating it standing at the counter. He studied the sky while he munched. It looked a little chilly out there, although the forecast was for sun and warm temperatures in the afternoon.

Maybe they could go to the museum. The boy loved the museum. He especially liked going into the old-town section, prowling through the sailing ship display, sniffing the cinnamon smells in the old-fashioned kitchen, and sitting in the little theatre watching the silent films and giggling about the pratfalls of Laurel and Hardy. Jordie smiled to himself. He couldn't count the number of times he'd taken him there.

Then they could go to Fisherman's Wharf for a lunch of fish and chips and ramble around looking at the boats. Neal liked to peer into the windows of the houseboats and speculate about what it would be like to live on one. They'd talk to the fishermen, ask them about their catch. Once they bought a live crab and Neal took it home with him. But he complained that his mum threw it out.

Jordie left a note for Jenny, saying he had to work today but would call in the early afternoon. She could reach him on his cell if she needed him for anything. Brad would be over at ten and she wasn't to leave the house alone. Then he grabbed his windbreaker and headed out the door.

His first stop was his own house. He hadn't been home much for three or four days, since Jenny got hurt. He needed to empty his mail box and make sure the food wasn't rotting in his fridge. Then he grabbed his keys and locked up. He didn't want to be late, Neal was always waiting for him to arrive with hungry eyes and baited breath, and he didn't like to disappoint the little guy. His eager anxiety always tugged heavily at Jordie's heart strings.

Slowing his truck on the crowded street in the centre of James Bay, he squeezed into an empty space. He spotted the boy leaning over the second floor balcony of the apartment he shared with his mother. He waved enthusiastically, his red curls bobbing on top of his head. Jordie laughed and waved back before heading toward the foyer of the four-story building. A couple of battered bicycles leaned against the front of the structure, and a tricycle was overturned on the walkway. The grass was worn down in a hard path across the front.

Jordie took the stairs two at a time and knocked softly on the scarred door of the suite. A little boy about waist high opened it almost immediately and leaped into his arms. "Hi, Neal, how are you, little guy?" Jordie's voice was husky with emotion.

"Hi, Dad," was the reply. "You sure took a long time getting here. Gosh, I've been waiting all day."

Jordie laughed. "It's only eight-thirty, son, the day's just starting. Let's say good-bye to your mum, and fetch a jacket, okay? It's a little cool out."

Neal untwined his thin freckled arms from around his waist and nodded his head, curls bobbing. He dashed through the door still standing ajar, and Jordie followed more slowly. Rita was not up apparently. The living room was strewn with magazines and overflowing ashtrays. A couple of beer bottles and glasses sat in dried rings on the coffee table he'd bought her. He looked in the kitchen. No sign of a clean dish. The boy probably hadn't eaten yet this morning.

Neal reappeared, his hair wet and combed carefully to the side, although it was already pulling back into its usual unruly shape.

"Is your mum sleeping?"

Neal nodded and looked doubtfully toward her closed door.

"Well, we'll just leave her a note." Jordie looked around and found a piece of paper. Neal produced a stubby brown pencil from his jacket pocket and they stuck the note under a magnet on the refrigerator.

Neal took his hand as they descended the stairs, chattering non-stop about his week, the dog he'd met on the next street over, and what they might do today.

~*~*~*~

It was nearly time for Neal to head home and he knew it. He lingered over his ice cream cone where they sat on the park bench, licking it slowly, making it last until his hands were sticky with chocolate. "You better eat a little faster, son, or there'll be more ice cream down your sleeves than in your tummy." Jordie leaned over and tickled him through his shirt, and Neal's face screwed up in a squeal of laughter.

"Besides, you don't want to let that ice cream drip on your new jeans, now do you?" Neal began eating faster, his tongue making precise scoops around the soggy cone.

"Why don't I go stay at your place tonight, Dad? I've never stayed at your place." His little face was hopeful, his eyes alight.

Jordie shook his head, and watched the small face fall. He looked away. "Not this time, son. I've got work to do. But maybe soon. Yeah, soon."

Idly he watched a woman with a baby buggy maneuver her way onto the sidewalk, a small dog trailing, his leash attached to the handle. A man walked a little behind holding the baby against his shoulder, patting it's back.

It should have been like that for him. When his son was born, it should have been that way. He would have pushed the buggy, or held the baby while his wife bought cones for them. Then they'd have sat in the sun, rocking the carriage and chatting as they ate, the dog lounging at their feet.

Instead, his wife had insisted she couldn't have children. Jordie still remembered how devastated he'd been by the news. He discussed adopting but she wouldn't entertain the idea. He finally locked his longing away in his heart and tried to create a family with just the two of them until she moved into her own room and even that fantasy was dashed. And he'd been duped. Duped out of his life as a parent, as a father.

His gaze turned back to Neal who was feeding the last bite of his cone to the little dog waiting patiently by the baby carriage. Jordie would love to take Neal home with him. Linda wasn't there to go into one of her rages, or her cold sulks that lasted weeks. Finally, he was free to have his son come home. Just as he was getting an opportunity with Jenny.

He thought of Jenny's bitterness toward her husband, toward Bobby's unfaithfulness and numerous affairs. All the hurt she had suffered for herself and her children was summed up in her harsh divorce.

How could he then bring home his son, born out of wedlock to a woman he had been seeing while married to Linda? Jordie's heart quaked at the thought. Yet he had to tell her, and soon. This little boy was a part of him, a part he wasn't about to let go, not for anything. But he was afraid, as he'd never been afraid before in his life. Just when it looked like there might be a chance for them together, Jenny might reject him out of hand, without letting him explain or taking the time to get acquainted with this little bundle of life who meant so much to him. He'd blown his first chance with her years ago, and now he was mortally afraid he might blow his last.

"Come on, scout," he said, pulling his thoughts together. "Time to go. You've eaten so much today, I doubt if you'll be able to eat one bite of dinner tonight. What have you eaten? Let's see, first there was the big plate of pancakes, with two glasses of milk."

"And one glass of orange juice," Neal added, skipping along beside him.

"Yes, and one orange juice. That must be why you had to pee three times while we were at the museum."

Neal giggled and hung on his arm.

"Then there was the burger and coke. Then there was the hot dog from the street vendor's cart, and the bag of popcorn."

Neal shrugged. "And the apple," he interjected.

He opened the truck door and boosted him up the high step. "Yes, the apple you found in the truck. I'm glad you didn't let that go to waste." Neal's face beamed as his dad buckled his seatbelt and slammed the truck door.

"Don't forget the gum you bought me," the boy said, fingering the crushed package from his pocket as Jordie climbed in the driver's side.

"Okay, although gum isn't really food. You're not supposed to swallow it."

Neal nodded in agreement. "And then the ice cream cone," he stated triumphantly.

Jordie grinned over at him and took his sticky little hand in his own big one. He remembered when Neal was born. By then the affair with Rita was long over. He'd realized what she was like and begun to despise himself for the sneaking, lying and side-stepping of the truth he had to do to see her. But when the baby arrived, he'd gone to the hospital and seen that little bundle through the glass and his heart had stopped. Literally stopped. He'd been afraid it wouldn't start again, but when it did, it was with an entirely new and painful beat attuned to the scrap of humanity that was his boy.

Now he said, "Listen, son, I know it's been hard not seeing much of me, but we've had most Saturdays together, haven't we? And things should slow down at work soon, so we can spend a weekend together, maybe next month. What do you think?"

His heart quaked at the wide grin spreading across the little guy's face. Well, maybe he could take him camping or something. Or maybe he'd get his nerve up and risk everything to tell Jenny about his son. Just maybe.

CHAPTER THIRTY THREE

The sky was clear pure blue overhead. It looked limitless, as if she could see through it to the heavens beyond. The gnarled branches of the Garry oaks made a frame around Jenny's hidden spot in the tall grass on the bank. Brad had finally left and Jordie called to say he would be gone longer than planned. It was wonderful to have some breathing space and she was determined not to waste it.

The trees around her were stunted by the relentless ocean wind, the bark broken with cracks crevassing across the trunks as if clawed by bears. They were shaped against the hill at an angle, looking pruned up and back by a giant hand.

Up close, the lichen encrusting the branches was whitish and feathery. An olive green fungi interspersed along the bark with spots of pollen-yellow mold, and a scaly, pale green growth. Brilliant green moss grew against the tree trunks in the crotch of the branches. She'd gotten to this spot by a little-used path wending its way through heavy brush between the Garry oaks clogging the hillside. The ground was seeded with a sparse covering of grass.

From the warm flat stone on which she sat, she could see straight down to the rocks below and far out across the bay. She picked out her house on the other side of the cove, her sundeck festooned with the big ceramic planters brought back from Greece, new greenery showing from their tops. Her windows reflected the sun back in a blinding glare.

Below, to her right shone Armadillo Rock, the low tide barely lapping at its base. The ocean was still, must be slack tide. The breeze was so mild it barely stirred the twisted olive green leaves, leaving her hidden spot sun-soaked. She settled her back against a tree trunk and closed her eyes.

The seagulls wheeled and soared overhead, issuing forth plaintive demanding cries. In the far distance arose the raucous clamour from Bird Island far out in the bay. Sometimes when the wind was right she could smell it from here, that unbridled colony of seagulls, puffins and cormorants, weeping white guano over the rocks.

She sighed and let her mind wander. But it didn't wander far. Always, when she caught herself daydreaming, or 'mooning' as her mother used to call it, her mind turned to the hopelessly tangled puzzle of the money and Frank's death. What had really happened? Sometimes she was so frustrated she would scream out loud, stamping around her living room and shouting at Frank for leaving her in this mess.

Or she would be overcome by a helpless anger, sure that Frank's death was no accident but unable to prove anything else. Anger at those who would attack him, and now her, for no reason that she could see. If it was the money, then why was it in the Sentinel Security account in the first place?

And always there was a thought niggling at the back of her mind. Jenny frowned ferociously across the bay below. It was something Frank had said. Early on in the business relationship, they'd argued several times about how he conducted business. Jenny thought it needed more structure and he wasn't willing to give an inch. He'd told her in no uncertain terms that those were the guidelines of their partnership. He would continue to handle a handful of clients, the way he had always done. She wasn't to interfere.

But the later arguments had come about because Frank not only had more 'special' clients, but there was a difference in that the profit margin was low. She remembered his explanation. These new accounts were clients from other security companies that had closed. But when they came to Frank, it was because of a recommendation. And that recommendation was from Bernie Olsinger! Bernie was the common denominator.

There was something sinister about that circle of events. Bernie referred clients from other firms to Frank. The clients brought their own security agents. Frank took the pay from the client, booked the agent and took a fee to do the booking.

She shuddered and sat up, rubbing her arms and frowning down into the bay. The waves were starting to move again, the water was higher around Armadillo Rock. Slack tide was over. Suddenly she was chilled. Jordie would be looking for her, he'd be back from the store soon. She was starting to chafe under the controls he kept on her. It was irritating to report to someone all the time, even if that someone was Jordie.

Rising, she brushed off her jeans and crawled back through the bush to the narrow trail. As she jogged along the path, hoping against hope that she'd beat him home, she grinned to herself. There was one obvious advantage to having Jordie around. He liked to cook. It was a welcome change from her own feeble efforts.

And she liked to spend time with him. She liked everything about him, how he looked with his tightly curled red hair cut short, his grin when he teased her and managed to get a rise out of her, the way his body moved as he prowled the kitchen or reached past her to help lift or carry. Things had been a little tense after the attack, but he'd pulled back to the same old relaxed guy with the same hot gaze that followed her wherever she went.

As she topped the hill at the back of her patio, she spotted Jordie's truck pulling into her driveway. She sprinted onto the deck and wrenched open the patio doors. Racing into the kitchen, she grabbed the note she'd left for him and tossed it in the garbage. Then she seated herself on a lounge chair on the deck, stifling her giggles and trying to control her breathing from the run. What Jordie didn't know wouldn't hurt him.

~*~*~*~

Jordie paced the living room, occasionally stepping around the cat as Guts paced by his side. Jenny was in the bathroom. He heard the water running, then it stopped, then began again.

He ploughed his fingers through his hair in frustration. He couldn't keep doing this. Jenny needed security and he was the first to volunteer, convinced no one would do it as well, no one would be as attentive. Hell, no one would care as much. But it was killing him. Just being this close to her for such long periods of time was literally killing him.

Last night he'd barely slept. If he wasn't hearing things that bumped in the night, he was thinking about her being so close, just a room away lying naked or wearing a flimsy little nightie hiked up to her waist as she slept with legs sprawled under the quilt. His own body hadn't been nearly as relaxed.

Now here they were getting ready for bed, another night of torture. He turned around at the muffled sound of a door opening, imagining her leaving her bathroom and moving over to the bed, her nightie translucent in the light from her bedside lamp. He watched her bedroom door, but it remained closed. He turned back and continued pacing.

"Jordie?"

At the soft sound, he whirled around. Jenny stood in the hall, her housecoat clutched tight at the throat with a white-knuckled fist. "Jenny? What is it?"

Her hair was pulled back from her face as if she'd just washed. The scrape by her temple still showed as a bruise but most of the discolour had faded to little more than a shadow. Her eyes were dark, like emeralds in her pale face. Then her lashes swept down. She shrugged lightly. "Aren't you going to bed?"

"In a minute." He twisted to face the window, seeing her image reflected there. She turned uncertainly, watching him over her shoulder before she went back down the hall.

He rubbed his face, running his hand roughly over the stubble of his beard. God! How was this going to go? He didn't know how much more he could handle. Maybe he'd get so tired he'd fall into a stupor and it wouldn't matter. He bent to give the cat one last swipe down her back and headed for Margaret's room. As he passed Jenny's bedroom, he saw her door ajar. A soft beam of light fell across his socks as he stopped in indecision.

He nudged the door open with a finger. Jenny stood with her back to the room, her face pressed against the glass of the window. Her head was tilted downward, hands clasped in front of her resting on the sill. He moved silently across the room before he had time to second guess his motive.

"Jenny." His big hands rested lightly on her shoulders, then ran down her arms in a slow caress. "Are you all right?"

She shuddered under his grasp. Her body leaned back against him and he pulled her closer. "Are you crying?"

She turned in his arms, her face pale but no tears showed on her cheeks. She rubbed his chest through the cotton shirt, then moved her hands higher to caress his neck above the collar. "No, I'm not crying. I'm just... I don't know." Her gaze fell indecisively to the front of his shirt. "I can't sleep these days. I'm so restless."

He lifted her chin with his fingers, focussed on her generous mouth as determination suddenly solidified in his chest. "Me, too. I think I know what's wrong," he said, and laid his mouth over hers.

He kissed her with heat and desperation, with everything he had. Placing his hand behind her head, he cupped her scalp as he increased the pressure of his mouth. Then his tongue slipped inside, licking and tasting.

Ah, this was Jenny. She was new but familiar, as if he'd known her flavour a long time ago and had merely forgotten momentarily. His heart pounded heavily against her hands trapped between them, his breath coming fiercely through his flared nostrils. He felt like he was running a race. And he had to win.

She was definitely kissing him back. Her hands slid around his shoulders pulling him in tightly against her breasts and tugging fiercely at his shirt to clear the waistband. Then her fingers were on his skin, exciting him even more.

Ah, Jenny. A lifetime of waiting, summed up in a single kiss. His arms wrapped tightly, hands moving across her flesh to caress her hips. Those lovely hips that he'd watched swing away from him so many times in that sassy walk of hers.

He breathed into her throat and heard her answering sigh as his palm found her breast beneath the robe, moulding and shaping until her nipple rose up urgently against the fabric. Oh, he wanted her. Had wanted her for what seemed forever. His pulse jumped. Swinging her around, he backed her against the bed.

"Jenny, I need you," he mumbled into her neck, nudging the edge of her robe aside with his chin. His lips followed the line of her collar bone, pressing hot slow kisses along her skin. Placing one knee on the mattress, he lowered her to the sheet, following with the weight of his body.

"I've wanted you for so long, sweetheart. I don't think I can wait. God knows I've tried, but I'm only a man." He realized he was begging, but didn't care. When he kissed her again, he felt her quick response as she pressed upward against him, her breasts flattening against his chest.

He tugged at her robe and parted it to find her naked beneath. Her breasts were full, the nipples standing up like pencil erasers. His mouth was there in a flash, sucking her in like sustenance for his body.

Her gasp was barely audible above the blood-roar in his ears. "Jordie, ah, yes. Do that again." The echo of her voice vibrated inside his ribcage. His hands were all over her now, feeling the swell of her hips and the contour of her belly. Her legs parted and his hand slipped between, pressing through the concealing curls to find her wet and ready for him.

He heard a moan, didn't know if it was her or him. He was like a man on a desert who'd just come in sight of the oasis, within smell of it, that rich earthy aroma of new life. He reached for his own clothes, only to find his pants were already undone, the belt buckle hanging. He looked back at Jenny, her face flushed and mouth swollen.

Then he paused, hoping for his head to clear, to read her expression. "I want to make love to you. Sweetheart, say yes..." She returned his stare, her hands pushing the shirt off his shoulders and tugging it down his back.

That was all the encouragement he needed. Pulling her farther up the bed, he followed, parting her legs with his knee and sliding into her. He caught her moan with his mouth, ravishing her with his lips and tongue. She wrapped her arms around his back and hung on.

It was over much too fast. Jordie thought his heart would burst through the wall of his chest. He was afraid to move, he couldn't absorb any more sensation, his very skin too sensitive to bear it. His big hand seized Jenny's wrist to keep her from touching him until his heart stopped leaping against his ribcage, until his breath could come in gasps instead of gulps.

Smoothing her hair back from her sweaty cheek, he murmured, "I'm sorry, sweetheart. I didn't mean to attack you like that. I wanted... It's just..." He took in a swift breath and rolled her over with him to lay on her side, then pressed the tear from the corner of her eye with the pads of his fingers. "Did I hurt you?"

She covered his mouth with her fingers. "No, you didn't hurt me. Not in the way you mean. Isn't it strange, after all this time?"

Her eyes were luminous, a clear green shining up at him. He ran his hand down her breast, grazing her nipple and watched it leap to attention under his fingers. "Well, I wouldn't call it strange. More like kismet, or destiny. God must wonder what took us so long. I blew it."

"*We* blew it," she said. "I was in such a hurry. I thought Bobby was the one. And all the time, I was angry that you'd left me here..." She broke off, reached up to kiss him. Her hand slid down to his muscular thigh pressed tightly between her legs. He shifted and she placed her fingers on his manhood, feeling him already starting to rise and fill for her.

"It doesn't matter now, Jordie. Just now, we're the only ones who matter. This is what matters."

He felt the blood begin to roar again in his ears, to carry him along on that turgid swift-moving stream. But he'd hold back this time, he promised her silently. He'd take his time and take her time. They'd be slow together, no more misunderstandings, no more waiting and longing for what wasn't and maybe could never be. Not anymore.

CHAPTER THIRTY FOUR

Angus Murdoch's voice boomed through the receiver as Jenny held it away from her ear. "So, they're at it again. Another Writ and Notice of Motion. Fred Austin wants to start an action requesting Relief from Oppression of a minority shareholder. They're alleging that there's a large amount of profit in the company which you refuse to pay out as dividends."

Jenny stirred in her chair but said nothing.

"Well? What do you say?"

She sighed. "To begin with, Angus, Fred sent a formal request to see the books about a month ago. I sent back a letter saying that Alita was free to come in and look them over. I asked for the courtesy of twenty-four hours' notice. She never called. So they can't say I've refused them access to the books."

Angus grunted, but remained silent. She envisioned him making notes. "I'll fax you a copy of the request and my response." Jenny motioned to Queenie who was hovering in the doorway, and she went off to find the file.

"Fred is right, there's profit in the company. But we haven't had a year-end yet. I don't know how the year will finally shake out, and I don't see how she can force me to declare dividends before I'm ready."

Angus mumbled something. "Just a minute," he said before the phone was muffled for a minute. "Sorry." He was back. "No, she can't force a declaration of dividends. Even at year-end, if you have reason to think the profit is extraordinary and there'll be expenses against it, you don't have to pay them out. Well, I'll do up a response. Come see me Friday so I can confirm with you. We'll be in court in two weeks, short notice and all that. Talk to you soon."

Jenny punched the intercom button and rang Dave's desk. "Guess what? We have proof that Alita knows about the money and it's making her nervous. She wants access. Do we have two people working together to get the money out, or are Bernie and Alita working separately? Do they each know what the other one is doing?"

~*~*~*~

The next day Jenny looked with loathing at the letter laying on top of the pile of papers on her desk. She felt like there was an adder loose in her office and it had just raised its lethal head right in front of her. The letter was from Ms. Kramer, Area Manager, Special Licenses Branch. Ms. Kramer was writing to inform her that her license had been recommended for suspension pending certain actions being taken on behalf of the company.

Jenny re-read the body of the document, then put through a call to the lawyer. "Angus," she wailed, "they're doing it. They're threatening to pull our license unless we give in and hire Adam Schwartz! I don't believe it. It will be an unmitigated disaster if we have to take him on." She was in a dither, marching around her desk as she shrieked into the phone. The cord tangled until she was forced to bend over from the other side of her desk to keep the receiver to her ear.

Angus asked her to read him the letter.

"They say they'll suspend our license if we don't do a list of things, and they've given us four weeks to comply. They want us to satisfy the Branch that we've acted responsibly with any profits. They say that's in response to a complaint from a shareholder. They want us to withdraw from the investigations area until we can show we have the other departments of our business under control. And most importantly they want us to hire someone of their recommendation who has more experience than the present CEO.

"In other words they want to take over the business. I know of people with *no* experience who have gotten licenses and opened their own security business. And for them to try to delve into the books, it's outrageous. They can't do that unless they suspect some kind of fraud, and then it's the police who look into it.

"They also want to get rid of Dave Powers, if they want us to shut down his department. Maybe with his police background, he'd get in the way of what their appointee wants to do. And I don't have to hold my breath to figure out who their recommended person is going to be. Bernie Olsinger has all but ordered me to hire that slime ball, Adam Schwartz. I want to fight this tooth and nail. Till the last dollar is drained from the bank."

Angus laughed. She looked at the phone in amazement, then put it back to her head. "What are you laughing at? My business is going down the tubes!"

"It's okay, Jenny," he managed. "I know how serious this is. But it's too ludicrous to be upheld in any court of law. I read the regulations when their first letter arrived, and spoke to a friend who's handled a couple of administrative hearings when a license has been threatened. And they need good solid grounds to suspend you.

"Not only that, they don't have any administrative power to tell you what you have to do with regard to profit. Shareholders have their own remedies. Just calm down. Fax me the letter and I'll respond. I'll send you a copy before I send it, then we'll fire off the first salvo. Okay? But you have to admit, there's something very strange about all this. If you know what's behind it, maybe you should come and talk to me. I might be able to save you more trouble or head off further interference."

"Just do up a letter to stop them. Thanks, Angus. I feel a little better now." Jenny slammed down the phone, then marched into the back room. "Dave," she called. "Things are definitely heating up. There's no doubt Bernie and Alita are working together. Time for another summit meeting."

~*~*~*~

As Jenny shoved a hanger haphazardly into the sleeve of her coat, she looked around her house for signs of Jordie. She hadn't seen his truck outside, but sometimes he got one of his manager's to drop him off. She'd used her own car today but was used to having him there when she got home. Her face flushed as she thought of how they'd spent the last two nights. She'd been lucky to get any supper, but the alternative had been infinitely more appetizing, and certainly more satisfying.

She thought of his hands, those big hands caressing her skin. God, he liked to do that, and she just wilted when he started in on her. Her legs went weak and her heart set on fire, her mouth dry. Until he began to kiss her. Then…

The cat strolled down the hall toward her, curling his furry body around Jenny's leg and purring contentedly. "So, Gutsy, you're glad I'm home. Well, I am too. These days at work are so long. Come here, baby. I think you've been neglected the last few nights." She leaned down and picked up the little beast, rubbing his ears and smoothing his glossy black and white coat. Her hand quickly stilled as she picked up the sound of footsteps thundering up the stairs from the basement. The cat turned her head toward the noise, purring louder.

"Hi, Mum! Are you home?"

Jenny paused. "Rob? Robbie? Is that you?" She ran into the long-armed embrace of her son. "Rob! Why didn't you tell me you were coming? How did you get into the house? You look wonderful!" Her glad eyes drank in his tall lanky frame. He was leaner than when he'd started out on his journey. Well, she'd fatten him up. He was taller too. Maybe he'd grown a bit while he was away, or maybe it was his new leanness. He seemed to have put on a bit of muscle in his shoulders and arms. And his face was different. Older, more confident. His eyes returned her gaze, a little smile crinkling the corners. His mouth had a new firmness about it, a determination and assurance that hadn't been there before. He'd grown up. Her boy had become a man.

Jenny laughed and hugged him, ruffling his hair, long and shaggy at the back. "You've grown, Rob. It suits you." She let her pride and happiness beam from her face. "I'm so glad you're home. How I've missed you! You look like you filled out a little."

He flexed his arms, displaying his new form for her appreciative gaze. "Yeah, I had work in Germany for a month or so," he said as he dropped his pose and took the cat gently from her arms. "Swamper on a truck. Then in Spain I worked on a farm for a couple of months. Plus, some odd jobs here and there. It's easier to do manual labour when you don't have a work visa. They feed you and pay you a few dollars in cash. It helps out and it helps the farmer." He rubbed the cat's ears and held him against his chest. "How are you, Gutsy? Did you miss me? Hey Mum, what's for dinner? I'm starved."

"Well, come into the kitchen and we'll see what there is. How did you get into the house? I didn't leave it unlocked, did I? Jordie will kill me. He's my bodyguard these days." Jenny opened the fridge and peered into the interior dubiously. She hadn't expected to have to feed anyone but Gutsy tonight. Jordie always looked after dinner. *Always?* She laughed to herself as heat swept her body. *How had a few nights turned into always?*

Robbie perched on the counter, still holding the cat. "Jordie let me in, he came home at lunch. I was lying on the back lawn having a snooze. He came over and demanded to know what I was doing loitering on private property. Then he recognized me. He said to tell you he'd be late getting back tonight. What's going on, anyway?"

Jenny startled guiltily, nearly smacking her head as she pulled out of the fridge to search his face for clues as to how much he might know.

"He said he'd been keeping an eye on things, and that it would be good to have me here to help out. Is there suddenly a crime problem in the neighbourhood, or what?"

Jenny felt silly and juvenile, but tried not to show her relief at his comment. *Apparently he wasn't referring to what was going on between her and Jordie, at least not yet.* She proceeded to fill him in on events at the office, without being too specific about details of Norman's attack or the huge amount of money sitting in the company bank account. Telling him of Frank's death was the hardest, and Jenny shed a few tears as she told the story. Robbie looked shocked and even more amazed by the fact that Frank had left his mother shares in the company.

Meanwhile she found a package of frozen pork chops in the freezer and put them in the microwave to thaw. Rob put some of his old music on, then started cutting up vegetables and ripping lettuce for a salad. He offered to mix up a batch of biscuits. Jenny hid her amazement and readily agreed. This was a new Robbie. He'd always been pretty good about helping out in the kitchen when asked, but Jenny had to spell out in detail everything she wanted done. He had never actually offered to cook anything before.

They worked happily together, pausing to gossip or laugh. Jenny found herself touching him often, on the back, on the shoulder, mussing his hair, just to reassure herself that he was actually there. She hugged him at one point and he stopped setting the table to turn around and hug her back. "Oh, Mum. I had a grand time, I really did. But it's so good to be home. I found all my old things down there in my room, my drum set still sitting in the corner. My car collection on the shelves. All my books, my clothes. They aren't even that dusty. You must have looked after it all for me. I'm glad to get the clothes. The ones I brought back with me are pretty worn."

"Well, I had the feeling that you might be back in the next month or two, so I went down and tidied up a little." She grinned. It had been fun dusting off his books. He had always been an avid reader. Sorting out the drums and sticks, putting clean sheets on the bed just in case. She'd spruced up the bathroom, fresh shower curtain, towels and soap.

"Grab the biscuits, I think they're ready. Do they ever smell good. I'll get the salad. The pork chops are under that lid on the stove." Jenny bustled about and got them seated at the table. Applesauce, salt and pepper, fresh butter and glasses of milk appeared on the table. Jenny said grace, holding Robbie's hand in hers and giving heartfelt thanks for her son's safe return. She had tears in her eyes as she began to eat, and smiled at Robbie through the misty haze.

"Ah, tears. You do cry more, don't you? You told me that in Paris, and I couldn't believe how different you were."

Jenny laughed and sniffed. "Yes, it's great. But a lot has happened since we saw each other. It's so strange to be going to work, knowing that Frank isn't there. I could bounce ideas off him, I need someone like that. Queenie and the whole crew are still there. They all stayed on. And Dave's pretty good, you haven't met him. We took him on just before I left for Greece. He's ex-police, a former detective. He runs our investigations department." Jenny told him about the threat to their security license and a few details about the lawsuits launched by Alita.

Robbie ate in silence, listening, glancing up between bites. "That's amazing, Mum. It sounds like things have just gone crazy since Frank died. You're fighting off attacks from all sides. Maybe I can help somehow. I don't know what, but surely I can do something. I was going to start looking for a job Monday, but that can wait. I still have a bit of money in the bank for emergencies."

Jenny stopped chewing and focused on his bearded face for an instant. "I was just going to ask you what your plans were. That's not such a bad idea. No one knows what you look like now, especially with the beard. Maybe Dave or Esley can use you in surveillance. Let me work on it."

She smiled to herself as Rob served the rest of the food onto his own plate. At her last count he'd had four pork chops, five biscuits, and two heaping plates of salad. She mentally scanned the contents of her cupboards for desert and snacks for later. She was probably going to be all right for the moment but would definitely have to hit the grocery store in a big way before tomorrow night.

"Maggie's coming home Tuesday, Rob. I'm picking her up at the ferry. She'll have a load of stuff with her so I'm borrowing Jordie's van. This will be wonderful, to have you both here at the same time. We missed you at Christmas. The house was full of people, so we weren't lonely, but we still missed you."

"Little Mags is coming home. I can't wait to see her. Do you know, it'll be nine months since I've laid eyes on her? I won't shave my beard. She'll be surprised! Don't tell her I'm home and I'll come out to the ferry with you to pick her up."

Jordie knocked on the glass doors of the dining room, and Rob rose to open the door for him. "Hi, Jordie. Come on in. I guess you're going to let me stay, now that Mum has given her okay to it. You were a little hot there, this afternoon." He grinned.

Jordie laughed and his face flushed. "Yeah, well. Just watch yourself."

Jenny snickered. "I hear you tried to run the bum off the property."

"Yeah, young ruffian. Laying about, sleeping in the sunshine, backpack all banged up. He looked like he'd been on the road for a while, and I couldn't figure out what he was doing here on this dead-end street stretched out on your lawn." He gave Rob a fond look, but his expression was desperate when he turned back to gaze at Jenny.

CHAPTER THIRTY FIVE

Jenny went to change and the two men meandered into the kitchen. Rob began to stack the dishes in the dishwasher as Jordie cleared the table.

"Gee, you're a handy guy to have around," Rob said. "You're helping out with the dishes and you didn't even eat the food.'

Jordie began filling the sink to wash the pots and pans. "I don't mind doing dishes, Jenny's always wiped when she gets home. She's under a lot of stress right now, Rob. Anything you can do to help would be appreciated."

Rob looked serious. "Mum told me some of it. What's behind all this? It sounds really strange. I mean, Mrs. Jensen is probably mad that her husband left Mum enough shares to control the company, but the way to deal with that would be to challenge the will, wouldn't it?"

Jordie turned, his wet hands wrapped in a tea towel. "I'm sure they've explored all avenues. They did challenge the will and that failed. They can't get control of the company back. What they can do is harass her, and they're certainly doing that."

There was silence. Jordie studied the young man. It was apparent Jenny hadn't told him about the money. This was her decision. She'd tell him what she wanted him to know and decide when, if ever, he should be told the rest. But Jordie was determined that her son should know there was a physical danger. Rob was a grown man, he could be a big help in keeping Jenny safe, if he was forewarned.

"There are other concerns, Rob," Jordie proceeded carefully. "Your mother was physically attacked a month ago. I don't know if she mentioned it."

Rob nodded, then shook his head, his face intent.

Jordie continued. "A man attacked her while she was out walking. It was dark, and she couldn't see him, but she's sure of who it was. She was able to identify him for the police. Did she tell you any of this?"

The younger man shook his head, his face pale.

Jordie put his hand on Rob's shoulder and lowered his voice. "Well, you need to know. She's trying to protect her children by keeping this to herself, but you're a man now, and she needs your protection. So listen up."

His face felt like it had turned to stone as he continued. "She can't go out alone. Period. I see her to work in the morning and usually pick her up but Brad dropped her off tonight. I carry my cell phone with me so she can call anytime. But especially at night, she can't go out alone. If she wants to go for a walk, go with her. If she wants to visit friends or see a movie, take her there. Her car is right outside. I'm totally serious…"

Jenny rounded the corner and stopped in her tracks when she saw the two of them, heads huddled together in front of the sink. She'd changed into a jade green shirt with a pair of blue palazzo pants, her hair tied back with a scarf.

"Gee, Mum," Rob blurted, "you look so pretty."

She looked totally disarmed, and colour stole up her face. Her smile was tender. "Thank you, Rob, that's sweet."

His colour matched her own.

Jordie grinned, realizing Rob had successfully turned her attention from the conversation they'd been having. His grin slowly faded. She did look lovely, completely desirable. And he read in her eyes that he'd be sleeping in his own bed tonight.

~*~*~*~

"Dave, I think I've solved one problem. Who to trail Norman when he gets back."

"Who did you have in mind, Jenny?" Dave's attention was deep in the files in front of him, and he didn't look up.

"Robbie."

Dave looked up. "Who's Robbie?"

"My son, he just arrived home from Europe. He's been gone since last fall, and before that he was off at university for two years. Norman wouldn't know him if he tripped over him. He's grown a beard, his hair is long. You'd have to give him some training, but he's a natural. And most important, we can trust him."

Dave gave her his full attention. "Okay. I like that. He's a stranger who knows all the characters in this scenario. Actually, I'll come over to your place tonight, if that's convenient. I'll bring Esley and we'll set up a schedule. Esley is out watching the airport and Brad is taking over this evening."

~*~*~*~

The next day at the ferry terminal, Jenny pointed. "There she is, in the red shirt. Doesn't she look good?"

"She looks great. Let's go."

Maggie had reached the luggage rack at the ferry dock. As she glanced through the boxes and bags tumbling on the rotating conveyor belt, she began to pull pieces off and stack them behind her. She was struggling with a large box, when a tall young man with a heavy beard reached past her and grabbed the rope wrapped around it. "Here, let me help, Mags," he said.

She pulled back as if she'd been stung. "Pardon, what did... Rob? Robbie!" He grinned and opened his arms and she flew into them, squealing as she wrapped her own arms tightly around him, "You're here! I can't believe it. Oh, this is so great. Where's Mum?"

"I'm right behind you, Maggie. Doesn't he look good? He's been home three days, and I've been dying to tell you but he wouldn't let me. He wanted to surprise you." Jenny laughed and was engulfed in a group hug.

"Better pay attention here, or your luggage will go missing." Jenny pulled them back to the moment, realizing they were blocking the baggage belt. She looked around to see the grinning faces of other passengers patiently waiting. She pulled her children out of the traffic flow. "Show Rob which ones are yours, Maggie, so he can pull them off."

"Oh, Mum, guess what?" Maggie carried on before Jenny could answer. "I've brought Horsey back with me, Horsey, come and say hi to Mum. And you remember my brother. Robbie. Remember Horsey, in Nelson? He used to go swimming with us."

"I remember." Rob's hand shot out in greeting. "You were in the same year as Maggie at school. I might even have recognized you, actually." Rob and Jenny looked the young man over, trying to visualize the old Horsey they'd known years before. He was medium height, shorter than Rob and heavier built, with muscular shoulders and arms. His hands were large and capable, Jenny noticed as she took one in hers, and calloused. He had done some hard work in his young life.

She smiled into a pair of shy gray eyes surrounded by thick short lashes. She remembered those eyes. He had always had a disconcertingly direct stare for a youngster. And the expression had seemed to say, *I know you mean well, but I don't expect you to do what you say you will. Life has taught me to watch out for myself.*

Now something of the same expression was there, but the vulnerability was better hidden. He was eager but guarded. "I know Maggie didn't warn you in advance that I was coming over here, Mrs. MacDougall. I hope this isn't too much trouble. But I'll only be staying one night. I have to get back to the Kootenays. There may be a job waiting for me there. But Maggie said you wouldn't mind." His eyes watched carefully.

Jenny hung onto his calloused hand. "Welcome, Horsey. Call me Jenny. I'm not your teacher any more. I'm thrilled that Maggie brought you. I told her to bring you over to spend some time with us when she could." Maggie and Rob had begun pulling boxes and suitcases off the belt and piling them in a stack.

"You're welcome to stay as long as you want. We have room and the house has been empty for ages. How's your aunt? Maggie said you lived with her after we left Nelson."

He smiled shyly. "Auntie Emma is fine. She'll be seventy-four this summer. But her health is good."

They bundled the luggage into the back of the van. Rob drove with Horsey up front and Jenny sat in back with Maggie to catch up on news while they headed for home.

"I hope you don't mind, Mum," Maggie began, her voice lowered. "But Horsey was going home to an empty house and no job. His aunt has gone down to the States to nurse her sister who had a heart attack. So I just brought him along for a few days. He'd been talking about meeting you again, so I knew he'd want to come. He didn't decide until this morning and by then you'd already left the house. You know I can't get any cell phone reception on the ferry."

"That's fine, Maggie. And I think it's very thoughtful of you. He should fit in quite well. He's the same age as Rob, I think."

"A year older," Maggie inserted.

"Right. And they can share the basement. Who knows? Maybe he'll find a job out here for the summer. I wouldn't mind him staying, as long as everybody pitches in."

CHAPTER THIRTY SIX

D ave stopped at Jenny's office door. "Rob's doing well, by the way. He's a natural. We can certainly use him for the summer. Now we just need to find someone to keep an eye on Bernie Olsinger. Someone Bernie won't recognize."

She nodded. "I think I've solved that problem too. This guy is new to town, never been here before. And we can trust him."

Dave had a quizzical look on his face. "Who did you have in mind?"

"A man named Horsey."

Dave's expression became more curious. "Horsey?"

"Well, I'm sure he has another name. He used to be in my class when I taught elementary school in Nelson."

"You were a school teacher?" Dave came through the doorway and sat down, crossing his legs.

"For a few years. Anyway, Horsey is perfect for the job. And very trustworthy."

Dave's mouth puckered in an attempt not to smile. "You think because you taught this boy in elementary school that he'd like to come here and do surveillance work for us?"

"He's already here, living at my house. And he's very attached to me. Thinks I helped him out when he was a kid. I'm sure he'd be willing, and he's very clever."

Dave did smile then. "So that makes two. How many people do you have living at your house now? Last time I was there you lived alone."

"Well, there are four of us now. Maggie's home, as well. And I think we can use her, too."

Dave laughed out loud. "How can we use Maggie? She can tackle Adam Schwartz, trail him around for a while?"

Jenny grinned. "Don't get flippant, Mr. Powers. I think Maggie would be a big help over the summer. It would free Brad up for more demanding jobs that you and I both load on him. She could also interview Alex Martin the Deputy Minister. Martin is Bernie Olsinger's boss, and I think we need to know more about him. Maybe he'll be able to help us reign Bernie in.

"She could pretend to be a student reporter from the university newspaper. That way she could record the conversation without him getting suspicious. Martin likes publicity, and he loves beautiful women. She could ask specific questions about how security licenses are handled, and who gets them, how they're reviewed. All cushioned in a more general context, of course. All the information we need to fight this license suspension they're threatening us with. And we'd have him on tape."

Dave's mouth dropped open. He promptly closed it and stared at her. "You're right, he likes beautiful women. He wouldn't let go of your hand the night we met him at that

Ministry function. Kept rubbing your fingers and smiling his shark's smile."

Jenny blushed. "Why, Dave Powers. I think you just paid me a compliment. He did have a shark's smile, didn't he?"

~*~*~*~

Jenny sat on the sundeck, poring over the company accounts. Court was next week and she worried about the documents she might be asked to produce. Her hand dragged at the hair on the back of her neck, clenching in a tight fist. How was she going to explain these huge deposits?

She gazed sightlessly out at the ocean as it glittered like a tame pond below. *On the other hand, I'll bet quite a wad of dough that Alita isn't going to question those deposits. She doesn't want to have them explained before a judge. All she wants to do is get her hands on as much of it as she can.*

Besides, what judge would understand a shareholder questioning why there was so much money in the account? Jenny's lips pouted in a frown. Alita was just after money, any way she could get it. The court action was solely to find out how much was there.

She straightened and looked out toward Bird Island. Clouds of gulls flew in complicated maneuvers around the rocky point. Loons waddled vaguely near the water.

She should probably go do some baking. With three young people in the house, food never lasted for more than a day. She could maybe do a marathon session and save a little for when the kids got home this afternoon from their excursion up Island. Jordie would likely eat the rest.

She missed Jordie. She'd thought of sneaking over to his house in the middle of the night, but it was impossible. He'd be furious with her for being outside alone at night.

And anyway, the kids never settled down early enough to contemplate such a move. She always flagged and headed for bed long before they wound down. Oh, the energy of youth!

It had only been a few days since Rob had arrived and although she was thrilled to have a houseful again, it just seemed very bad timing. She'd followed Jordie out onto the sundeck as he left last evening, and he promptly pulled her into the shadows and kissed her senseless. "How long are we going to wait?" he growled. "Until they head back to university for heaven's sake?" His arms were fiercely wrapped around her body, caressing her wherever he could reach as he kissed her throat. "God, Jenny! I've never lived a longer week in my life. What are we going to do?"

She didn't have an answer for him.

Was that his truck? Her head swung around at the sound of a motor, but she didn't see anything in his driveway. It was Saturday, and he always worked on Saturday. Although she could seldom reach him at his store if she phoned. She usually could catch him on the cell in his truck.

Her body was starving for him, her arms seemed so empty and her bed was cold and uninviting. They'd had some hot conversations on the telephone with her in her bedroom and Jordie at his house.

How had she managed all this time without a man? Those years after Bobby left when she felt like her heart was frozen solid and her body had shut down like a dead battery. Now she was so alive, every nerve ending tingled as if it had been shot with an electrical charge.

It was torture to have him come over in the evening to dinner and not be able to walk into his arms. She could see that same hunger in his eyes. Sometimes she thought he didn't even hear what the kids said. They treated him like they always had, good old Jordie next door. They looked to him for help if there was a problem. None of them seemed to notice that Jenny and Jordie were living in a separate world when they were in the same room together, each nerve yearning toward the other, hearing only the words and underlying messages that were subliminally sent.

She shuddered, a delicious ripple of sensation down her spine. She and Jordie would have to find a way to handle this. It was ridiculous. After all, they were both adults and these kids were not kids any more. Rob and Maggie were definitely old enough to understand that their mother had needs. It was just that... Well, it was awkward. She hoped Jordie would be patient.

She went back to the financial sheets spread out on the wooden deck, red ink scribbled here and there in the margins. She'd get Queenie to run off a new set of the accounts for Angus Murdoch to look at on Monday before the hearing.

Jenny heard footsteps echo hollowly on the boards and looked up to see Jordie come around the corner of the house, his jacket slung casually over one shoulder. She smiled up at him, the sun in her eyes doing little to hide the delight shining there. "Hi, stranger. You're back early," she said.

She became aware of movement near the corner, and squinted to see a small figure come out from behind Jordie's long legs. "Who have you got there?" she inquired, putting her cup on the papers to anchor them against the light breeze and rising slowly. "You brought a friend."

Moving into the shadow of the house to shade her eyes from the glare, she saw a small boy, maybe five or six, smiling beguilingly up at her. His body was thin, stick-like arms and legs protruding from his too small tee-shirt and navy shorts.

His hair was a mass of red curls and freckles covered every inch of visible skin.

Jenny laughed and held out her hand. "Hi, I'm Jenny. Who are you?"

"I'm Neal," he said, taking her hand in a firm, if sticky, grip and then hanging on, turning the handshake into a hand holding. "Dad said we'd come to see a friend of his today. Are you his friend? I really like your place." His eyes sought out the chairs without waiting for an answer, and he quickly peeled his hand from hers to settle into a padded lounge, his feet graced with giant grubby runners sticking straight out in front of him. "This is great, Dad. Oh, wow, a hot tub!" He darted off the lounge and around the corner to inspect his new find.

"You can't go in there right now, Neal. Just have a look, first," Jordie called, never taking his eyes off Jenny.

She whirled around to gaze at him with shocked surprise. "Jordie," she whispered, "Dad? What does he mean? Have you adopted a child?" She smiled mistily, but Jordie looked more embarrassed.

He opened his mouth to speak but she continued, "That's wonderful! I mean it, what a sweet boy. He looks just like you did when you were that age. Just like you." Her gaze followed Neal thoughtfully, then raised to meet Jordie's, a troubled look on her face. "Is he yours, Jordie? Why, with that hair, and those freckles, a person would almost think... And the same name as your stepfather..."

Jordie took her hand in his to stop the flow of words. "He's my son."

She felt dizzy. "What does that mean? Just give me a minute." She put her free hand up to her eyes to shield her from his gaze.

"Jenny, he's my natural child." Jordie gently pulled on her hand to get her to look at him. "I didn't know how to tell you, and he was pushing to come over, so I just brought him. I knew you'd know the truth after one good look at him. He's the spitting image of me when I was little."

"Oh, Jordie." Her voice was low. Pulling out of his light grip, she walked unsteadily over to watch Neal lift the lid of the hot tub and peer inside.

"Have you ever been in a hot tub?" she asked.

The little boy dropped the lid and whipped around to face her. "Nope, but I sure would like to. Can I?" His face screwed up with wanting as he looked hopefully at her, his eyes half closed against the sun's glare.

"Not this time, Neal." Jordie's voice cut across the silence. "We'll go over to my house and I'll show you around. You can pick out which room you want to sleep in. He's staying with me for the weekend," Jordie added, his voice slightly defensive in the face of her silence.

Neal leaped to attention and nodded for emphasis at Jordie' remarks. "I'm staying with my Dad for the weekend. He promised."

"Well," said Jenny, drawing a deep breath and looking the little boy over with a practiced eye. "Why don't you get settled in over there, and then come back here for lunch? I'm going to do some baking this afternoon. We've run out of cookies. Maybe you'd like to help me bake them, Neal."

His dark blue eyes gleamed up at her in eager anticipation, and Jenny felt like she'd been transported back to her own days in elementary school, when such a look from Jordie, that dark-eyed excitement of his, would always entice her into an adventure of some kind before the day was over.

As Jenny watched the two walk along the path to the house next door, looking so alike, the small one a miniature version of the bigger, her mind whirled with questions. So Jordie had a son! If he was five, then Jordie had been with his mother six years ago… And possibly ever since. Her heart quaked in her chest at that last thought, her breath coming with difficulty.

Maybe this was the woman Izzy had told her about. *But there was a son?* This affair wasn't finished, then, in fact would never be over. After all, he had visiting rights if Neal was spending the weekend. And he'd certainly stayed involved. *Was this why he disappeared on Saturday?*

CHAPTER THIRTY SEVEN

Jenny felt herself go cold. Would she have to face the possibility that Jordie was involved with another woman, one who had a powerful hold on him in the form of his child? The muscles in her chest squeezed until it hurt to breath. She leaned weakly against the doorjamb. There might not be a future for her in this situation.

The thought brought her up short. *A future?* When had she started thinking she had a future with Jordie? After all these years, they had become lovers. Was there going to be anything more to it than that? And for how long?

Heat washed her cheeks as she remembered how he'd made love to her that first night, a hot quick coupling that left them both awed and wildly hungry for more. He'd held her and caressed her with unspoken tenderness, used such attention and care. *Did he make love like that with Neal's mother? When was the last time?* She cringed, physically nauseated by the thought.

The night she was attacked, he'd helped her remove her clothes as matter-of-factly as if he did it all the time. And he'd dressed her again in the hospital emergency room before he led her out to his truck. Somehow over the weeks and months since Linda left, she'd begun to think it was possible for her to be with him.

And then when they'd made love, she'd begun to imagine... But of course Rob had arrived right away, then Maggie and Horsey, and he'd stopped staying over. There was no apparent need for him to be there, with other people living in the house, and now the possibility that he had another woman who could look after his physical needs...

She felt unexpectedly foolish. Jordie had never said he wanted them to be together, not on any permanent basis. That first time he kissed her in her dining room, a kiss like thunder in her blood. But he'd apologized, gone home and never alluded to it again. In fact, he'd been embarrassed. *Did he feel embarrassed about them making love, as well?*

She turned her head to gaze down the path toward his house. Jordie had always wanted children. He would never give up the opportunity now to keep his son in his life. *Did that mean he'd never give up his child's mother?*

Jenny felt ill. She shook her head in silent agitation, her cheeks hot, her mouth dry. The child's high-pitched voice floated over from next door. And she'd invited them to lunch! Now she had to face Jordie and his son over a meal and cookie-making while she wallowed in her own private hell.

By the time Neal had slurped his last spoonful of soup and eaten his fourth section of grilled cheese sandwich, Jenny felt like her face was frozen into a parody of a smile. Her heart ached for the little guy. She had stopped counting the number of times he said *Dad*, and she guessed at the uncertainty in his little breast that prompted it.

After Bobby had left, her children called her constantly until she thought she'd go crazy. *Mum,* they called, *Mummy, Mother,* like a litany. As young as they were, the absence of one parent had made them over-anxious about the presence of the other. She was sure that having his dad only on weekends, and then maybe not absolutely *every* weekend, had made Neal worry.

She avoided looking at Jordie, but managed to chat with the little boy as he devoured all the food in front of him. Immediately he swallowed the last mouthful, he asked when could they make the cookies.

"Right now, if you want," she said, rising to stack the dishes.

"I'll get them, Jenny."

She looked up, then quickly away. She couldn't read that inscrutable expression in Jordie's shadowed eyes. "Okay." She picked up the milk and took it out to the kitchen to put in the fridge. "Come on, Mr. Baker," she called, "let's see how good you are." Dragging a chair up to the counter for him to stand on, she pulled the heavy mixer forward so Neal could reach. Then she got out her recipe box and began pawing through the cards. "What kind? We can do chocolate chip, oatmeal chocolate chip, peanut butter…"

"Chocolate chip!" Their voices came in unison, and Jenny looked up, laughing, to see two faces looking at her with the same expression in those dark blue eyes, so much alike in their eagerness. Her gaze was riveted on Jordie. He sobered and the look that stole across his face made her breath catch. Vulnerability, pleading and love all seemed to shine from his eyes. *Please accept us. We need you.*

Jenny lowered her gaze and busied herself finding the ingredients as Jordie located some measuring cups. The child was beside himself with excitement. He danced on the chair on his toes, waiting for instructions. With her help he carefully measured the flour, his tongue caught between his teeth as he drew a knife across the top of the cup.

Jordie's eyes met hers above the curly red hair. "Neal was very excited at the idea of spending the weekend with me," he said carefully. "He wasn't able to come before, but now the way is clear for us to spend a little more time together. It's what we both want."

He was quiet for a minute as he helped pour the second cup of flour into the sifter. Then he looked over at Jenny, measuring butter on the other counter. "We want to be like a family, Jenny. Other people have that, and now's our chance. Right, Neal?"

Neal looked up and grinned but quickly went back to his task. He didn't take his eyes off the sifter as he grabbed it by the handle and squeezed, watching the ingredients drift into a bowl.

"Do you understand?" Jordie said.

He reached to steady the child on the chair and she placed her hand reassuringly on his heavy arm. "I understand Jordie. I don't know what I would do without my kids. Believe me, I understand."

He grinned in relief, and walked around to give her a hug. "She understands, Neal. I told you she would." There were tears in his voice as he hid his face in her hair.

"Yikes!" Neal shrieked, and they both turned to see a spoon spinning madly around the bowl, hitting the mixer and flinging butter and sugar onto the counter. They both yelled and grabbed for the control button.

An hour later, they rested on the sundeck drinking coffee and munching cookies. A plate of cookies sat on the edge of the deck, and every now and then a small hand reached up to take one, then disappeared below the boards again. "Here, Gutsy," they heard, "come on, Gutsy. Here kitty."

Jenny leaned close to Jordie's ear. "I don't think Guts likes cookies. He's never developed a taste for them."

Suddenly the cat shot out from under the deck and raced around the side of the house, Neal in hot pursuit. Jordie laughed, his head thrown back against the chair. Jenny looked at him with affection. She hadn't heard him laugh like that for a long time. He'd been very sober, almost grim, since she'd moved back to the Island.

She was pleased for him but also terrified about this new development. She worried it around in her mind for a minute. "What about Neal's mother?" she probed, trying to keep her voice light. "Does she object to you taking Neal for the weekend?"

He shook his head, his face becoming closed. "She's fine with it. She likes him to see me as often as he can."

And do you still see her? The question trembled on the tip of her tongue. But she didn't ask, just sat there watching the gulls wheel in the air above the sand, wondering what it all meant.

"What is it?" His voice was gentle.

"Does his mother know that Linda left?"

He nodded steadily. "Yes, she knows. That's why I'm able to have him for longer. She knows that wasn't possible when I was still with her." His mouth was set in a grim line now as he looked at her with fierce determination.

"So, does she... I mean, will she be coming over too?" Jenny flushed. What was she doing with her questions? Jordie didn't have to explain his life to her, but she couldn't leave it alone. It was like a sore tooth, she kept going back to see if it still hurt as much as the last time she prodded it.

"I imagine so." Jordie looked across the water as he spoke. "She wants Neal to come and she'll be bringing him over from time to time."

Jenny thought she was going to choke on her coffee. She sat there willing the last mouthful to go down, and not get stuck in her throat, or worse, embarrass her by coming back up. Tears popped into her eyes. She told herself it was because of the discomfort in her throat.

Getting up, she walked into the house and hung her head over the sink, willing the muscles in her chest to relax. There were big warm hands on her back. "What is it, Jenny? Let me help." She sobbed then, a huge gasp that struggled to escape the obstruction in her throat.

"I'm sorry. I need that little guy and he needs me. But I need you, too. And I'm deathly afraid that I can't have both, that I'll have to choose. And I can't." His voice broke, and he tightened his arms around her. She felt his chest heave against her back.

"Jenny, tell me I don't have to choose. I love you so much. I always have. And now I have my son. Tell me I don't have to choose between you." Jenny leaned back against him feeling the heavy muscles of his chest heave under his shirt. His big arms were around her, just like the morning she awoke in bed broken and sore from the attack. Jordie had been there looking after her ever since she'd returned to this house.

She had liked to pretend they were just friends, with an attachment that stemmed from the strong bond that formed when they were young. But Jordie looked after her. And she would be lost without it.

"No, Jordie," she said, turning to hug him, her arms locking around his back. "You don't have to choose." She laid her head against his solid chest, listened to his heart beating, and wondered if he wanted to keep his son's mother too.

CHAPTER THIRTY EIGHT

Norman climbed off the crowded hotel courtesy bus in Seattle, moving easily around the other passengers who were stopping at the foot of the steps to pick up their luggage. He already had his, a small carryon bag, and it had never left his hand during the ferry ride from Victoria or while he made his way to the downtown hotel. He walked into SeaTac airport jostling through the crowd as he had done countless times before. He could relax now. He was on familiar territory and he was out of reach of the Canadian authorities.

The Canadian police were busy staking out Alita's house in Victoria. He smirked in satisfaction. Let them wait, those provincial lawmen. It had been ridiculously easy to get back into Victoria, meet with his mother at the house, stay for a couple of days to rest and pick up his luggage.

Alita had been hyper, but she was always that way. She lost her nerve if she got a phone call that was a wrong number. She'd swear it meant the police were tapping their line. She didn't like having him in the house, sure they had the place staked out.

Norman wasn't worried. He'd entered the house by watching from two lots over. When he realized the surveillance team seldom left their vehicles and there was no one at the back, he'd climbed the hill from the next street, pushed through the bushes in the park and dropped easily into their yard. He'd waited until the cars were moving, indicating a change of patrol, before he eased forward and through the basement window.

Alita was worried for him. Mothers were like that, and it couldn't stop a man from doing what he had to do. If she'd done it right the first time they wouldn't be in this fix. He'd be secure within his father's business, not on the outside trying to prove himself and carve a niche in the organization. And she would still be with his father, living well in Panama. Norman wouldn't be stuck in a backwater town, making his living in this cold northern country she'd moved to, married to that dour-faced old man.

She'd been too good for Frank, just as well he was gone. He'd been a liability, asking too many questions, examining all the bills and querying the amounts. Bernie had had to pay him a visit and pull him into line. But even that hadn't worked well. Not the way things had been when they'd had Stouffer to rely on. That had been like clockwork. The glory days, when everything fell into line, like ducks in a shooting gallery.

But all of that was gone. Best to pay attention to the business at hand. He wouldn't come back to Canada, not for a long time, if ever. He hadn't told his mother that. She would have cried and clung, called him her baby. He hated that. He was no baby. He was a man, man enough to work for his father, be accepted as his lieutenant. That's what he was after, that family position. And he was close, so close.

He'd left the house, sneaking out the way he'd sneaked in, after Alita made the contact. She'd gone shopping, buying a few items, then stopping in a change room and picking up the package that had been left there, carrying it out in her shopping bag. Norman packed his case that night, giving Alita a one-armed hug and peck on the cheek as he went.

He walked with a jaunty swagger through the airport, arriving at the Air Mexicana booth. Was the agent familiar? He couldn't remember if he'd seen her here before. "Hi, sweetheart," he grinned. "What have you got going to Mexico today? Doesn't really matter where, although down the west coast is my favourite. Cabo or Mazatlán, maybe Puerto Vallarta."

He always said the same thing. Alita had told him to go low profile, use a different airline every time. But he was too good-looking to go unnoticed, especially by these sex-starved flight and terminal attendants. They were all hot for him, ready to go anywhere with him if he but asked. So his approach was to act like a tourist. Loved the sun, loved Mexico. He'd take a flight to any of the tourist destinations down the west coast. Those airports were always busy, full of feather-brained travellers. Norman could just disappear in the crowd.

"Well, sir. We have one going to Puerto Vallarta at five this afternoon, returning in a week. It's a charter, but there are still a couple of seats available. Would you like me to book you on it?"

Norman flipped out his Canadian passport and a bundle of cash. "Sounds good, what's the damage? It must be on discount, right?" They usually were when he was purchasing a last-minute ticket.

The attendant glanced at his passport and copied the number. "That's right, Mr. Jensen, it's on discount. You're lucky to get such a good price for this flight." She studied the picture a moment too long and then looked back at his face as if for verification. Norman's smile stiffened. He placed his hand on the passport and she reluctantly relinquished it.

Taking his ticket, he sauntered away. He stood near a concrete tower and watched the ticket desk as he pretended to scan a magazine. She seemed to be acting normally, no frantic phone calls were made, so he left and spent the afternoon in the Upper Deck lounge at a table by the window, drinking martinis and watching the planes take off.

He glanced at his watch. Check-in was two hours prior to departure because it was international, but he had no intention of checking in at three o'clock. No point in giving them that long to decide if they should remember something. He paid his bill at quarter after four and walked with a measured stride to the gate. There was a small lineup of hurrying passengers at security and he waited with a calm that belied his inner turmoil. All he really had to do was get on that plane and he was free. They'd be taking off in minutes, too busy to worry about someone like him.

Finally, he placed his bag on its side on the conveyor belt to go through security and dropped his watch, wallet and change into the basin. He added his shoes to the pile and stepped through the detector gate. As he did, the alarm went off. It usually did, and his heart always leaped into his throat. It was probably his belt buckle. Once it had been the metal studs in his jeans. It went off for most men, a security guard had told him. Yet his hands sweat and his heart thumped heavily at the sound.

The guard waved him over to the side, had him remove his sports jacket and passed the wand over his body. "Just your belt, sir," he said courteously. Norman nodded and shrugged back into his coat, checking the inner pocket to make sure everything was in place.

His bag had not come through the camera check yet and he waited impatiently. But still it didn't show. A security supervisor wearing a firearm in a holster pushed through the crowd and moved behind the camera operator as both of them peered into the viewer. They murmured to each other, the supervisor nodded and the bag appeared on the now moving exit belt. Norman reached for the handles at the same time as the armed guard.

"Sorry, sir. We're going to have to ask you to open your bag. Please unzip it right over here." He indicated a table to the side, and ushered Norman with a firm grip on his elbow.

Norman pulled back, trying to think rapidly. "What are you talking about? There's nothing in there but my shaving kit and a change of clothes. Show me what you see on the camera."

"No, sir, sorry. Please bring the bag over here and open it, or I'll have to call backup security. I'm trying to be courteous, sir. If I can just have your cooperation."

Norman nodded, his heart thudding. "Absolutely, of course. Just give me a moment here and I'll be right with you." He could hardly breathe, and his mind seemed to be churning thickly, mired in fear and the need to run. This had never happened before. There was nothing in that case but his overnight things. What was the problem?

That ditzy ticket attendant had recognized him! There must be a warrant out. This was just a ruse, to get him away from the group moving at a steady pace through security. This was a ploy, to pull him aside before they arrested him.

Norman gripped the bag in his left hand and edged around the conveyor belt as if to comply with the guard's request. The guard half turned away to meet him at the table, and he ran. Sprinting through the crowd, he pushed and shoved, knocking a child over. He heard its sudden outraged cry.

There was shouting behind him, a cacophony of confusion and noise. He dashed clear of the crush of passengers and headed down the hallway, running flat out, his heart pounding in his ears, his lungs ragged. All he had to do was get out of sight! He could blend with the crowd, go to a different gate, swipe a ticket to another destination. He'd find a way. He wasn't helpless. The last thing he needed was money. He had lots of that.

The noise receded in his head as he started to feel in control again. Chuckling softly to himself, he reached into his inside jacket pocket with his right hand, fondling his second passport. He laughed out loud. They'd never figure it out.

He felt a sudden tug at his back and then he was slowly falling, as if he was a balloon man and the wind was knocking him over. Well, he'd just get up. But where was his case? He looked around in concern. There it was, just ahead of him, skidding down the rubber-lined walkway. Thank God. He thought he'd lost it. He'd have to be more careful, keep a better grip on the handle.

But he was tired. It wouldn't hurt to rest for a minute. He had plenty of time. There were lots of flights leaving and he could take any one of them, any one he wanted.

CHAPTER THIRTY NINE

The security guard stood over the prone figure lying on the floor of the airport passageway. He was panting heavily, partly from the run and partly from the adrenaline surging through his body. He'd just shot a man. For the first time in his life he'd had to shoot and the guy appeared to be dead.

What choice did he have? There were people everywhere in the terminal hall. He'd shouted for him to stop, pleaded with him to stop and then the runner reached inside his jacket for a weapon. His backup was racing behind him, but he'd already gotten the call from the ticket agent upstairs, and he'd seen what was in that case. It was a gun or he'd turn in his badge. The man had to be stopped.

Security spread out, cordoning off the area and ushering shocked and nervous passengers past the site. Portable screens were erected to hide the scene from view. The medical attendants worked on the man, but it was readily apparent that it was too late.

Airport police arrived and took over, expertly measuring, photographing, drawing diagrams. They searched the man's pockets. He'd been reaching for a Panamanian passport carrying his photo under a different name. When they opened the case, the security guard hovered anxiously. There were overnight things, a change of clothes. He pawed through, looking for the item he's seen on the camera, then held it up. A sideburn trimmer. The guard shook with shock. A sideburn trimmer! One of those little gadgets that were hand held and bought by every kid for Dad on Father's Day. It had showed as a gun-like shape on the camera. And it had cost this man his life. The guard went to the side and quietly vomited.

Police cleared the site and supervised removal of the body, escorting the security guard and other witnesses away for questioning. They had been back in their office for fifteen minutes, answering questions and filling in forms when a junior officer burst into the room. "Guess what, Sergeant. We found a false side in the guy's case. It's lined with metal so nothing in the cavity shows on the security camera if it's laid on its side when it goes on the conveyor belt. And it's loaded with money, cash. Canadian, you know that funny-money they use, all different colours. Mostly fifties and hundreds. Must be more than a quarter million dollars. Good thing we had that tip about a cash ticket for anywhere in Mexico. Wonder what the RCMP have on him?"

~*~*~*~

Dave flopped down on the couch in front of Jenny's desk. "I've just gotten an update from my friend in the police. Alita's talking alright, but not about Sentinel Security. She denies any knowledge of cash in our bank accounts. Says as far as she knows it's all legal. But what she *is* talking about is Stouffer and a couple of other companies in Vancouver, as well as suitcases of money leaving with Norman for Mexico every couple of weeks. She knew he was involved in money laundering and that it involved Olsinger. Can you believe she's turning Bernie in? I think she blames him for her son's death. So if she's going to go down, so is he."

When the Police Chief arrived at the Sentinel offices the next afternoon, they crowded into the back room to listen to what he had to say. "This is all off the record," were his first words. Jenny winced. She knew she'd never get anything out of him that was *on the record*, but she was anxious to hear anyway.

"Alita admits being involved with Norman only in the sense that she took phone calls for him. So she was aware of what was going on, but not directly involved. We think her goal is to nail Olsinger, so she has to admit to knowledge in order to have evidence that would convict him. She says Bernie gave Norman his orders and funnelled the money to him."

Jenny gave a gasp.

The Police Chief glanced at her. "That's right. At any rate, Stouffer was involved and didn't choose to be suspicious, so Norman didn't have to work very hard at using different fictitious agencies to bill him. That seems to be why the Ministry interfered when Stouffer came under investigation. This was Bernie's domain, and he insisted he was doing an internal investigation. He managed to stop the police action, telling his superiors he was doing his own very sensitive look at several security companies and didn't want any interference with the evidence. But when nothing came of it and the story hit the newspaper, Bernie had to come out as the guy who'd clean up the industry. His own boss was looking at him and he had no choice but to shut Stouffer down. Alex Martin, the Deputy Attorney General, demanded it."

"And Martin is nothing if not a politician when it comes to these things," Jenny inserted. "He's always landing on the right side of public opinion."

Dave said, "You're right. Martin takes the hard line whenever something from his ministry comes up in the press looking less than respectable. But we've never seen the report of the investigation, have we? The commission that Martin headed never saw the light of day."

The Police Chief clamped his lips shut on that comment, but added, "Alita says Bernie had a boss, so we think the threat to you may not be over. Even though Olsinger is under arrest, we recommend you continue with personal safety measures, Mrs. MacDougall. We'll make an officer available to help with that. Then there's this."

The Chief pulled a court order out of his inside breast pocket and laid it on the desk in front of Jenny. "We served it on your bank this morning, freezing the funds in your account, as there's evidence to suggest that they may come from illegal activity."

"You can't do that!" Jenny gripped the arms of her chair. "We haven't broken the law. You've just signed the death warrant of Sentinel Security Group if you cut us off from access to our bank account." Her face was hot, but there was a clammy sensation in her palms. Alarm bells rang in her head. She hadn't fought tooth and nail with Alita only to lose it to some over-assiduous police bungling.

The Chief nodded. "I'd be happy to sit down with you and your accountant to decide what portion of the account should be frozen. We want to be reasonable. You've certainly worked with us and our intention is not to cripple the business, simply to seize proceeds from organized crime. But for the moment the account is frozen."

Jenny glowered. "We haven't just cooperated with you, Chief. We've *given* you this investigation. We've cracked the case and practically delivered all the evidence, other than Alita's statements. We deserve better than this. We're already hurting. This could kill us."

Her jaw was rigid and Dave recognized the glint in her eyes. His gaze swivelled to the Police Chief to see how he was going to take the verbal lashing he was confident Jenny was about to deliver.

"I expect to be back in front of this Justice," Jenny gestured at the warrant, "tomorrow morning and I want you to meet me there in full cooperation. I don't mind transferring money out of the company account into another account that can remain frozen pending trial. But you can't get away with freezing my whole account."

The Chief cleared his throat and nodded, his neck red above the tight collar. "Fine. Well, we can certainly, uh, cooperate in, uh, whatever way..." He paused, his gaze flickered sideways. "Well, that about wraps it up. We'll keep you informed as things move along. I fully expect Alita will cut a deal with the Crown in exchange for evidence against Olsinger. But that remains to be seen."

"What about Frank's death, Chief?" Jenny had calmed, the high colour receding from her face to leave her skin pale. "Are you going to re-open that case?" Her voice choked.

The Chief nodded. "We'll certainly look into it, Mrs. MacDougall."

Discussions between Jenny, her accountant and the staff sergeant resulted in an agreed order the next day in court. Jenny transferred five hundred thousand dollars into a separate account which was then frozen pending the outcome of police investigations. She asked that it be deposited into treasury bills. If some of that money was coming back to Sentinel, she wanted interest attached.

Dave laughed. He didn't see any of that money coming back. In fact, he was astonished that she'd been able to keep the total that low. "I thought it was closer to seven hundred thousand," he commented.

"No," said Jenny, her expression innocent. "The rest can be accounted for in increased activity in the company, partly because of the new Investigations Branch that you've headed up."

Dave grinned.

CHAPTER FORTY

Jenny's heart leaped at the sight of Jordie in her office. "What are you doing here in the middle of the day? Have you got time for lunch?" She leaned back in her chair, smiling as a warm tingling started in her belly.

He closed the door. "I have to admit I'm hungry." When he advanced purposefully, skirting around her desk, his face sported a grin.

"Jordie?"

Seizing her wrist, he pulled her out of the chair and wrapped an arm around her waist. His other hand brushed the hair away from her cheek. Then his mouth was on hers in a slow languorous kiss that successfully removed her smile and slammed her eyes shut. When he lifted his head sometime later, she remained immobile.

"Jordie?" she murmured.

"That's me. And yes I have time to eat, but I don't know if it'll be lunch. Queenie tells me you don't have another appointment till three o'clock. So I'm taking you home. To my house." Her eyes popped open, the green glinting in a wide-eyed look.

"You are?"

"Yes. This situation has gone on long enough." One hand came around to cup her chin and his tone said he would brook no argument. "I can't hold out any longer. I know you don't want me to push things at home with your kids, and I'm willing to give it time, but..." His fingers worked their way down her blouse, undoing buttons as he went. When they found her nipple and began to work that little button, he was suddenly even more persuasive.

"Are you ready to come, or do I have to carry you out of here over my shoulder? I don't mind doing that. If your legs are as weak as mine feel, you might need a little assistance." His voice vibrated with humour but his eyes were intense.

"Why, Jordie. I do think this macho disguise suits you. I can't imagine what took so long. I was beginning to think I'd have to take things into my own hands..."

He shut her up with his mouth.

~*~*~*~

"Call from Fred Austin, Jenny. Can you take it?" Later that afternoon, Queenie poked her head around the corner of Jenny's door, then gave her a wide grin. Dave and Esley looked across the paper strewn table as Jenny hesitated in surprise, then blushed frantically at Queenie's look. Damn her, although Jenny knew she'd come back to the office looking much more relaxed than when she'd left. Irritably she reached behind her for the telephone. Was there no privacy in this world?

"Hi, Fred," she said. "What can I do for you?"

"Hello, Mrs. MacDougall." Austin's voice sounded reedy through the connection. "How are you?"

"I'm fine, thank you." She raised her brows at the men and punched the speaker button.

"Well, that's good. Listen, as you know I still act for Alita Jensen. Not in criminal matters, of course," he added in hasty disclaimer, "but in her business interests. She's asked me to contact you and request a meeting. There are some matters outstanding that could, perhaps, be ironed out."

"A meeting with Alita? I thought she was in jail." Jenny was sure she heard him wince on the other end. Esley smirked. "Didn't she make a deal with the Crown," Jenny went on, "in exchange for her testimony against Bernie?"

Within days the police had laid charges against him, much to Jenny's relief. Alita had been promised immunity to some charges and the recommendation to the judge of a lenient sentence on more minor ones.

"Yes, she did, as you well know." he barked. "However, she's asked me to meet with you to sort out some business issues. Are you able to come to my office sometime this week?"

"I'm not able to come to your office at all, Fred," she snapped back. Flushed with indignation, she tried to reign in her temper. She really had to get a handle on her hair trigger responses. Except with Jordie, of course...

"However," she continued more calmly, "if you want to see me here in my office I could free up some time on Friday, or else we're looking at one day next week."

Esley hid a smile behind the bristle of his moustache. She didn't feel like cooperating but it was, after all, better to see what he and Alita were up to. She'd just cooperate on her own terms.

"Very well." Austin's voice had become acerbic. "I'll be there at eleven, Friday." He rang off.

"Fred wants a pow-wow," Dave said.

Jenny nodded. "I wondered when he'd come calling," she said. "Probably looking to set himself up to represent Alita's shares. Which means I'll have him dogging my trail and questioning every decision I make from now till Doomsday." She looked gloomily down at her paper, doodling squiggles into the corner of the sheet.

"Maybe not," Dave interjected. "She might just need cash. I heard this morning that she got more of a sentence than she counted on. It's my bet that she'll want to appeal. That costs money. Maybe she wants an advance on dividends. You might be able to buy some of her shares in exchange for a chunk of change."

~*~*~*~

When Fred arrived Friday he hemmed and hawed until Jenny lost her temper and told him she had exactly fifteen minutes before she went on to her next appointment. He flushed angrily but finally got down to the business that had brought him to her office.

"Alita's interested in raising funds for her appeal," he stated flatly. "She wants to have dividends declared early."

"I'm not declaring them early," said Jenny in an identically flat tone.

Fred squirmed. "When will you be declaring them? Your year-end comes up in another month."

"I realize that," said Jenny.

"Then, what are your plans for the dividends?"

Jenny gave him a level look and let her breath out in a gust. "Fred, I don't have to give this information to you now. But I'm going to take pity on Alita. Five hundred thousand was removed from the corporate account by the Attorney General and is being held pending a police investigation.

They think it's traceable to the proceeds of crime. So we're unlikely to get it back."

Fred boggled. "How did they decide that? Alita didn't give evidence that would tie this company or any of its assets to crime."

"No, Fred, but the police aren't as stupid as she seems to think. A similar thing happened with Stouffer's company. It's just a matter of time before they turn up evidence that will link that money to the laundering scheme."

He nodded, making notes in a small book.

"So, there isn't as much money as Alita thinks," Jenny continued. "The balance of earnings for the year looks alright. I'm not going to declare it as dividends for several reasons. One, we may have to defend ourselves against criminal or civil charges. Frank was the majority shareholder and CEO. So anything he did, whether wittingly or not, leaves the company liable.

"Two, we have just begun the start-up of an investigations department. It's costing us, and will continue to cost us in the next year or two. Vehicles have become a major expense, along with cell phones and laptops.

"Three," and she ticked them off on her fingers, "I want a reserve for uncertainties. Things such as fighting off attacks on our license, keeping in mind that our managers haven't had a raise in more than two years. There's also the matter of three or four legal challenges from shareholders that we've had to defend." She gave him a look that should have curled his hair. "So there's not much left to provide for dividends."

She had Fred's attention. He'd been listening intently and writing furiously in his book, but at her last comment he looked up with his mouth open, ready to protest. She forestalled him with her hand.

"Year-end is about a month away, and then we're allowed three months to get the books in shape. I'll declare any dividends at that time."

There was silence, disturbed only by the scratch of Fred's pen. He finally lifted his head and they gazed at each other. Finally, Jenny wriggled and looked away. "Well I suppose I could float a loan to Alita of fifty thousand, to be paid back at the time of dividend disbursement. But I'd rather not. I'd rather use that money to buy some of her shares." Jenny folded her hands in her lap. *Let him take that back and see how it went down.*

Then she shifted slightly, and relented again. "I could probably give her a further loan against next year's earnings, Fred, if she really needs it. I'd have to think about it, but it's possible. I would imagine, though, that she has other assets Frank left her that she could liquidate. Surely she doesn't need to rely solely on this company to fund her appeal."

Fred ignored her for a moment, finished his notes and stood up. He gave her a measuring look. "How much do you think the company is worth?" he said.

Jenny's mouth opened in surprise, then closed. "I'd have to have an appraisal done," she finally said. "Is Alita interested in selling?" She tried not to sound too eager.

Fred turned and left. Jenny sat in astonishment, staring after his retreating back. What an extraordinary meeting. He simply left. Not "Good-bye. Thank you for your time." Nothing. And left her with that parting shot. *How much do you think the company is worth?*

Jenny's mind whirled. She pulled the phone forward and dialled her accountant. "Who do you know that does business valuations? I'll probably want two independent numbers, but I want to start with the best person in town. And now, not tomorrow."

CHAPTER FORTY ONE

Jenny negotiated with Fred, who pursued every dime and nickel until she threw up her hands in total frustration and told him she would not speak with him again for a month so he could get some perspective. They settled within minutes and Jenny signed an offer to purchase Alita's shares.

"Minus fifty thousand for what she's cost us because of her activities," Jenny insisted. Alita had cost the company plenty and Jenny was not going to swallow it all herself. She visited Frank's wife in jail to discuss the final details.

Alita was housed in the federal women's jail in Vancouver. She looked thin and slightly disheveled, all the more noticeable because of her formerly impeccable appearance. The prison clothes hung shapelessly on her slight frame. Her hair was growing out at the roots and she self-consciously passed her hand over it several times when Jenny first sat down.

"Alita, surely someone can get you supplies here. Things like makeup and hair colour. What's Fred thinking of?"

Alita flushed and raised her chin haughtily. "I don't think that's the role of a lawyer."

"Well, it's certainly his job to look after you. There must be a service for that. Don't you have anyone to do these things?"

Tears sprang to the woman's eyes, and Jenny found herself in the incongruous position of sitting with her arms around her, offering comfort to the same woman who'd hated her for the last four years. "There was only Norman," Alita sobbed, "and now I don't even have him." She cried in a piteous wail, and Jenny held her tighter, smoothing the fine hair back from her unlined face.

"I can only imagine," she said. "If I lost one of my children, I think it might kill me."

Alita nodded and leaned on her. "I did it all for him," she said softly. "Everything. He was so unhappy when I left his father. He was always trying to prove himself. And he needed money. So I helped him, the best I could. Now I see it was the need for money that killed him." She fell silent and finally pulled away from Jenny's arms, but stayed beside her on the bench. She wiped at her eyes with the backs of her hands. Jenny handed her a tissue.

"Frank didn't know. He didn't know the money was illegal and that it was being laundered. He'd done the same thing many times before. A company would close down, and some of the security people would come to him bringing clients. Frank would book the service and get paid a fee, usually a percentage. He did it more as a service than anything else. Sometimes he knew the guard and wanted to help him out. Sometimes it was Bernie who wanted a favour. The security guys needed an office to take the phone calls and they didn't mind paying Frank for that."

She was quiet for a moment then looked deep into Jenny's eyes, her own unnaturally bright. "I made him do it. He was a kind man, and an honest one. He began to get suspicious about the money that was piling up, and the invoices coming in. He'd come home and grumble that he didn't know who these people were. But it was usually a favour for Bernie. If he started getting stubborn, I'd call Bernie. We were stuck, you see. Norman needed cash flow, and so did Bernie. And I was in between. I had to look after Norman and I was the key to Frank."

Her eyes turned crafty as she focused on the window. "Bernie always made it very clear, that if we couldn't rely on Frank for a certain amount of put-through, then he couldn't use Norman. He was going to drop him like a hot brick. And I couldn't let that happen."

Alita seemed in her own world now. She'd obviously turned this over and over in her mind. She spoke carefully as if trying to justify exactly why each step she took had been absolutely necessary.

"The real problems began when Stouffer shut down. He was a big part of the deal and he'd cooperated. There were others, but they were small operations in comparison. You see, Norman wanted to get in good with his father. He needed to prove he could be trusted, and he blamed me for the hard time he had in that quarter. His father told him he was worthless, called him a playboy."

"Where does Norman's father live, Alita? Is he in Mexico?"

Alita blinked as if suddenly aware of Jenny's presence. "No." She shook her head. "We lived in Mexico for a long time, when Diego and I were first married and Norman was a baby. But then he moved us to Panama. I left him then. I knew he was going back to the old business, although he'd promised me that he never would."

"I thought he was Mexican."

"No, Diego's Panamanian. He lives on the Isla de Coiba, although he has a base in Colon as well."

"Well, that explains Norman's Panamanian passport, although it's not in his name. It was in the name of Diego Rodriguez."

"That is his name, Jenny. Norman Suffron is his Canadian name. But he was baptized Norman Diego Rodriguez. That was his name and he never forgot it."

Jenny sat on the hard metal bench as Alita rambled on about meetings with Bernie where he threatened to take Norman out of the picture. He made sexual advances on Alita, and she was petrified Frank would find out. She complained to Norman but he told her to stop being a sissy. All Bernie wanted was a little excitement, she didn't need to act as if she'd never done it before. She'd been appalled and mortified at her son's attitude and felt it was just another example of the way his father was corrupting him.

"Alita, where did all the money come from? Was it Diego's? Is he the head of this whole organization?"

She looked at Jenny blankly for a second, then seemed to come out of her reverie. "No, not Diego. He's not the head, but one of the lieutenants, you might say. It's part of his family. I don't know for sure any more. But I know that most of it was drug money. The main problem was there was too much. They needed to take it physically out of the country into Panama, or launder it through some legitimate businesses. They couldn't just put it in the bank. Norman took a lot down in cash. He made a trip every couple of weeks.

"But it wasn't enough. They must have dozens of businesses they funnel the money through, but Bernie was one of the bag men, so he used his influence in the security field."

"And is Bernie the top guy here, or is there someone else? Someone he takes orders from?"

Alita smiled. She looked at Jenny calmly. "Does Bernie look like the boss to you?" Her voice was contemptuous. "How do you think he got away with running those licenses like he did? Stouffer stayed in business for a good year and a half after the police recommended charges. You almost lost your license because you weren't cooperating with him."

"Not just mine, Alita, yours! Yours and Frank's." Jenny's tone sounded loud in the bare echoey visitor's room. She strove to speak calmly. "You were watching your own business going down. How could you do that?"

Alita smiled, a calm flat smile as if looking at a child who doesn't understand. It was a strange expression of detachment. "My son's livelihood was at stake. There was no question of what to do. You understand."

Jenny's gaze dropped to her hands. She was starting to feel a little out of touch with the outside world, locked in this small room with a woman who had never liked her and now seemed to be hovering on the very edge of sanity. A feeling of panic knocked at the back of her mind. She had to remind herself that she was not the one who's focus had become skewed. She pulled in a slow breath and let it out to steady herself.

"So, who's Bernie's boss? The police hint that you've said you know, but you're not talking. Are you afraid? Should the rest of us be afraid?"

"No, you don't need to be afraid." Her face was serene. "His hands are tied now. He can't make a move without tipping his position. If he tries to get to Bernie or me, the police will know." That calm detached smile was back on her lips. "If the police get evidence on him, he'll simply run. What else can he do?"

Suddenly her face crumpled. "If only Norman hadn't run! If only he'd stayed with me. I begged him!" Tears slid down her cheeks.

"Alita," Jenny said, "who visits you, besides Fred Austin?"

"There's no one. Fred's only come once, he's a busy man, you know."

Jenny felt suddenly terrified. What would she do, facing five years of prison and nothing to look forward to, no one to visit her?

She burst into speech. "I don't get over here that often, but I'll come to see you when I do. I can send you supplies, personal items that you can't get here. Write to me and let me know what you need. Do you feel up to talking about business? Fred had some final details we need to agree on."

When they had settled everything, Jenny left. Alita had proved surprisingly hard-headed about every item they negotiated. Jenny's opinion was revised once again, and by the time she rose to go, she had more confidence that Alita would survive the prison experience.

And if she was lucky, she'd win her appeal. With a sentence of under two years, she'd be transferred to a provincial women's prison and only serve maybe eight or nine months.

~*~*~*~

"Well, Chief," said Jenny, "I understand the wheels of justice grind exceeding slow. But it's my opinion that if you find out who's been Bernie's guiding light in the public service, you'll have his money laundering boss. Because Bernie was moving up fast in a ministry where everyone else in those positions was a lawyer. Who was helping his rapid advance?"

The Chief shifted in his chair. Dave hid his grin. Jenny was always right on target, and the Chief squirmed under her pointed remarks. "Well, I don't know about that," he finally said. "But we're following up on the order to halt the Stouffer investigation. We're also looking at who ordered the review for you folks, but that seems to dead-end with Olsinger. And Alita is still talking around the issue. I'm starting to suspect, however, that she knows less than she hints at."

Dave's watched Jenny's face and noted her incredulous look.

CHAPTER FORTY TWO

Y ou know, Jordie, you're starting to remind me of Frank, the way you're always telling me we have to go to this, or show up at that event," Jenny grumbled. "You'd think you held an interest in the business."

She adjusted her jacket with a jerk and led the way into the hotel lobby. She was dressed in a pale green suit of light wool. The skirt was a simple sheath in a nubby texture, the jacket a faint weave in the same colour, fitted and held closed in front with a single gold button. She wore a blouse of off-white silk beneath it. Jordie was decked out in a well-fitted suit that she'd never seen before tailored perfectly to his broad shoulders.

He took her elbow to escort her up the steps and into the large room where the reception was being held. "It's important to come to these events, and you know it," he said. "You're just being stubborn. If I hadn't said anything, you would have come anyway. The invitation was hand-delivered, for heaven's sake. You can't ignore that." She whined a little more and he gave her a look of strained patience before negotiating their way across the room to greet the Deputy Minister.

Alex Martin looked sharp in a designer suit. He broke off his conversation with another man to smile warmly and extend his hand to Jenny, ignoring Jordie altogether. "Mrs. MacDougall," he breathed in his rich, full voice. "How good of you to come. I was hoping you'd be able to attend. I'd like you to meet the new Assistant Deputy Minister." Martin turned smoothly to the man beside him. "Jenny, this is Shane Bureau. Shane, this is Jenny MacDougall, owner and operator of Sentinel Security Corporation, one of the largest and most respected firms in Victoria." She shook hands and Martin pulled her aside with a firm grip on her arm, leaving Jordie to introduce himself to Bureau.

"Thank you for coming to our little reception. I hope you've forgiven us for the shameful treatment you received at the hands of the Special Licenses Branch. It was outrageous and totally unprofessional. Luckily no harm was done. Your business was able to carry on uninterrupted during the fray." He smiled engagingly, holding her hand in a firm grip between both of his warm ones.

"If it hadn't been for you, we may not have caught Olsinger. Our province is lucky to have upstanding citizens like yourself. You keep the rest of the populace honest and accountable and that can only be for the good."

Jenny smiled back and carefully disengaged her hand. She saw Jordie watching and mentally debating whether he was needed. Turning, she looked up into Martin's attentive gaze and thought, not for the first time, what a remarkably attractive man he was. He certainly liked women. And well he might. She was sure they threw themselves at his feet.

"Well, Alex," she began with a small smile. "I've forgiven you. I never took it personally and I don't now."

His smile relaxed and seemed to grow in magnetism.

She was starting to feel dazzled. "Rather, I take it on a business-like basis," she continued, drawing her eyes away from his gaze to better gather her thoughts. "And damage *was* done, both to the business and its reputation in the industry. I'd like those issues addressed. We sustained substantial expenses defending ourselves from the attacks of the Branch. And our reputation amongst the members of the industry was tarnished. I'd like to come by your office one day soon and discuss it further."

She trusted herself to look back at him then, and he burst out laughing. "You've got it, Jenny. Call my secretary Monday, and come and see me. I very much look forward to that encounter."

She flushed, smiling, and walked back to stand beside Jordie.

"Well," he said, "what did he say? Formal apology?"

Jenny gave him a big smile. "That's right, but I told him that wasn't going to do it. I'm to see him next week about damages at the hands of the Branch."

Jordie narrowed his eyes. "And here I was thinking maybe I better get over there and rescue you."

She spotted the glint of approval in his eyes, before she took him firmly by the arm. "We can't let them off lightly. They acted outrageously, and they know it. He said so himself. Now, come and meet some of the other people here. I don't know everyone but a lot of the Victoria owners seem to have come."

~*~*~*~

"No, I'm sorry," said the voice at the other end of the line. "Mr. Martin isn't in. Can I take a message?"

"I don't need to speak to him, just his secretary." Jenny plucked a dead leaf off the plant on the low table beside the bed and leaned over to drag it slowly through the curly red hair on Jordie's chest. He caught her hand, holding it prisoner for a moment before bringing it up to his mouth to lick her fingers. She grinned, the heat rising up her throat.

"This is his secretary speaking."

"Oh, of course." Jenny tugged her attention back to the phone. "Well, I spoke with Alex Martin at the reception Friday, and he asked me to call to set up an appointment with him. I know he's busy, and I'll be happy with a time next week if that's all you can manage."

There was a pause. "I'm sorry. I'm not able to set up an appointment at this time. Can someone else help you? Perhaps if you told me what it's about..." The woman's voice trailed off uncertainly.

Jenny frowned into the phone. "He asked me to make an appointment with him personally. It's regarding damages suffered by my company from certain actions taken by the Special Licenses Branch. Alex Martin is the only one who can address these issues. How is it you can't make an appointment? He specifically requested to see me."

"Just a moment please." There was a muffled sound, then the line was placed on hold. Jenny waited. Jordie rubbed her shoulders, kissing a line down her belly. Too soon, the line clicked live again, and another voice came on the phone.

"Yes, can I help you?" a masculine voice inquired.

"Who am I speaking to?" Jenny struggled to keep her voice even, pushing Jordie's head away with her other hand.

"This is the Minister's executive assistant, Bob Rainey. What can I do for you?"

"Well, Bob, this is Jenny MacDougall of Sentinel Security Group." She explained once more. "Can you tell me what the problem might be?"

"Well," the voice drawled, "Mr. Martin is unavailable and so we aren't making appointments for him at the moment. Perhaps if you called back on Monday…"

"Listen, I don't want to wait till next Monday or even tomorrow. I've put up with a lot from your Ministry and I'm starting to lose what little patience I once had. Do you want me to go to the newspapers, tell the whole tale of how Special Licenses harassed and threatened us, tried to illegally suspend our license, and now they won't even talk to me?" Jenny's diction got more precise as her temperature rose. Jordie moved behind her and began to rub her neck and shoulders, working on the tension.

"Of course we don't want that. It's just that we have a problem, but I can see that you have one as well." Rainey paused, and then plunged on. "The thing is, Mr. Martin's whereabouts is unknown at the present time. He's not been in touch with his office. Now, this is entirely confidential. I hope you'll keep it that way, but we're simply waiting to hear from him before we carry on, business as usual. However, I can understand that you can't wait. I'll take your request up with the Minister in the meanwhile, and call you back tomorrow, by noon. Will that do? That's the best I can manage."

Jenny caught her breath. "Uh, that'll do fine, Mr. Rainey. I'll wait for your call."

"Jordie," she breathed, as she pressed the phone off. "Alex Martin has disappeared. Just disappeared. They don't know where he is."

CHAPTER FORTY THREE

Come here, sweetheart." Jordie reached out his long arms and enfolded Jenny against his chest. She sighed and leaned into him. "How are you, baby? I've missed you all day." His mouth came down on hers in a sweet tender kiss that took away all the stress and made her forget the office and distractions of the business. She kissed him back with all her love.

Finally, she rested against his shoulder, gazing into those dark blue eyes. "Jordie, I have a surprise for you."

He smiled a little. "You do? What kind of surprise? The kind I can feel rising up to greet you right now?" He nudged his body gently against hers.

She laughed and blushed, batting at his arm. He hummed, pressing a little harder. "This is nice," he whispered suggestively.

"I know, Jordie. But listen. What would you say to going to Greece for three weeks?" Her voice became tender. "You'd like it. I had a wonderful time there. And you can relax, just let go. No cares in the world."

He looked amused. "I know you had a good time there, Jenny. I'm not sure I want to hear about it, however. Greg still isn't my favourite person." His mouth firmed at the thought.

She twisted in his arms, running her palms up his chest. "Jordie, just listen." She took his face between her hands, kissed his chin softly, the corner of his mouth. "I love you, only you. Greg isn't part of this. And Greece really is wonderful. We could get away by ourselves. No kids, no business calls. We could be alone, just us. It would be heaven."

Jordie's face became still and he searched her eyes. Then he pulled her closer. "Jenny," he said, his voice cracking. "will you marry me? I know I'm not the world's best catch. And I've got other commitments." His eyes turned bleak, but he valiantly plunged on. "I love you. I've never loved anyone but you. You were always the one for me." His mouth claimed hers in a fierce kiss, his arms like steel bands around her, pulling her ever closer to his lean muscular body.

When he lifted his head, his gaze was keen on her face. "Will you?"

She leaned against him feeling his warmth seep into her, feeling the strength of him, both physical and emotional as he held her protectively. Looking into his face, she saw the love and caring so clearly, that for a long time had been hidden behind an aggressive stance and that hot look that she always associated with Jordie. And she saw the fear of what her decision might be.

"Yes, oh, yes Jordie. I didn't know if you'd want to..." She swallowed.

His eyes flashed, a glint of possessiveness in the dark depths. "If I'd want to? That's pretty well all I've wanted for the last twenty-five years. Even when I was little, I always imagined I'd marry you and we'd live together in a small house. We'd never be apart. It can't be like that I know, but this is our chance, and I have to go for it. There's no holding back now, is there?"

Jenny returned his fierce gaze as her heart beat hard in her chest. "No holding back." she vowed.

I would really like your help. Book reviews are the lifeblood of what I do and your review of my book would mean a lot to me. If you would take a moment or two and leave your review on Amazon.com or wherever you bought the book, that would be wonderful. If you want to send it to me, my contact information is at the bottom. I honestly thank you.

Last but not least, if you find an error in this book, please email me. This will help me fix things that my editors and I might have overlooked and make for a better read for others. In return, by way of showing my gratitude, I will send you a free copy of the next book with my sincere thanks.

Sylvie Grayson

You can learn more or contact Sylvie Grayson at her website- www.sylviegrayson.com
on facebook at www.facebook.com/sylvie.grayson
or email at sylviegraysonauthor@gmail.com

Be careful who you trust...

Katy Dalton worked hard to save her money. And investing it with her friend Bruno seemed like a safe bet. But her job disappears and she needs her money back, everything Bruno has already loaned to Rome Trucking. When Katy insists he return her money, Bruno stops answering his phone and bad things start to happen.

Brett Rome is frustrated. The last thing he wants to do is leave a promising career in hockey to come home and run his ailing father's trucking company. What he discovers is not the successful business that he remembers, but one that is teetering on the very edge of bankruptcy and a young woman demanding the return of the money she invested.

With the company in chaos, Brett hires her. But danger lurks in the form of Bruno's dubious associates. What secret are they hiding and why are they willing to kill Katy? Can Brett put this broken picture back together, and is Katy part of the solution or the problem?

A thrilling roller coaster of a story...

...when a police detective falls for his main suspect, life gets complicated...

When Chloe Bowman wakes to find her husband gone, never does she imagine it will take so long to find him, or that in the midst of the search she'll discover she doesn't really know this man at all. She soon realizes she has been left alone with her young son and a time bomb on her hands. Then the earthquake throws everything into question. Lurking in the shadows is the mysterious Rainman who travels under an unknown name.

Police Detective Ross Cullen was already investigating Chloe's husband when he disappears. Although he's powerfully drawn to Chloe, Ross also knows that when one member of a family disappears, the first place to look for the suspect is among those closest to him. No one is closer than Chloe.

But the deeper Ross digs the less he knows, and the more he's attracted to the young wife as she struggles to put her life back together. Can Ross break through the Rainman's disguises to solve the case so he can be with Chloe?

Sylvie Grayson has found her niche, you'll love this book...

SYLVIE GRAYSON

LEGAL OBSTRUCTION

Emily moves to a new town to hide her secret, but it follows her. Can Joe protect her from her past?

When Emily Drury takes a job as legal counsel for an import-export company, she doesn't make the decision lightly. She needs to get away to someplace safe.

Joe Tanner counts himself lucky. He's charmed a successful big city lawyer into heading up the legal department of his rapidly expanding business. But why would a beautiful woman who could easily make partner in the high profile legal firm where she works, give it all up to come to a place like Bonnie?

A mystery surrounds her arrival that wraps them both in ever tightening tentacles. As Joe realizes she has become essential to his happiness, his first reaction is to protect her. But he doesn't know the whole story.

Can Emily trust him enough to divulge her secret? Will he learn what he needs to know in time to stop the avalanche that's gaining speed as it races down the hill toward her?

...romantic suspense at it's best...

Sci-fi/ fantasy from Sylvie Grayson

The Last War series is a stunning portrayal of a new world created from fire and consumed at the edges ...- sci fi and fantasy at its best...

The Emperor has been defeated. New countries have arisen from the ashes of the old Empire. The citizens swear they will never need to fight again after that long and painful war.

Bethlehem Farmer is helping her brother Abram run Farmer Holdings in south Khandarken after their father died in the final battles. She is looking after the dispossessed, keeping the farm productive and the talc mine working in the hills behind their land. But when Abram takes a trip with Uncle Jade into the northern territory and disappears without a trace, she's left on her own. Suddenly things are not what they seem and no one can be trusted.

Major Dante Regiment is sent by his father, the General of Khandarken, to find out what the situation is at Farmer Holdings. What he sees shakes him to the core and fuels his grim determination to protect Bethlehem at all cost, even with his life.

Ms Grayson has created a fascinating new world with a lot of the same old problems. Sci fi and fantasy rolled into one with a sure hand and enormous imagination

From the mud and danger of the open road to the welcoming arms of the Sanctuary, from attacks by the dispossessed army to the storms of the open sea, Son of the Emperor takes us on a wild ride into danger and on to the dream of freedom.

The Emperor is defeated yet already unrest is growing in the north of Khandarken. After Julianne Adjudicator's father disappears, she seeks to escape the clutches of her vicious stepmother Zanata, and flees to the Sanctuary. This is the safest place for a woman in a hostile world of unrest and roving dispossessed. But when Julianne seeks asylum, it soon becomes clear all is not as it first appeared.

Then Abe Farmer arrives at the Sanctuary seeking medical help. Abe isn't interested in taking a young woman with them, as he and his injured bodyguard struggle to return to the Southern Territory. Yet when he discovers her fate if she stays, he finds he has no choice.

But the journey becomes more dangerous as they encounter the army of the New Emperor and are caught in the middle of a firefight as they flee toward the Catastrophic Ocean. Can Abe keep her safe till they reach home?

...a whole new world with the same old problems - fantasy at

its best...

TRUTH AND TREACHERY

THE LAST WAR
BOOK THREE

SYLVIE GRAYSON

When Emperor Carlton makes an offer to Cownden Lanser, can he refuse? Lanser has his own ambitions and Carlton may be offering everything he's dreamed of.

The Young Emperor has been backed into a corner. He holds a bit of land in Legitamia, but the skirmishes they've launched to expand his empire have had limited success. Now his ambitions are aimed at overthrowing everything Khandarken has cobbled together since the Last War.

Cownden Lanser, Chief Constable of Khandarken, is a private man with a close connection to the Old Empire that he doesn't divulge to anyone. Although he's dedicated to his position, things are not what they seem in the rank and file of the police.

Selanna Nettles is a sookie, healing the mine workers and the dispossessed in the Western Territory. But her life takes a startling turn when Chief Cownden Lanser hires her to attend a set of high-level meetings in Gilsigg.

When these three meet up in Legitamia, the result is explosive. Not just for them but for the future of Khandarken. The Emperor makes Cownden an offer that might be everything he's secretly dreamed of. How can he refuse?

The Last War series is a stunning portrayal of a new world created from fire and consumed at the edges... sci fi/fantasy at its best...

ABOUT THE AUTHOR

Sylvie Grayson has published romantic suspense novels, *Suspended Animation, Legal Obstruction, The Lies He Told Me* and *My Best Mistake*, all about strong women who meet with dangerous odds, stories of tension and attraction.

She has also written *The Last War* series, a romantic sci fi / fantasy set in a new world she has created. Although it's a series, each book stands alone.

She has been an English language instructor, a nightclub manager, an auto shop bookkeeper and a lawyer. She is a wife and mother, and lives in southern British Columbia with her husband on a small piece of land near the Pacific Ocean, when she's not travelling the world looking for adventure.